THE BOOK OF BETRAYAL

THE LAST ORACLE BOOK FIVE

MELISSA MCSHANE

Night Harbor Publishing

ISBN-13 978-1-949663-28-0

Cover design by Alexandra Brandt http://www.alexandrajbrandt.com

For Julie,
because if it's Portland, there have to be rhododendrons

1

Gray clouds filled the sky to the west, filtering the light of the setting sun and turning the new greenery lining the freeway even more lush and vibrant. Lightning, vivid and white, cut a jagged scar against the dark background. Wind lashed the car window, doing its best to push the car out of its lane, and carried the clouds tumbling toward us. It was hard not to feel we were outracing the storm, but I couldn't think of a better vehicle to win that race than Malcolm's Jaguar, slung low to the ground and purring like a cat.

"Did you know big cats can't purr?" I said. "Lions and tigers, I mean. I read it somewhere. And small cats can't roar."

"Is this apropos of a conversation I don't remember?" Malcolm said.

"Just thinking about your car's engine purring, and how a real jaguar wouldn't. We're not going to go rolling head over heels, are we?"

"Not with as low a profile as this car has. Are you afraid?"

"With you driving? Never." I leaned my cheek against the cold window glass and eyed the clouds. "Maybe a little afraid of this dinner."

Malcolm laughed. "Ashamed of me, or of your family?"

"Neither. I just want them to like you, and you to like them."

"I promise to like them and to be at my most likeable. I hope they don't think I've been avoiding them. It's been months since you told them we were dating."

"I'm sure they won't think that."

Malcolm changed lanes and exited the freeway, coming to a smooth stop at the top of the ramp. "I'm looking forward to your mother's cooking. I've only ever had her leftovers, and the real thing is sure to be spectacular."

"She's making lasagna. It's my favorite. You will *love* it."

He briefly put his hand over mine and squeezed before putting the car in gear and moving forward. "This is because I'm older than you, isn't it?"

"No. Maybe. It's stupid."

"Nine years isn't that big a difference. Remember that old fellow what's-his-name in *African Queen*?"

I laughed. "All right. I just can't help thinking my parents are going to think it's weird, when the truth is I never remember your age except when your birthday rolls around. And they're not going to think it's weird."

"*Your* birthday is coming around in a few weeks."

"I wish we could celebrate publicly." I let out a long, frustrated breath. "Maybe I should just tell the Board of Neutralities the truth. They seem to have faith in me, and I can't help feeling I'm betraying it."

"Don't," said Malcolm. "If they find out about us, you will certainly lose Abernathy's, and possibly your life. I haven't given up hope that you'll figure out an exception to the Accords. And since you won't let me break up with you—"

"What, and make decisions for me 'for my own good'? I told you that's what people in bad romance novels do." I rested my hand lightly on his for a moment. "Does it still bother you that nothing in the Accords would punish *you* for being in this relationship?"

"Of course it does. That's unfair if nothing else is."

"And everything about the Accords is unfair." I sighed again. "I'll keep looking." The truth was, I was discouraged. The Accords, the rules that governed all of magery and the Neutralities, said clearly that custodians of Neutralities had to maintain impartiality toward the two factions magery was divided into. They were just as clear that a custodian dating a Nicollien or an Ambrosite qualified as extreme partiality. But I loved Malcolm, and he loved me, and the thought of giving him up filled me with horror. So deception, and secrecy, were the order of the day.

I directed Malcolm through the last few streets and into my parents' driveway. The rambler-style house, with its beige brick façade and creamy white trim, looked drab this time of day, gloomy and gray. Even the rhododendrons, with their glossy green leaves, looked dispirited and droopy. I came around to Malcolm's side of the car and took his hand. "Ready?"

He looked down at me with an amused smile and a flash of his wonderful dimple. "*Morituri te salutant*, Helena?"

I slugged him in the shoulder. "I am not preparing to die, Malcolm!"

He kissed me quickly. "Then smile like it's a party, and release your death grip on my hand."

I knocked rapidly on the door before pushing it open. I might not live here anymore, but old habits were hard to break. "We're here!"

"Come in," Mom said from the kitchen. I pushed the door open farther and was greeted by a wave of hot air scented with tomatoes and herbs and half a dozen kinds of cheese.

"The smell alone was worth the drive," Malcolm murmured, helping me out of my coat. I hung his coat and mine on the hooks just inside the door, then took his hand again and led him into the living room, where my dad was just getting up from the couch. Jake, my brother, followed him a bit more slowly.

"Dad, this is Malcolm. Malcolm, my father, Roman Davies, and my brother Jake."

"Nice to meet you," Dad said, extending his hand to Malcolm, then catching me up in a big hug. "Hope the drive wasn't too bad."

"The rain held off," Malcolm said. "Though I enjoy driving in the rain."

"I've heard about your car," Jake said. "Vintage Jaguar, right?"

"1963 E-type coupe. It was my father's. Would you like to see it?"

Dad's eyes gleamed. "Louise, we'll be out front for a bit," he called out, and suddenly I was alone in the living room, blinking at the absence of men.

"Wait, I wanted to meet...they're gone," Mom said, emerging around the corner from the kitchen. "Boys and their cars."

"Well, it *is* a very nice car," I said, going to hug Mom. "I guess this means I have to set the table on my own."

"Jake did it before you came. Without being prompted. Sometimes I don't recognize my own children." Mom put her arm through mine and drew me after her into the kitchen, where both ovens were working hard. "Food will be ready in about ten minutes. How are things?"

"Busy, but dull, if that makes sense. I have a lot of customers who all want the same things." I couldn't tell my parents that I worked in an oracular bookstore, nor that most of my customers were capable of working magic to fight alien monsters invading our world. Fortunately, Mom and Dad were satisfied with my often vague answers.

"Dull can be nice. It beats tax season, which is what I've been wrangling for my business this last week. I want it over and done with."

"I'm glad I have an accountant." I also had Judy Rasmussen, who was a wizard with our accounting software and kept the books in perfect order for the accountant. I couldn't begin to imagine how complicated Abernathy's' taxes were.

The door opened, and shortly all three men trooped into the kitchen, their noses and cheeks rosy from the chill in the air. "I'd be afraid to drive that," Dad said. "The insurance premiums alone..."

"They are high," Malcolm said, "but it's one of my few indulgences."

I figured his expensive suits, his heavy gold watch, and his hand-stitched Italian leather shoes were more necessities of his job running a high-end security company than indulgences, and held my tongue. Today Malcolm was dressed in khakis and a lightweight black sweater that did nothing to conceal his excellent physique. It made me think about getting him home so I could get him out of his clothes as quickly as possible. I blinked away the image and smiled.

"It's nice to meet you, Louise," Malcolm was saying, shaking my mom's hand. "Your reputation as a cook has preceded you."

"I hope I'll live up to it tonight," Mom laughed. "Roman, why don't you pour the wine, and I'll serve the salad and bread."

It was the best meal I'd had in months: fresh, hot, crusty Italian bread with flavored oil and balsamic vinegar for dipping, a green salad rich with romaine and arugula, and the lasagna, pure heaven on a plate. I caught my mother's eye once and nodded at her, chewing vigorously. She flicked a glance at Malcolm and raised one eyebrow in an expression that clearly said *You done good, girl.* I blushed and couldn't meet anyone's eyes.

"So, Helena wasn't very clear on what you do. You...sell security systems?" Dad said.

"More specifically, my company handles the varied security needs of all its clients. That can mean alarm systems, but often it means private security personnel, bodyguards, transportation of sensitive material."

"*Your* company?" Mom said.

"It's an old family business. My brother and I run the organization. My mother is on the board of directors."

"So your mom is still the boss of you," Jake said with a grin.

Malcolm smiled back at him. "It never ends. As I'm sure you'll find out soon enough."

Jake shrugged. "I'm off to college in the fall."

"Where will you go?"

"University of Oregon."

"That's my alma mater. I hope you like it."

"I didn't know that. I would have thought you'd go to Harvard or Yale or someplace like that," I said.

"I was accepted to Princeton, but I decided I'd rather stay close to home," Malcolm said, giving me a look that reminded me he had a calling in life that mattered more than his university education. Though I would have thought he could fight invaders anywhere. I wondered for the first time how long he'd been a magus. Undergoing the Damerel rites for the implantation of the aegis that let humans wield magic was dangerous, and I couldn't imagine they'd let a teenager do it, but that was all I knew.

"So your mother, your brother...what about your father?" Mom said.

"My father passed away five years ago."

"Oh. I'm sorry, I didn't—"

"That's all right. It was quite sudden—he was only fifty-eight. But we remember him fondly, not sadly."

"I'm glad to hear that."

Dad cleared his throat. "Dessert, and then a movie? Helena tells us you're a fan of classic films."

"Yes, it's what brought us together. *The Philadelphia Story*, wasn't it? 'Unsuspected depth?'"

I laughed. "That's it exactly. I'd almost forgotten that."

"It certainly made me see you in a new light." His smile warmed me, and without any self-consciousness I kissed him lightly on the lips. It made his eyes light up, and suddenly I couldn't remember why I'd ever been nervous.

We carried our little plates of tiramisu into the basement, where my dad's shrine to the gods of entertainment lay. Surround sound, a flat screen TV filling most of one wall, leather recliners with plenty of cup holders...it was the most decadent way to watch a movie I knew.

Malcolm and I picked out a comfortable seat, and I curled up against his side the way I always did for movies. Though this was unlikely to end the way it did any time we watched a movie in my apartment, with the two of us kissing and taking each other's clothes off as the credits rolled. I caught my mother looking at me again with that sidelong smile, and snuggled in closer to hide my embarrassment. "I still can't believe you've never seen *The Thin Man*," I said. "And you such a big fan of *My Man Godfrey*, too."

"Well, as I recall, *you* had never seen *Notorious* until five weeks ago. That's a much greater omission, in my opinion."

"Helena's never seen *Notorious*?" Dad said. "Louise, we've failed as parents."

"The one you should see is *Hollow Triumph*," Malcolm said. "Helena and I watched that recently—Paul Henreid in a double role, psychological noir...it's not light watching, but it was compelling."

"I'll put it on my watch list," Dad said, pulling out his phone. Mom dimmed the lights.

"Movie time," she said, and the opening credits came up on the screen.

The Thin Man is one of my favorites, though I've always wished they'd given Myrna Loy more to do with her role and I've never gotten the appeal of Asta the dog. Malcolm chuckled in all the right places. When Nora Charles tells Nick she read he was shot in the tabloids, and my parents and Jake and I all said "It's not true. He didn't come anywhere near my tabloids" along with Nick, he nearly dislodged me, he laughed so hard.

"I have no idea who the real murderer is," he said near the end.

"That's all right, neither does Nick Charles," Jake said. "Want to take a guess?"

"My money's on Cesar Romero, but that's just because he's creepy in this part."

"I forgot who the murderer was the second time I saw this," I said, "so it was like seeing it for the first time again."

"Shh, pay attention or you'll miss it," Mom said.

We watched the dinner party unfold, the unmasking of the murderer, and the final scene where Nick throws Asta into the upper bunk so he and Nora can sleep together. "Not that they could do anything but imply that," I said.

"And you notice how they never move their heads when they kiss, in these old movies," Mom said. "They just press their lips together and hold still. Very awkward."

"I love old movies, but I wouldn't want to live in one," Malcolm said. His fingers curled around mine. "That was a really good one.

But I can't say I've ever seen quite so gin-soaked a movie. Odd how their code didn't prohibit displays of extreme drunkenness."

"It's true." Dad stood and helped Mom to her feet. Malcolm did the same for me. Handsome, and considerate, and funny, and polite... I wished I dared fling my arms around his neck and kiss him hard in a way that would have been wildly inappropriate in an old movie.

We went back upstairs to the living room, where Jake said goodnight and tromped off to his room. "He's going to text that girl," Mom said. "For hours."

"Which girl?"

"Her name is Claudia and they're in English together," Dad said. "And that is the extent of what we know."

"I don't understand the appeal of courtship via texting, but it seems to work for him," Mom said. "Remember before we had unlimited texting?"

"Remember before we had texting, period?" Dad said with a grin. "Back in the bad old days?"

"I don't know how I'd survive without being able to text people. So much better than calling and leaving a voice mail they might not get," I said.

"I prefer it, too," Malcolm said. "And it leaves a trail." Which reminded me of why I never texted Malcolm anymore, not unless it was something banal that anyone might send to a friend. We'd agreed not to leave evidence on each other's phones in the form of affectionate texts or voice mails.

"Well, back in *our* day, we were lucky to have voice mail," Dad said, intoning the way he always did when he delivered one of his "kids these days" statements.

"They don't want to talk about our day, Roman," Mom said affectionately. "Would you like anything else? More dessert? Coffee?"

"Actually, we should be going," Malcolm said, rising from his seat. "I have an early meeting tomorrow."

"Well, it was wonderful to meet you, Malcolm," Mom said. "I hope we'll see you again soon."

"I'd like that." Malcolm shook my dad's hand and hugged my

mom, who made the most outrageous face at me over his shoulder. I struggled not to laugh.

It was pouring down rain when we left my parents' house, a heavy, cold rain that beat down on my scalp like a thousand tiny frozen fingers. Malcolm's car was chilly, and the vintage Jag might have been a wonder to drive, but its heating system wasn't terribly robust. We sat in the driveway for a minute, me holding my hands over the vent to warm them. "I didn't know you had a meeting," I said.

"I do, but I might have exaggerated its earliness in my desire to get back to your apartment and practice kissing in a non-Hays Code-approved way."

"Mmm. I like the sound of that."

Malcolm backed out of the driveway and headed toward the freeway. We drove in silence; I felt too relaxed and full and happy for speech. It had gone well, my parents liked him—

"You had a good time, right?" I said.

"I did. You have a great family. You're luckier than you know, I think."

"What makes you say that?" I tilted my head to look at him.

"My family isn't nearly so pleasant to be around. My mother is... difficult, and Ewan can never decide whether to be a dutiful son or his own man, and I'm afraid I get irritated and snappish and make things worse. And then there's Andria."

Jealousy touched my heart. "I thought you dumped Andria."

Malcolm laughed. "Oh, love, Andria never came close to holding a place in my heart the way you do. But she's my cousin—second cousin—and my mother has never given up the hope that Andria and I will marry. One unfortunate side effect from having to keep this secret is that my mother believes I'm unattached, and has no trouble pushing Andria on me at every opportunity."

"But Andria has to know you're not interested."

A rueful smile touched his lips. "Andria knows. Andria is opportunistic and enjoys pushing my buttons. She is currently living with my mother rent-free and enjoying a lifestyle superior to what she would live at home in Quebec, so leaving doesn't benefit her at all."

He accelerated up the ramp to freeway speeds. This close to the road, I could almost see the rain as a wave pushed up by our passage. It was the strangest sensation.

"You're not jealous, are you?" Malcolm added. "Because I promise you—"

"I'm not jealous. Well, I sort of am, a tiny little bit, but more in the 'I've never met her and I have some small insecurities about how much prettier she is than me' way than anything serious."

Malcolm roared with laughter. "Helena, you are so much more beautiful than she can ever dream of being," he finally said. "She's pretty enough, but there's an arch self-awareness to her that makes it difficult to want to be close to her over time."

"'Arch self-awareness'? That's a sweet way to insult someone."

He glanced at me, flashing his dimple. "I hadn't thought—"

The smile fell away from his face, replaced by a look of confusion. Then pain creased his features, and he grabbed his chest. The car swerved across two lanes, and I screamed. Cars beside us honked, long and shrill. Malcolm cried out and took hold of the wheel again, his face still contorted in agony. We straightened briefly, skidded, and then the car was swinging in a huge weightless arc across the freeway. I screamed again. Something low and dark rose up fast before us. I struck the dashboard and everything went black.

2

Something hissed beyond the darkness, a loud, ceaseless sound. Rain. I blinked water out of my face and tried to sit up, but was restrained by...what was it? The seatbelt. Right. The car—

Memory returned. Malcolm's agonized face, the car swerving, the crash as the car plowed into the freeway's concrete barrier. One of the headlights was unbroken and pressed up against the concrete, making a white spot that illuminated the destroyed front end of the car. The windshield was shattered, and rain poured in on me. I wiped more water out of my face...except it wasn't water, it was blood. I must have hit my head on the dash. My hands were shaking. I had to get out.

Then I saw Malcolm. He hung limply in his seat belt, his head tilted at an unnatural angle. One of his arms, thrust toward me, was clearly broken, hanging awkwardly below the elbow. His face was bloody from a dozen cuts, all turning pink from the pouring rain. With trembling hands, I yanked at the seat belt, but couldn't get it to release. "Somebody help me!" I screamed, yanking harder.

Someone flung my door open. "Are you all right?" a man said.

"Help him—he's hurt—I can't get out—"

"Calm down, it will be all right," the man said, but I looked at

Malcolm's still face and panic bubbled up inside me. The man managed to unhook my seat belt, and I flung myself at Malcolm, feeling for a pulse.

"Call 911," the man said to someone over his shoulder, then to me, "Come out of there, and we'll see if we can get him out."

"No! You're not supposed to move him, he might have a spine injury, you can't—please help me!"

"I'm trying to. Come with me."

"No. I won't leave him." My hair and coat were soaked. The endless rain made everything so much worse. The ambulance was coming, it had to be coming.

Malcolm shifted. I grabbed his hand and squeezed. "Malcolm, can you feel that?"

He opened his eyes briefly, half-lidded, and looked at me with no recognition. Then he closed his eyes and sagged more deeply.

"*Malcolm!*" I shrieked. "No, no, no, no!"

Hands grabbed me, dragged me away. I fought them like a madwoman, clawing and shrieking, but they bundled me away from the car and into the passenger seat of a Suburban. "Let me go!"

"He's fine, he's just unconscious," the same man said. "Sit here and wait for the paramedics. It will be all right."

I gulped in rain-scented air and let out a sobbing breath. "How do you know?"

"I was a Boy Scout," the man said. "Is there someone you should call? Your family, maybe?"

"No, I—" There was someone I should call, someone better than the paramedics, but I didn't know how soon he could be there. "My phone's in my purse. In the car."

"I'll get it." The man ran back to the Jaguar.

I took a look around, pushing wet hair out of my eyes. Another car had plowed into Malcolm's, driving it farther into the wall. Good thing those old Jaguars had such long noses, or it would have been us smashed into the wall. As it was, the front end had crumpled, trapping Malcolm inside—I made myself breathe slowly. I couldn't help him by panicking.

The man returned with my purse. "Thanks," I said, digging through it for my phone. A couple of other undamaged cars had pulled up behind ours and had their hazard lights on, and the Suburban I sat in was parked across the lane in front of Malcolm's car. There was no shoulder, no way to pull out of traffic, and it all looked so unsafe I feared someone else would come barreling along, unable to stop, and add to the crisis.

I found my purse and dialed Derrick Tinsley's number. Derrick was a member of Malcolm's invader hunting team and a bone magus, capable of healing injuries, even severe ones. It rang, and rang, and I had to hold the phone with both hands because now I was shaking all over. Finally, Derrick said, "Helena?"

"Derrick," I said, then couldn't think what else to say. "Derrick, there was an accident. A car accident. Malcolm is—he's—"

"He's dead?"

I shook my head, forgetting he couldn't see me. "No, he's alive, but he's badly hurt, Derrick, I need your help—" Just in time I remembered my Boy Scout helper, standing nearby and watching me. "Can you come?"

"Where are you?"

"Somewhere on the Banfield."

"That could—"

"Hang on." Lights and sirens were approaching, and my helper ran toward the approaching vehicles. "The EMTs are here." An ambulance followed in the fire truck's wake.

Derrick swore. "Nothing I can do about that," he said. "Keep a close eye on him, and call me when you know what hospital they're taking him to. Probably Providence, but I don't want to take any chances."

His words confused me—why wouldn't he want the paramedics? —but I said, "All right," to a dead line—he'd already hung up. I put my phone away and staggered toward the ambulance and the fire truck, nearly falling when I put weight on my left foot. It hadn't hurt before, or at least I hadn't noticed it in my preoccupation with not leaving Malcolm. If a sprained ankle and a possible concussion were all I was taking away from this, I was lucky.

Three EMTs were clustered around Malcolm's car, and one had gone to check on the occupants of the second car involved in the crash. I hobbled over to that one, a uniformed woman who didn't notice me until I tapped her on the shoulder. Then she looked at me, did a double take, and swore. "Where did you come from?"

"From the car. Is he...he's alive, right? I told them not to move him. Was that right?"

"Come with me," the woman said, and led me over to the ambulance, where she found me a blanket and urged me to sit inside where it was dry, or at least drier than everywhere else. "You took a bad blow to the head. Is that your husband?"

"Boyfriend."

"Don't worry, everything's going to be fine." The woman had a very reassuring smile, and despite myself I smiled back. She blotted my face with a cloth, then did something to my forehead that hurt. "That will hold it until it can be stitched up. Are you dizzy? Nauseated? Head hurt?"

"My head hurts, especially when I move it quickly, but I don't feel sick."

"We'll watch you for signs of concussion, but I don't think you're in any immediate danger. Now, wait here and let us help the others."

I nodded, which made my head hurt again, and watched her hop out of the ambulance and run back toward the second car. It was a Ford Explorer that loomed over Malcolm's Jaguar. In the darkness, I couldn't tell how badly it was damaged, but the driver and his passenger were standing next to it with their coats held protectively over their heads, and the woman who'd treated me didn't look frantic. I hoped that meant they weren't hurt.

I clutched the blanket around myself and felt it grow damp from contact with my soaked body. Everything felt so distant, the headlights drifting past, the rain pouring down on the pavement, the Jaguar's one unbroken headlight adding to the street lamps and the lights from the emergency vehicles' headlights.

"Miss?"

I startled. A police officer stood nearby, growing gradually wet from the rain. "How are you?" he asked. "You look like you were injured. You were a passenger in the Jaguar?"

"Yes—no, I wasn't badly injured—is he all right?"

"Don't worry, he's being cared for. I just have a few questions, if you're up to it."

I nodded, regretted it when pain shot through my head, and said, "I guess so."

"Do you know what caused the crash?"

I swallowed. "Malcolm...something happened to him, a heart attack or something, and he lost control. He tried not to hit anyone, I promise—then we hit the median."

"Neither of you were drinking? Malcolm wasn't texting anyone?"

"No, of course not!" I exclaimed. "I mean...sorry. I guess you have to ask those questions."

"That's right." The officer glanced over his shoulder at the wrecked Jaguar. "Did he say anything to you before he lost control? Anything to indicate he knew something was wrong?"

"No. He just grabbed his chest and then swerved."

"All right. You just rest, and someone will talk to you again after you've been treated at the hospital." He smiled. "Everything will be fine."

I tried to smile back, but he'd already turned away. I stared after him, feeling even more adrift now than before. The Suburban was gone, and I hadn't even thanked my Boy Scout. I wondered what the other people thought, the ones in the Ford Explorer. Were they angry? Did they think Malcolm was a bad driver? He wasn't, he was a good driver, but he'd...

...what *had* happened, really? He'd been looking at me, and his face had changed, like he was in extreme pain, and he'd grabbed his chest like he was having a heart attack, just as I'd told the officer. But Malcolm was only thirty-one, surely not old enough to have a heart attack. Or was I wrong, and those could happen to anyone? I just didn't know. But it sure looked like he'd suffered some kind of attack, something that would make him lose control of the car.

A couple of EMTs came back to the ambulance to get a long, flat board like a giant tongue depressor and some other equipment my fuddled brain couldn't recognize. I leaned against the side of the ambulance and tried to control my shaking. Maybe I was in shock. I couldn't remember the symptoms or what you were supposed to do to treat shock, but lying down someplace warm was almost certainly part of it. I could lie down on the floor here, maybe. But I'd be in the way when they brought Malcolm back, and I didn't want that.

My eyes slid closed, and I forced them open. I remembered when Jake had had a concussion after some incident in football practice, how one of the things the doctor had said was that he needed to stay awake. Maybe I didn't have a concussion, but I didn't want to take chances. I shouldn't sleep. I wanted to sleep. Maybe if I slept, all this would go away. I should call someone else and get them to talk to me, keep me awake, but who? My addled brain couldn't think. I took out my phone and scrolled through the contact list, looking for inspiration.

Viv.

She answered right away. "Hey, sweetie, what's up?"

She was so cheerful it made my heart hurt. "Viv, Malcolm and I were in a car accident. He's badly hurt. I don't know what to do."

Viv gasped. "Helena, *no*. Are you all right? Where are you?"

"Still at the accident. They said I might have a concussion."

"Talk to me, sweetie. Stay awake. Was anyone else hurt?"

"I don't think so. We spun out, and hit the barrier, and another car hit us." Tears choked me, spilled onto my cheeks. "Viv, he's hurt *really* bad."

"Did you call 911?"

"The ambulance is here."

"So they're taking care of him. Don't worry, it will be all right. Do you know where they're taking him?"

"Not yet."

"Tell me when you do, and I'll come for you. Now, stay with me. Tell me about your night."

I let out a shuddering breath. "I can't. It was so nice, and now it's not, I just don't want to remember."

"Then I'll tell you about mine. I played a great gig, and Jeremiah came. You know, I don't think he's ever going to get my music, but it's so sweet that he tries."

"I know. You're so lucky."

"I feel lucky. You know why else today was a great day for me? This is officially the longest I've ever been with one man."

"Viv, that's so great!" I wiped tears out of my eyes, clearing them so the blur of EMTs huddled around the car turned into individual men and women and a stretcher that— "Viv, they're bringing him back. I can't believe they got him out of the car, it was so crushed—"

"Don't cry, Helena, it's going to be all right. Ask where you're going."

I moved back and out of the way so they could trundle Malcolm into the ambulance. He was immobilized on the big board and covered from the chest down with a heavy blanket. "Where are we going?" I asked.

"Providence," the woman who'd helped me said. "Sit back. We'll take care of you, don't worry."

"Did you hear that?" I said to Viv.

"I'll meet you there," Viv said.

I found a bench seat and strapped in, gripping it hard with both hands, feeling tremendously unsafe despite the seat belt. With a couple of squawks, the siren went off, and the ambulance accelerated until it felt we were flying along. I looked at Malcolm's still, horribly damaged face and prayed for the driver to go faster.

Malcolm's eyes flew open, and he convulsed against the straps. "Watch out," another woman said, and followed it with a string of instructions I couldn't understand. Once again blind with tears, I pulled out my phone and texted Derrick our destination. Trying to converse with someone felt like an impossible exertion. I put my phone in my pocket and wiped away tears, trying to make myself as small as possible in the corner so I wouldn't distract them. Malcolm would be all right. He had to be.

By the time we reached the hospital, I'd started pinching the fold of skin between my thumb and forefinger to keep myself awake. I'd begun to, not hallucinate exactly, but make bargains with God. If I could stay awake, He'd save Malcolm. If I could keep count of my breaths, He'd save Malcolm. My religious beliefs were so unformed, I had no idea if it worked that way, though I felt it probably didn't. But there was nothing I could do for Malcolm but pray and make irrational bargains.

The ambulance came to a stop. The EMTs slid the stretcher out with practiced efficiency, popped the wheels down, and ran with Malcolm through the doors into the emergency room. The woman who'd helped me guided me out of the ambulance, and I followed the others more slowly, leaving my sodden blanket behind. My ankle throbbed and felt like it was twice its normal size. Maybe somebody here could take care of that.

I hadn't been in very many hospitals in my life, and never in the back rooms of the ER, which was what this looked like. At least, the ambulance had pulled up at a door marked AMBULANCE ONLY and I could see the driveway went on up a slope to where I guessed the front of the hospital was. It was bright, too bright to my dark-adjusted eyes, with fluorescent lights lining the ceiling and walls painted some light color that made everything brighter. Probably the doctors needed all that light to see their patients clearly, but it just made my head hurt. I knew people always said hospitals smelled of antiseptic, but I couldn't smell anything but rainwater and blood.

A woman in hospital scrubs came toward me and put a gentle hand on my shoulder, nodding at my helper. "Let's get you fixed up, shall we?"

"Wait, where's Malcolm? I need—"

"Your husband will be just fine. You need to let the doctors take a look at him." The woman steered me toward one of the doors and into a small room with an adjustable bed and a curtain on rails half-circling it. "You've taken a bad blow to the head and it looks like your ankle is damaged. Let's just check your eyes, all right?"

She shone a penlight into my eyes without waiting for my assent. "Hmm, I don't think you have a concussion. Do you feel dizzy? Headache? Maybe double vision?" I confirmed all but the last. "Let's get this cut taken care of, and we'll check that ankle, make sure it's nothing more serious than a sprain. Then you can rest, and in a little while they'll take you to be with your husband."

"Boyfriend."

"Ah. Your boyfriend, then."

Her eyes went distant suddenly, as if she were listening to something. "I guess they're calling me," she said, to my confusion. "It will just take a minute, if you don't mind waiting." She left the room, drawing the curtain to encircle the bed.

I sat back farther on the bed, letting my legs dangle, and closed my eyes to dispel the dizziness. That had been strange. Or maybe my symptoms included selective deafness. My ankle hurt badly enough now I didn't worry about falling asleep; it wouldn't let me.

The door opened. "We don't have much time," Derrick said, making my eyes fly open in surprise. "Lie down so I can assess the damage."

"That woman will come back any minute."

"Quincy sent her on a wild goose chase, following the sound of pages all across the ER. Now, don't speak." Blessed pain-free numbness filled my entire body, making me want to weep with sheer joy. "Okay, there's the cut, the sprained ankle, a couple of strained tendons, and that lump where you hit your head, but nothing else. I have to do this fast, Helena, and it's going to hurt, so hold my hand and don't be afraid to crush it."

I took his hand, my addled brain marveling at the contrast between his dark skin and the pallor of mine. Almost before I'd gotten a firm grip, pain struck me as rapidly as the numbness had. I bore down on Derrick's hand and bit back a scream. Tears flowed down my cheeks. After an eternity, the pain subsided, and I let go of Derrick and wiped my eyes. "Thanks."

"I'm sorry it hurts, but you can't look like you were in a car accident. And you have to get out of here *now*."

"I thought the woman was going to be gone for a while."

"It's not her you have to worry about. Campbell's car has a signal in it that goes off if anything happens to it. It notifies Campbell Security that he needs help. It's only going to be a matter of hours, possibly a lot sooner than that, before somebody shows up wanting to know where Campbell is. And they absolutely can't find you here, unless you feel like having your secret shouted to the world."

"Derrick, I can't leave him! What if he..." I couldn't bring myself to say it.

"You can't help him now. I swear I'll call you the second we have news. Now, do you have a ride?"

I shivered again. "Viv's coming for me."

Derrick cursed. "That thing she drives is extremely recognizable. Call her and have her meet you at the top of the ramp, in the back of the parking lot." He took my elbow and hustled me out the door as I fumbled with my phone.

The rain had almost stopped, faded to a drizzle that depressed me more than the pouring rain had. Derrick hugged me, cursed, and said, "You're soaked to the bone, and you're covered with blood. Go home and get warmed up. I will call you." He took me by the shoulders and made me look at him. "Campbell's done tours of duty in places that make Afghanistan look like the Rose Parade. He will survive this. Don't worry about him."

"All right," I said, though privately I thought *How can I* not *worry about him?*

The little driveway led up to the back corner of the parking lot. I huddled against the building and hoped no ambulance would come in before Viv arrived, no crew of EMTs asking helpful, maddening questions. My mind wouldn't let go of my last glimpse of Malcolm's still, bloody face. If he died...I wouldn't even be able to mourn him publicly. Almost no one would ever know what he'd meant to me. He couldn't die. He just couldn't.

Headlights flashed, and I shrank back, hoping I could avoid

notice, but it was Viv in her old Econoline van, pulling up to a halt beside me. "I feel like I'm driving a getaway car," she said. "Hurry, let's get you home."

For once, the erratic heating in Viv's van was working, and stepping into the cab was like entering a warm, comforting bubble. Viv turned off the radio, which was playing something by Motion City Soundtrack, and said, "Are you all right?"

"Derrick healed me, but—" I burst into noisy, messy sobs, curled up on the seat and cried while Viv tried helplessly to calm me down. There was nothing she could do. All the fear and misery I'd had bottled up inside me came out in a river of tears. I pressed my wet face against the window and shook with great, shuddering breaths. "Better now," I gasped.

"You were totally entitled to that crying meltdown," Viv said. "Can you tell me what happened?"

"There's not much to tell that I didn't say already. Malcolm had some kind of heart attack, the car went out of control, we crashed, and then someone ran into us. It's just the reality of those things that give them such weight. Telling you about it is anticlimactic."

"Isn't Malcolm too young for a heart attack?"

"I don't know. I think so. But it couldn't have been anything else, could it?"

Viv's brow furrowed in confusion. "A stroke? But you'd think he'd be too young for that, too. Some kind of poison?"

"Not in my mom's food. And I ate everything he did, so I'd be poisoned too."

Viv pulled into the parking lot behind Abernathy's. "Do you want me to come up with you?"

"...Yes?"

Viv sighed, then hugged me hard. "I'm so sorry," she whispered. "It's going to be all right."

"I wish people would stop saying that. If it isn't all right, it's going to be so much worse if I had my hopes up."

"I know. But the truth is, even the worst things pass. And there's no reason to believe Malcolm won't have the best of care, and he survived to reach the hospital, so I think saying it's going to be all right isn't unreasonable." She patted my head. "Let's go upstairs, and you can take a hot bath, and I'll make some herbal tea, and I'll sit with you until you fall asleep."

"I don't think I can sleep until Derrick calls." I unlocked the back door of Abernathy's and let us both in to trudge up the stairs to my apartment.

"*I* think," Viv said, "you'll fall asleep in the tub."

Which I almost did. I dozed off in the hot water, woke before I could drown, then curled up in my pajamas and bathrobe under my covers and let Viv rub my feet until I fell asleep for real. My last thought, as I drifted off, was *Derrick's taking an awfully long time to call,* but I was too exhausted to let it disturb me.

3

My ringtone woke me out of shallow sleep in which my dreams were disjointed memories of slewing across the freeway and flying into the concrete barrier. Fumbling around, I finally snatched my phone up. "Derrick?"

"No," Lucia said, "but that tells me half of what I need to know. Are you all right?"

"I'm fine. Why are you calling at—Lucia, it's four in the morning!" That was nearly six hours after the accident. Why hadn't Derrick called yet?

"I'm not going to ask you details about what you were doing earlier," Lucia said. "You don't want to tell me and I don't want to know. Just answer yes or no: were you in a car accident around ten?"

"Yes." What was she getting at?

"Were you with anybody else?"

"Yes."

"Was he driving?"

"Yes."

"This is the important one, Davies: did he have some kind of heart attack that caused the accident?"

"Yes, but how did—"

"I'll call you later." She hung up.

I stared at my phone, my fingers curled around it like a life line. I was fairly certain Lucia knew Malcolm and I were together, in contravention of the Accords, but she'd never asked and I'd never told. I suspected that she, as another custodian of a Neutrality, was unwilling to turn me over to the Board, either because we were friends or because she didn't like the Board much. But those questions were oblique even by Lucia's standards. It sounded like she already knew about the accident and was going for confirmation.

I put my phone away and lay curled up on my side, staring at it, willing it to ring again. Maybe I should call Derrick—or would that be bad? Surely he and Olivia and Hector, the rest of Malcolm's team, weren't the only ones waiting at the hospital for news. Derrick wouldn't be able to speak freely in front of Malcolm's mother, for one. I wiped away a couple of tears. There was nothing I could do but wait.

My short sleep had refreshed me, though I was still achy from Derrick's healing. I slouched into my living room, dragging my quilt with me, and curled up on the couch, setting my phone on the end table where I could keep an eye on it. I could watch a movie—but everything reminded me of Malcolm. I wiped away a few more tears and cursed myself for being stupid. Derrick would call.

I rested my head on the arm of the couch and closed my eyes. In six hours, the store would open, and I would have to behave as if nothing were wrong. No, not exactly; the world knew Malcolm and I were friends, and of course I could be upset at my friend being so badly injured. But I needed to control myself. Which would be easier if Derrick would *just call already*.

I cursed again, this time aloud, and sat up. I couldn't sit here alone with my thoughts. I got up and put in *Vertigo*, which wasn't my favorite Hitchcock film, but had the advantage of being one of the movies I'd never watched with Malcolm. I made myself some popcorn and a big mug of hot chocolate and settled in to watch.

Right when the truth about Madeleine Elster is revealed, my

phone rang. I spilled what was left of my popcorn and snatched it up. "Where are you?" Judy demanded.

"A...at home?" I stammered.

"You weren't with him when he crashed his car?"

"I was. Derrick got me out. You heard about that?"

"Reports have been coming in all night. All Nicolliens, of course, until the news broke that Campbell was taken to the ER. You're all right?"

"I'm fine now. Is Malcolm all right? What have you heard?" Tension gripped me in a tight fist.

"Nothing more than that. It's all the deaths that everyone's worried about."

"Deaths?" The tension increased.

Judy let out a deep sigh. "Something happened around ten o'clock last night that killed dozens of magi. Father's still sorting through the reports. They just collapsed, like—"

"A heart attack?"

Judy paused briefly. "So Campbell experienced it too? But he survived."

"So far." Tears choked me. "I don't know if he's still alive."

"Is Derrick with him?"

"I think so."

"Then he'll let you know when there's news. You shouldn't worry about it. That won't help him."

"*Nothing* I can do will help!" I found myself on my feet, shouting at my phone. "I can't be there for him, I can't work magic, all I can do is sit here and *wait*!"

"I know. I'm sorry. I wish I could help. Do you want me to come over?"

"No. I'm sorry I yelled. Besides, your father probably needs you." The strangeness of Judy's news struck me. "Did you say *dozens* of magi?"

"All of them steel magi, too. We think something might have gone wrong with their aegises. Thank God it's not just the Nicolliens."

"You *want* more magi to die?"

"Of course not!" Judy sounded exasperated, as if she, too, was near the breaking point. "I'm just saying we don't need any more friction between the factions, after what happened with the familiars at Christmas. Father was frantic right up until we heard about Campbell. Then he gave Parish a call and learned this thing struck both sides equally."

"But Malcolm survived."

"So did a lot of people. And not all the steel magi were affected."

I dropped onto my couch. "What do you mean?"

"Once it was clear it was the steel aegis that was the problem, Father had his people start calling all the Nicollien steel magi. And some of them were just fine. So maybe it's the batch of aegises, or who performed the Damerel rites to implant them—"

I swiveled to lie back on the couch. It was a relaxed pose, but I felt nothing like relaxed. "That makes sense. I guess Mr. Rasmussen won't know until he's got more information."

"He's got people working on that. The house is full of them, which is why I'm awake to call you. I'm really glad you weren't hurt. We heard Campbell's car was totaled and there were three other cars in the pile-up."

I shook my head, though she couldn't see me. "There was only one other car, and I don't think they were hurt badly. I hope they weren't. I was in shock, and it was raining so hard, and...Judy, he looked dead. I don't want that to be my last memory of him."

"It won't be. He's going to be fine. There were a lot of steel magi whose aegises failed who didn't die."

"I bet most of them weren't on the freeway when it happened."

"No." Judy let out a deep breath. "I really can come over if you want company."

"I'm just trying to relax enough to sleep again. I keep waking up thinking my phone is ringing."

"I won't keep you, then. I'll come over around eight and I'll bring breakfast, so don't worry about that."

"Thanks, Judy."

I put my phone down and closed my eyes. Derrick would call—

The phone rang. Not Derrick—Lucia. "Have you heard anything?" I demanded, sitting up abruptly.

"Not about Campbell. I take it no one's called you either."

"No." My voice shook, and I swallowed to get myself under control.

"Sorry to hear that, but I've got worse problems. And so do you."

That chilled me. "What do you mean? Did someone see me with...someone they shouldn't?"

"Not that kind of problem. A lot of magi died tonight just after ten, all of them experiencing some kind of heart trauma. Not just here—all over the world. Lots more than that had heart attacks that didn't kill them outright. All of them were steel magi."

"I know. Judy told me."

"Did she tell you not all steel magi were affected?"

"Yeah. She said they think it's a flaw in the aegises."

"Maybe. I'm not so sure." Lucia's Italian accent was stronger than usual, her words slow and deliberate.

"What else could it be?"

Her words became even more deliberate. "Think about it, Davies. Only steel magi, the front line fighters in the Long War, are affected, but not all of them. And every one of them was hit at the exact same time. To me, that doesn't sound like an incident. It sounds like an attack."

It took me a moment to understand. "You mean...something by the invaders? The ones the Board and I encountered last Christmas?"

"Or their human allies, more likely. They wouldn't have included their own steel magi in the attack. I'll bet you my next month's paycheck we won't find a single magus with the marker among the victims."

I nodded. "I wouldn't take that bet." Intelligent, monstrous invaders had contacted the Board and me almost three months ago and revealed the existence of a shadow cabal of magi that had infiltrated the Wardens. The Board had discovered a neurological marker that indicated someone had made deals with the invaders and was a traitor. Unfortunately it was a marker that occurred naturally in about one in three people, so it wasn't a useful test on its own.

"If I'm right," Lucia said, "it's going to be nearly impossible to keep the shadow cabal a secret. Bad enough not being able to purge the Gunther Node without giving everything away. It's getting harder to keep track of who's allowed to know what."

"What would you do if you were allowed to...purge?"

"Imprison a lot of people. Have trials. Execute some people."

I shuddered at her casual tone of voice. "I couldn't do that."

"If it came down to a choice between the life of an innocent and the life of a traitor, you could." Lucia's cold, flat statement disturbed me, the more so because I couldn't say she was wrong. "Anyway, I called Ragsdale after I talked to you last and let him know my theory. He's going to gather the Board and come up with a plan. That plan will almost certainly be 'figure it out, Pontarelli.'" She sighed. "I almost wish they'd never brought me in on this."

"You were a natural choice, once they'd cleared you of complicity. And they know you don't like them and aren't likely to just tell them what they want to hear." Lucia had been the first person the Board brought in on the secret, before me, who'd encountered one of the intelligent invaders personally. She'd spent the last three months slowly and secretly cleaning house at the Gunther Node and had been about to start in on the factions. This would certainly change her plans.

"Yeah, well, that doesn't mean I have to like it. I'm telling you because I'll be sending over a bunch of augury requests in the morning and I want you to be prepared. You're to give those priority over anything else, understand?"

"I will. Is there any other way I can help?"

"You don't think that's enough? Davies, I'd go crazy if I thought the oracle might be corrupted. Just knowing you know the secret is a reassurance."

I sighed. "I hate not knowing which of my customers is a traitor. But I hate even worse knowing there's a possibility that some of them could be invaders wearing human suits."

"We've almost got a solution for that. The problem is installing it without Campbell Security getting suspicious at us doing an end-run around them."

Her mention of Campbell Security sent a new pang of fear through me. "You ought to investigate them. They're powerful enough that if they are corrupt somehow, they could do a lot of damage. Not that I believe they're corrupt."

"Don't take this the wrong way, Davies, but at least you know for sure a certain someone isn't one of the shadow cabal."

"Thanks, Lucia, that's *so* cheering."

"Hey, I did tell you not to take it the wrong way. I'm looking at it as having cleared over two hundred local magi of complicity with the invaders. Unfortunately, far too many of them lost their lives in the process."

"That's sort of cold, even for you."

Lucia gave a humorless snort of laughter. "I'm not saying I wanted this to happen. That's far too high a price to pay. Right now I've got my trusted people working on figuring out *how* it happened."

"I didn't know magic that big was even possible."

"Possible, yes. Practical, no. There are no records of magic on that level ever being done. I'm also grateful they didn't try this a month ago, when I still didn't know which of my people I could trust. I'd have been completely incapable of running this investigation." She cleared her throat. "And speaking of trusting people...you should probably know Ewan Campbell was not among the victims last night."

Ewan. Malcolm's younger brother. "That doesn't mean he's one of the bad guys."

"No, but it doesn't automatically clear him, either. Just be aware."

She hung up abruptly, leaving me gaping at the phone. If Ewan were a traitor...he and Malcolm weren't close, but family was family and Ewan was high up in the hierarchy of Campbell Security. Which could mean the company wasn't safe, after all.

I'd left the movie paused in the middle of a scene transition, one picture overlapping the other. It felt appropriate for how I felt now.

There was the world everyone knew, the one in which magic was imaginary and monsters a thing of story. There was the magical world, where men and women fought the Long War against monstrous invaders from some other reality. And then there was the shadow world, in which some of those men and women concealed their true natures as they worked with those invaders to defeat those who called them friends.

I was one of the few who could see all three worlds, and it was an enormous burden. I hadn't even been allowed to tell Malcolm the truth. Maybe that would change now it was clear he wasn't one of the shadow cabal, as the Board referred to them. Assuming he...I dropped my phone on the couch and buried my face in my hands. *Derrick, call.*

The phone rang.

I snatched it up and saw Derrick's name. My heart started pounding like a timpani. "Derrick?"

"He's all right," Derrick said, and the room swam in my vision. "He was in surgery for a long time. The surgeon said—actually, he said a lot of things, but they had to operate on Campbell's heart and it was tricky. But he'll be fine. He'll be in the hospital for a couple of weeks, but I'll start healing him as soon as he's in recovery. Once we get him home I can finish the job and he'll be walking around like new. I promise."

"Thank you." I wiped my eyes. "Have you seen him?"

"He's still in the ICU. I thought I'd call you first. There's...it's not all good news."

"You said he was fine."

"He is, for someone recovering from emergency open heart surgery. But that's where the bad news comes in. The reason for the surgery was his aegis became fully physical. Not permanently—it was phasing in and out and causing a hell of a lot of damage. But they had to take it out. Thought it was a sliver of metal from the crash."

The dizziness returned. "They took it out?"

"Yeah. It saved his life, but...Campbell's no longer a magus."

4

"But...that's what he *is*," I said. "He can't not be a magus."

"I know it's hard to imagine," Derrick said, "but he's lost his aegis, and that's what it means. And you know that's not everything he is. He's still a Warden, even without his magic."

"I know." I let out a deep breath. "All that matters is he's still alive."

"Quincy has an idea to get you in to see him, but it will be in a few days, once things calm down and he's not quite so closely observed."

"I'm so glad. Thank you. For everything." A horrible thought occurred to me. "What if he blurts out my name when he wakes up?"

Derrick laughed. "No worries. He's on a breathing tube that keeps him from talking or swallowing. It will keep him from saying anything incriminating before he comes to his senses."

"All right. Would you—"

"What?"

"Never mind. I'll tell him myself." What I'd actually meant to say was to ask Derrick not to leave Malcolm alone with Ewan. If Lucia was right that this had been a shadow cabal act, and if Ewan was one of the traitors, he might decide to finish Malcolm off personally. But I realized in time there was no way to explain all that without giving everything away, and much as I hated it, I couldn't assume Derrick wasn't a traitor himself.

"You'll visit him as soon as we can manage it. I promise," Derrick said. "They tell us we can go in to see him in a couple of hours. I'll keep you posted."

"Thanks, Derrick."

I disconnected and dropped the phone into my lap. It wasn't a total relief, but my hands weren't shaking anymore. I couldn't imagine Malcolm without his magic. Practically the first thing he'd done when we met was set something on fire with magic. He used it as naturally as breathing—though it sounded like right now, his breathing wasn't natural. It hurt, thinking of him in that condition. But he was alive, and—I curled up and cried great tears of relief and joy. Alive, and I would see him soon.

I abandoned the movie—I didn't really need to see Scottie Ferguson make over poor Judy Barton—and dragged my quilt back to my bedroom. Maybe now I could sleep. In a few hours, Judy would be here, and then my day would start. A day filled with Wardens tromping in and out of Abernathy's, filled with theories about what had happened and why. I would be very surprised if any of them came near the truth.

"I'M JUST SAYING it's weird that they all had heart attacks at the same time," Doug Schrote said. The Ambrosite treasure hunter had been hammering that point home for half an hour, and I was ready to beat him senseless with my copy of the Accords. Doug wasn't the sharpest knife in the drawer, but he was a dedicated conspiracy theorist and it was just bad luck he'd happened on a conspiracy that was real. Not that he knew this. Not that I intended to tell him.

"If the aegises were defective, they might have responded to a pulse of magical energy," Evelia Duclos said. Evelia was a lot smarter than Doug in every respect but one: she thought she could win an argument with him. "And those happen more frequently during storms. Or it could have been the storm itself. Electromagical energy is powerful."

"We get storms this time of year, every year, and it's never happened before."

"That's not a reason to go looking for a mystery, particularly when Mr. Parish is still investigating. So is Lucia."

Doug stubbornly shook his head. "If someone wanted to strike at the Wardens, taking out our steel magi would be a good first step."

"Someone, who?" Evelia exclaimed. "The mundanes don't know anything about us, and even if they did, they can't work magic. Unless you're suggesting it's invaders."

I successfully kept from cringing at Evelia's words.

Doug's jaw firmed up squarely. "No one knows where the intelligent ones went, but they have to be around somewhere."

"*Doug*." I put some force into his name. "I told you, it's $625. Pay me so I can help someone else."

"Oh. Right." Doug pulled several crumpled bills from his pants pocket. "You see it, don't you, Helena?"

I handed him his augury. "I think an electromagical pulse makes more sense than a conspiracy."

Doug scowled, but he left without saying anything more about intelligent invaders. I looked past him through the window, down the sunlit street at the spot where one of those creatures had abandoned the human body it was wearing and revealed its true self. What if Doug were one of them, and he was hinting at the truth as part of their cunning plan, whatever it was? I made a mental note to have Lucia check him out.

"Doug's a good man, but he lives in a fantasy world," Evelia said. "Don't be too worried about his fanciful ideas."

"I won't, Evelia."

I took her augury slip and retreated into the oracle. Had I looked more disturbed than I should? Most people today had put my distractedness down to my distress over the many, many deaths that had rocked the magical world to its core. Everyone was in mourning today, except maybe Doug, who didn't have a lot of friends. I'd had few customers, and those auguries they'd asked for had been variations on the theme of "what would So-and-so want us to do with his possessions?" It was a reminder that death could touch anyone. Maybe I needed a will. I didn't have a lot to leave behind.

Ahead, I saw the blue glow of an augury, and quickened my step. Evelia Duclos was the only one left waiting for an augury, and it was just after five. If I was lucky, no one else would come in, and the last hour would pass uneventfully. Probably I shouldn't entertain thoughts like that, tempting fate and all.

But the store was still empty except for Evelia and Judy, just emerging from the back of the store. "$475," I said. "Judy, will you take payment?"

"Sure," Judy said, pulling out the receipt book. "The accountant called. He wants to set up a time for him to bring over your taxes for you to sign."

I made a face. "Better now than later, I guess. It just feels wrong to worry about something so ordinary when so many people are dead. See you later, Evelia."

I went to my office, put my feet up on my desk, and pulled the office phone toward me, a putty-colored lump that was probably twice as old as I was. I'd caught Malcolm using it one night, while he was on the run for murder, and the memory made me close my eyes and hug the phone tight to my chest. I wanted to see him so badly—well, I'd just have to practice patience, something I'd mastered in the five months we'd spent apart. Mostly mastered.

I called the accountant and set up a time for the next day, then hung up, but I didn't return to the store. Could the oracle communicate on behalf of a dead person? It almost seemed like spiritualism, asking for the motives of someone who'd passed away, but the oracle hadn't rejected any of the auguries and hadn't charged much for them, either. It was things like that that made me think the oracle was alive, though not in any way that made sense to a human. It was a comforting thought after the day I'd had. So many of the dead had been friends, or at least acquaintances.

My phone rang, startling me off my chair. "Tell me you haven't heard rumors that this is some kind of enemy attack," Lucia said.

"Just from Doug Schrote, and nobody listens to him."

"Well, I've heard it from two sources more reputable than him. It's only a matter of time before I have to confirm it. When I do, I want you to be prepared for the fallout. I'll send some trusted enforcers over to maintain the peace. For now, I want you to send Judy Rasmussen to the Gunther Node tonight. Make up some errand. Tell her...I've got some confidential paperwork you need and I don't want to trust it to a flunky."

"I can't tell her that. She'll want to know why I don't get it myself."

"Then come with her. Just get her over here. I want her cleared before things go south."

"All right. In an hour."

Lucia hung up. "What can't you tell me?" Judy said. I spun around to see her standing in the doorway, her black-fringed eyes narrowed suspiciously.

"Um...nothing?"

"You are such a bad liar. It's a good thing no one on the Board has ever asked you point-blank about your relationship with Campbell. Who was that?"

"Lucia. She wanted you to pick up some confidential paperwork. I told her you'd make me do it. I just don't want to go alone."

"You're still not telling the whole truth, but that one's more plausible." Judy rolled her eyes. "Honestly, I don't want to go home for a while. It's just a reminder of death. Let's pick up Lucia's incredibly important paperwork, then get something to eat. Maybe Viv will want to come."

"I'd like that." The thought of spending the evening with friends cheered me. I felt some niggling guilt at enjoying myself when so many people were dead, but my being miserable wouldn't bring them back. "Let's just hope no one else comes in."

No one else came in. I called Viv and arranged to pick her up after our business at the Gunther Node. Lucia knew Viv was in on the secret of the magical world, and her only response had been,

"Why don't we just sell tickets?" which I guessed meant she wasn't going to kill me outright. But I didn't think Lucia's acceptance would get Viv a free pass to the inner workings of the biggest Neutrality in the Pacific Northwest. So I locked up the store at 6:02 and Judy and I got in my old Civic and headed toward the Columbia.

I let Judy drive. I'd never yet been out to the Gunther Node, or rather the entrance to the node, under my own power, and I only had a vague idea of where it was. "This isn't about paperwork," Judy said.

"Of course it is."

"There's nothing so secret that Lucia can't entrust it to Dave or Martin. What are we really going out there for?"

"Lucia just said paperwork. If she wants something else, she didn't tell me," I lied. I didn't know the details of the procedure that confirmed the presence of what Laverne Stirlaugson, chairwoman of the Board of Neutralities, persisted in calling the "traitor's mark," just that it was non-invasive and left the subject unaware they'd been tested. But Judy was smart enough to figure out something was off. What was I going to do if she wasn't clean? I trusted Judy with my life, and if she did have the mark, I was certain she was just one of the one in three who were innocent carriers.

Mostly certain.

"It better not be some kind of surprise party. It's not even close to being my birthday. And I hate surprise parties anyway."

"It's not a surprise party. I wouldn't do that to you, not after what happened the last time."

"Good."

We drove along a bumpy road paralleling the river, passing warehouses and barnlike structures. Planes passed overhead, taking off from the airport several miles west of us. A small white van I recognized as belonging to the Gunther Node passed us going the opposite direction, and then Judy pulled up to a small airplane hangar and parked just inside the door. It was completely empty except for us and another of the white vans, and colder than a March evening could account for. I stood next to my car, shivering and rubbing my arms despite my fleece-lined jacket. "How do we get in? There isn't anyone here."

Judy strode across the concrete, the tapping of her low heels echoing off the corrugated iron walls. I followed her toward a white circle painted on the floor. It wasn't perfectly round, but had squiggly lines and curves emerging from it. In an abstract way it looked like a flower wreath. Judy walked across it; I followed more carefully, not liking to touch the white paint.

An electrical box hung on the far wall, but Judy opened it and revealed an old-fashioned telephone handset. She removed it and put it to her ear. "Helena Davies and Judy Rasmussen," she said. She listened for a moment, then hung it up and motioned me to join her in the circle. "Hurry," she said, and I stepped inside just seconds before the world blinked, and we were elsewhere.

The new place was cavernous and made of poured concrete, easily three stories tall, lit by long fluorescent bulbs hanging from the walls and ceiling. It made me think of some Cold War military facility, or a nuclear power plant, but I doubted either of those would smell faintly of gardenias. Men and women hurried across the cavern, some of them pushing carts, others carrying papers or briefcases or strange equipment that might have come from a UFO.

Judy shooed me out of the circle we'd arrived in, which looked nothing like the one we'd left. "Ms. Davies," a woman called. I knew her only as Sue, one of the unaffiliated bone magi who worked for Lucia. "Come this way."

Judy and I followed Sue into a narrow passageway, lit not by fluorescent bulbs but by red-tinted LEDs. It wasn't the same route I'd taken the last time I'd visited the node, but then I had no reason to believe we were going to Lucia's office. Or maybe we were, and there were half a dozen routes to her office. The place was certainly big enough for that to be possible.

The passageway snaked along, taking us deeper into...it felt like we were underground, deep underground. There were no doors, nothing but the ruddy concrete walls, rough-finished, and the polished concrete floor that reflected the lights like tiny suns.

We walked for nearly three minutes, and the passage curved and doubled back on itself like some kind of intestinal system. I started to get nervous after one minute. This couldn't be a normal welcome. Judy had been to the node several times, and she had to guess something was wrong. I glanced quickly at her, striding along beside me; she looked cranky, but then she often looked cranky when she was hungry, which she probably was. She turned her head to look at me, and I smiled, hoping I didn't look suspicious. I needed to be a better liar if I wanted to keep myself safe.

Finally, we came to a door at the end of the passageway, matte-silver with a simple latch. Sue opened it and gestured for us to go through. It opened on a long, straight hallway lined with more metal doors, and now I felt confident, because I remembered this hall. I didn't need Sue's aid to find Lucia's office, but I let her go first anyway. Judy followed close behind me.

Lucia's office looked like a '50s bomb shelter, with a desk matching mine back at Abernathy's and a metal bookshelf crammed with papers and oddly shaped equipment. The plastic milk crates stacked against the back wall, also full of papers, had multiplied since I'd been here last. Lucia sat behind her desk, her fingers interlaced and resting on its top. Behind her stood her assistant Dave Henry. Dave held a strange-looking gun that looked like it had been made by the Tiffany Company from a design by Nerf.

"Took you long enough," Lucia said. "Henry?"

Dave took a manila envelope from the shelf and handed it to me. "That's it?" I said.

"That's it."

"Well, you sure wasted our time," Judy said.

"Judy—"

"Well, she did! Martin could have brought this to you."

"Maxwell's busy," Lucia said. She caught my eye and nodded, the faintest movement—Judy was clean. I felt like cheering. Something had gone right today.

It had been the faintest movement, but Judy caught it. "What's really going on here?"

"Aside from wasting your time? Nothing. This is important paperwork I need the custodian to sign off on."

"So do it, and let's get out of here." Judy scowled at Dave, who smiled pleasantly at her.

I opened the folder and took out the papers inside. As far as I could tell, they were pure gibberish, so I kept them away from where Judy could see them and said, "Can I borrow a pen?"

Lucia dug around in the top drawer of her desk and came up with a pen with a Hello Kitty bobblehead on it. I tried not to let the sappy cat face put me off.

"Hurry up, Helena," Judy said, coming to my side. I awkwardly shielded the paperwork with my left arm. "What's the big secret?"

"It's private, um, custodian business," I said, signing rapidly without paying attention to where I was signing.

Judy craned her head. "That's a set of instructions for Monopoly! What the *hell* is going on?"

"Here," I said, thrusting the papers at Lucia. "Judy, let's go."

"I'm not going *anywhere* until you tell me what's really happening here!"

I sagged. "Lucia..."

Lucia sighed. She held out her hand for the pen, then flicked the bobblehead, making it jiggle. "She'll know soon enough," she said. "You want to tell her, or should I?"

"*Somebody* tell me *something!*" Judy demanded.

"I don't know where to begin," I said.

"Take a seat, both of you," Lucia said. I promptly sat. Judy moved more slowly, keeping a wary eye on Lucia. "There's a group of Wardens who are working with the invaders. They're behind all the steel magi deaths. I had Davies bring you here so we could prove whether you were one of them. That's all."

I blinked at her. "I guess it was easier to explain than I thought."

Judy was wide-eyed and silent. Finally, she said, "I only believe you because if you were going to make up a story, it would be more plausible."

"Thanks. I think," Lucia said drily.

"You thought I was working with the enemy?"

"I didn't," I said quickly. "But we had to know, not just believe."

Judy blinked. "*You* knew about this? And kept it secret?"

"I had to. I'm sorry." Her tone of voice made me feel guilty.

"I'm just amazed you were able to lie so well. How do you know I'm not a traitor?"

"The traitors have a physical alteration," Lucia said, "a change in brain topography. If you don't have it, you're not a traitor."

"But some people naturally have it," I said, "so if you have it, you might still be innocent. And then there are other tests. Not nice ones."

"Is that why we walked down that insanely long corridor?"

Lucia nodded. "And why Henry is armed to take out the most powerful wood or steel magus. If you had the mark, we would have done a more...invasive procedure."

I shuddered. "How many people have you done that on?"

"Not many. The survival rate isn't good yet. We're working on that." Lucia stood up. "Sorry about the secrecy, Rasmussen, but Davies and I are both bound by the Accords on this one, and it's not the sort of binding you break."

Judy scowled. "I get that. It doesn't make me happy."

"Your happiness isn't my top priority. Now, both of you...get."

We found ourselves in the hallway before either of us could protest. Judy glared at me. "You could have said something."

"You don't really think that."

"...No. But I was trying to hold on to my righteous indignation for a while longer. How long have you known about this?"

"Since Christmas. I haven't told anyone. Not even—"

Judy held up a warning hand. "Don't say it here. Did you tell Viv?"

"I said I didn't tell anyone. Viv is part of 'anyone.' And the secret has been eating at me since then."

"It's almost too much to believe. Everything I've thought my whole life...how can I look at my friends and not wonder which of them has been lying to me? And what about my father? He can't possibly be a traitor."

"Lucia will prove the truth."

Judy sighed. "I need food. Something fattening. Let's get out of here. The smell of concrete is seeping into my clothes."

We found our way back to the cavern and collared a black-jump-suited tech to send us back to the airplane hangar. Safely in my car, I gave Judy the details: how an intelligent, monstrous invader had come to Abernathy's encased in a human body. How it had told me of the existence of Wardens working with its kind to defeat our side in the Long War. How the Board had sworn me to secrecy while they gathered their forces. "It's not a secret Lucia thinks we can keep much longer," I said. "Doug Schrote's not the only one who thinks the incidents with the steel magi weren't coincidence. And when the Board confirms the truth—"

"There will be a witch hunt," Judy said. "If Lucia can't prove whether someone's brain has been altered or is just naturally that way, people will start executing vigilante justice. Nicollien versus Ambrosite will be nothing compared to that."

I shook my head. "I'm officially overwhelmed. I'm done thinking about this. Let's get Viv, and eat, and talk about things that aren't death and treachery and magic."

"I'm having trouble thinking of anything else," Judy said.

5

On Tuesday they moved Malcolm out of the ICU. "He's recovering quickly," Derrick told me Tuesday night with a chuckle. "They have no idea why."

"But you can't just heal him outright. They'd notice that."

"I'm repairing his internal injuries, slowly. His heart is fully healed. He took some damage to his spine that I'm in the process of repairing. I think the nurses are under the impression I'm some kind of priest, with the amount of time I spend in there with my head bowed."

I laughed. "I think that's the first time I've laughed since the crash. Derrick, when can I see him?"

"In a couple of days. It's complicated. Try to be patient."

"I hate being patient."

But I didn't have much choice, unless I wanted to walk into the hospital in full view of everyone and ask to see him. It was tempting, but I hadn't completely lost my mind. I busied myself with auguries, though the number continued to drop off as the week progressed and news came in from all over the world. So many dead steel magi, and so many theories as to why. The popular one in Portland was that the magic on the victims' aegises had failed the way the alterations to the familiars had last December. Lucia told me the Gunther Node was swamped with magi wanting their aegises checked for flaws.

"They could have their own glass magi do it," she told me Wednesday morning, "but we have a reputation for excellence, so of course they have to come to us. And I don't mind, since it gives me an excuse to run them all through the test."

"You make them all walk that corridor? Doesn't that take a long time?"

"Beats thinking the node is full of traitors. What's worse is checking the ones who fail the first test. Like, for example, Ryan Parish."

I sucked in a startled breath. "He failed?"

"He's a steel magus who wasn't affected by the attack. And he's resisted everything I've done to get him in here. It's not looking good."

"Mr. Parish can't be a traitor. Imagine the damage he could do!"

"Already have," Lucia said grimly. "I'm going to have to take more drastic steps."

"Like what?"

"You don't want to know. I'm sending Maxwell over with some more augury requests. I just wish the damn oracle would answer questions beginning with 'who?' This whole nightmare would be over if I could ask for a list of names."

"What about that invader detector you were talking about?"

"For the front door? I don't dare install it until I know whether Ewan Campbell is a traitor. I wish—" Lucia sighed. "I need his brother back in action. Be ready for Maxwell." She hung up. *She* needed Malcolm back in action? I selfishly believed no one could possibly want him well more than me, but Lucia was right: with Malcolm proved not to be a traitor, Campbell Security could be brought in on the problem. If Malcolm were up and running the company, of course.

The bells over the door jingled. I made my way to the front of the store, taking my time about it. I was feeling a little tired from a couple of sleepless nights and wished more than ever I'd put a couch in the office so I could get a nap sometimes. Besides, Judy was probably there to entertain whoever it was while they waited for me.

"Welcome to—oh," I said, stopping as I emerged from the stacks. "Detective Acosta. How can I help you?"

Detective Acosta turned from where he'd been reading the titles on the spines of the books and smiled at me. "Ms. Davies. Good morning."

"Where's your partner?"

"I'm on my own today. I'm sure he sends his regards."

"That's nice."

The silence that fell ate at me like acid. Acosta and I weren't friends. He'd suspected me of being involved with murdering the previous custodian, Mr. Briggs; he'd suspected me of being involved in the disappearance of my ex-boyfriend Chet; he'd as much as accused me of being a fence...well, all right, there'd been some truth to the last. The point was he suspected me of crime, period, and I was pretty sure he had me on some kind of watch list down at the precinct, or wherever he lurked when he wasn't harassing me.

"So," Acosta said, "did you have a nice Christmas?"

"You came all the way down here to make small talk? Detective, I can't believe this is the best use of your time."

"Staying at a fancy hotel like the Grandison. That's got to be outside your budget."

He was smiling a little half-smile, the kind that says someone knows a secret and wants you to wheedle it out of him. I wasn't going to be drawn. "I'm frugal."

His smile widened. "So it *was* you at the Grandison. I didn't think there were any other Helena Davies in town, but it might have been some visitor. Thanks for confirming that."

Too late I realized my mistake. The Conference of Neutralities, which I'd attended last December, had posed as a conference of heating and cooling system salesmen. "How did you know I was there?" I said, opting to go on the offensive.

"I think I'll ask the questions, if you don't mind."

"I do mind, actually. Why are you prying into my business? I haven't done anything wrong."

"What was a bookseller doing registered as an HVAC salesman for a conference that brought attendees from all over the world?"

"Again, none of your business."

"I'm sorry. I should have begun by expressing my condolences over the loss of your colleagues to that rabid dog attack. I hope you weren't hurt."

"Detective, do you have a point?" My heart thudded painfully against my ribs, but I managed to sound casual and maybe a little impatient.

Acosta's smile fell away. "Ms. Davies, let's just stop dancing around. This bookstore, and by extension you, are at the center of something illegal. You and I both know it. I'm offering you the chance to confess to the truth. If you give evidence that will convict your employers, I can guarantee a reduced sentence for you—possibly even no sentence at all. If you refuse, you'll go down with them. Do you understand?"

"What I understand, detective, is that you're harassing me. You have no evidence and you have no warrant. You don't even have a partner. Does Detective Green know what you're up to, or are you on your own time?"

Acosta took a step closer. "Last chance, Ms. Davies. Tell me the truth. If you're involved with the Mob—"

I laughed. It felt good to laugh, even if Acosta had my insides tied up in knots. "I'm not with the Mob, Detective Acosta. Abernathy's isn't a money laundering business or a fence. We cooperated with the police over those stolen books last summer and they proved we were innocent recipients of stolen property. I don't know why you're so obsessed with Abernathy's, but I think you should consider whether it's really healthy to keep pursuing us."

His eyes narrowed. "Is that a threat?"

I blinked at him. "Um...no. I meant..." I didn't actually want to come out and suggest he was emotionally unstable. "I'm just concerned for your well-being. Since you were so kind as to ask after mine."

"All right, Ms. Davies. Just remember, I offered you a chance." He put up the collar of his coat and left the store, ducking his head against the intermittent drizzle.

I dropped onto the stool behind the cash register and buried my face in my hands. I so didn't need this right now. Or ever. How had Acosta learned I was at that conference? I'd thought their security was excellent—well, it was Campbell Security, so it had to be. Somebody needed to know we were compromised.

I pulled out my phone and called Timothy Ragsdale's office. I thought of him as "my" Board of Neutralities member because he was always the one who showed up when things went wrong around here. Ragsdale's secretary answered the phone after three rings. "Ragsdale's office."

"Hi, Monique, it's Helena Davies. Can you put me through to Mr. Ragsdale?"

"He's busy. Can I take a message?" Monique had a nasal Brooklyn accent and always sounded like she was chewing gum. I'd never met her and my mental picture of her was probably totally incorrect.

"Would you ask him to call me?" The door opened, and Jeremiah Washburn came in, smiling his brilliant smile. "It's about the last Conference of Neutralities."

"Will do. Later, Helena."

I put my phone away. "Hi, Jeremiah. Augury, or safe deposit box?"

Jeremiah blinked. "Wow, that was abrupt. Are you in a hurry to get me out of here?"

"No, I just...no. How are you?"

"That's more like it." Jeremiah unwrapped a scarf from around his neck and unbuttoned his jacket. Underneath he wore a red T-shirt that said NEVER TRUST AN ATOM, THEY MAKE UP EVERYTHING. "I'm going to take on a new familiar tonight, so I need a few things out of my box."

"I thought you said you wouldn't have another familiar, after the problems with them last December."

"I can't afford to stick to my principles with so many steel magi dead or incapacitated. I'll be more efficient a hunter if I have a familiar." The smile fell away from his face, making him seem a stranger.

"Wouldn't you be even more efficient if you were part of a team? That's not snark, I genuinely want to know. You and Becky Randall are the only magi I know who hunt alone."

"Hmm. Interesting question. I guess I've always felt more comfortable not having to coordinate with other people. And when you work alone, you're less likely to become careless." Jeremiah leaned casually against the countertop. "It's probably mostly because I'm a loner at heart."

"You seem gregarious enough to me."

"Just trying to keep up with Viv. She's a true extrovert, and I love it."

I hopped off the stool. "She's my best friend, but sometimes I find her exhausting. I'm glad things are going so well with you two. Um... they are, right?"

Jeremiah laughed. "Very well, for two people who are so very different."

"Different is interesting. You never run out of things to talk about."

"That's true. We need to find you someone so we can double date sometime."

Jeremiah wasn't privy to the secret. Even Viv and Judy knowing sometimes made me nervous. "If I find the right guy, I'd love that."

I took the keys off the wall. No one but I could touch them, but I couldn't help thinking, as I always did, that they looked like a security risk, hanging there in the open. I unlocked Jeremiah's enormous box and let him heft it onto the table in the center of the room. "I'll leave you to it," I said, and retreated upstairs.

My phone rang when I was halfway up the steps. Ragsdale. "Ms. Davies," he said. "Do you have information, or questions?"

I went into the office and shut the door. "A police detective—actually, Detective Acosta, you remember him?—anyway, he just came to the store accusing me and Abernathy's of being part of some kind of

Mob operation. The worrying thing is, he knew I'd been at the Conference of Neutralities."

"I take it he didn't know what the conference actually was."

"He knew I wasn't a heating and cooling salesman and thought it was suspicious that I'd been there, but I think that means he believed the cover story was a lie. He just didn't know what it was covering up."

"Interesting," Ragsdale drawled. "Do you think he might be a tool for our enemies?"

That was an interesting thought. "I doubt it. I think he really does believe he's going to crack this case wide open and bring a bunch of mobsters to justice. The other odd thing was his partner wasn't with him. I don't know why."

"We'll have to pay closer attention to our friend Acosta. He's not dangerous, but he is an annoyance, and he needs to be brought to heel. Thank you for the information."

"Wait!" I exclaimed before he could hang up. "What should I do if he comes back?"

"Ask him for a warrant, and refer him to the store's owners for any other demands. We'll watch out for you, Ms. Davies. Good day."

Well, that was sort of helpful. I tucked my phone away in my pocket, where it barely fit, thank you, girl pockets, and went back to the front of the store, where I sat on the stool again and wondered where Judy was. She'd made a bank run this morning, but it didn't take her that long to go to the bank and back. It was coming up on noon, and I was getting hungry.

Ten minutes later Jeremiah came trooping through the stacks, carrying a duffel bag full of things that made strange knobby lumps on its surface. "That's a lot of stuff for one familiar," I said. "What does it take to...what do you call it? Bonding?"

"Binding," Jeremiah said, setting the duffel on the floor. "This stuff is just to get the familiar used to me. Most of the hard work is done before I get there. A bone magus alters the invader's body to make it a little more terrestrial, then another magus puts the harness on it and seals it shut. The harness acts like an aegis in reverse, preventing the familiar from being able to use magic."

"All magic?"

"It can only use magic as directed by its owner. The binding attaches a familiar—technically, its harness—to a magus. That will let me wield its magic on my behalf. It also keeps the familiar from wandering too far away if it gets off its leash. Not that it matters, because it can't hurt anyone regardless of whether it's leashed, but tracking down a lost familiar could otherwise be a huge pain in the ass." Jeremiah buttoned his coat back up. "You really don't have anything to worry about."

"I killed half a dozen familiars who were trying to suck the magic out of my body. I know, it's different, and the bindings won't fail again, but I'm not going to like familiars no matter how safe you promise me they are. You don't let yours near Viv, do you?"

"I don't. But that's as a courtesy to you, not because I think she's in danger. They're just tools, Helena. We may make them look like animals, but they don't feel or think the way we do."

I remembered the malevolent gaze of ruby-red eyes in a face that saw me only as an obstacle to its plans. "I believe it."

Jeremiah picked up his bag. "See you later," he said, and bumped his way through the door, holding it open for Judy, whose cheeks and nose were pink with cold.

"Sorry that took so long," she said. "I met some friends and we..." She wiped her nose, and I realized she'd been crying. "We were talking about a couple of people who died, remembering them."

"I understand," I said, giving her a quick hug. "Look, if you need to go home early—"

"I'd rather not be home right now. Father's got analysts going over all the information he has on the steel aegis failure, and I'd have trouble not telling them the truth. When will Lucia let it all come out?"

"I don't know. She did say she proved your father innocent of treachery, isn't that something?"

"A small something." But she looked suddenly more cheerful. "What did Jeremiah want?"

"Safe deposit box. He's taking on a familiar tonight."

Judy glanced over her shoulder at the door. "Oh, I wish I'd known, I would have wished him luck."

"I didn't think it was all that complicated a ritual."

"It's not. It's just traditional. More now than before, given what happened with the familiars. I thought he'd sworn not to take another."

"That's what I said. He said he needed to be a more effective hunter."

Judy shrugged. "Let's have lunch. I'm starving."

The rest of the day wore on uneventfully. It was one of those quiet days I treasured as a memory for the days when it wasn't so quiet and the Wardens drove me crazy with their demands. The gray skies cleared around four, filling the air with sunlight that warmed the store physically and emotionally. I swept the floor without resenting it, for once; I felt contemplative, at peace with myself and the universe, and even my worries about Malcolm were at a distance.

I swept my way out of the stacks just as my phone rang. Derrick. I let the broom fall and snatched my phone up with trembling fingers. "Is everything all right?"

"Everything's fine. I'm calling to have you clear your schedule for tomorrow night. We can get you in to see him."

I gripped my phone more tightly. "What do I have to do?"

"Meet us at the far side of the main parking lot at Providence at 9:30. We'll show you what you have to do from there."

"This sounds ominous. Will magic be involved?"

"Of course. You'll be going in after normal visiting hours and... well, you won't look like yourself."

"I guess I might have expected that. You'll disguise me?"

"Sort of. They were looking for you at first—the brown-haired girl who came in with him."

"I don't have brown hair."

"Your hair looks darker when it's wet. Anyway, Madeleine Campbell became a teensy bit obsessed with finding you—who was Malcolm with and why was she so ashamed that she snuck away, but really she wants to know who he's dating that isn't Andria. But half the people who encountered you couldn't remember what you looked like, and the other half didn't think it was such a big deal. So she's backed off, for now."

"What did Malcolm say?"

Derrick chuckled. "He gave a good impression of a man whose memory was fuddled by head trauma. Said you were a girl he offered to give a ride to on account of the rain and he didn't remember your name. It was clear to everyone but Madeleine that he enjoyed rattling her cage."

"It sounds like he's regained his sense of humor."

"More or less. I did mention what a crappy patient he is, right? He's impatient and cranky as hell and I hope and pray seeing you will settle him down a bit. If he could get away with rising from his bed like Lazarus from the grave and walking away, he'd do it."

"Have you told him what's been going on?"

"Some of it. The general details, not all the mess about trying to figure out why the steel aegises failed. I don't want him more riled up than he already is, and knowing the truth...he'll just get more antsy to be well and out of there."

"I can't wait. You're sure it can't be tonight?"

"Quincy won't be ready until tomorrow afternoon. It's a powerful illusion and a complicated one. 9:30, all right? Don't be late."

I said goodbye and hung up. I wasn't going to be able to contain myself until 9:30 tomorrow night. I wanted to go *now*...but I could be patient. I'd have to be.

6

The clock on my dash read 9:27. My phone said it was 9:26. My impatient heart told me it was well after 9:30 and Derrick and Olivia were late, I wasn't going to see Malcolm tonight and.... I checked my phone time again. 9:27. I scanned the parking lot, which was about half full. I was the only car parked at the top of the lot, and I had a clear view of the front door as well as any other cars that might, for example, pull up beside mine and contain magi who could get me in to see Malcolm without being noticed.

The orange-red brick of the Providence Portland Medical Center was darker at night and the pillars in front of the main entrance seemed thicker than in the daytime, as if they were sentries guarding the patients' rest. Off to one side was the entrance to the emergency room, not the ambulance entrance but the one for ordinary people. As I watched, someone dressed in scrubs came out of the ER entrance and strolled up the sidewalk toward me. I shrank down, then sat up, unsure which action would make me look less conspicuous. But he just turned the corner and got into a sporty little Kia parked off to my left and drove away. Hopefully this meant no one would care that I was sitting here in my car, doing nothing.

I thought about just going in. Who in the hospital would care about an ordinary woman visiting a sick friend? But no, Derrick had said this was outside normal visiting hours, not that I knew what those were, and I was pretty sure the hospital would care about that.

A black SUV pulled into the parking lot and drove up the incline until it noodled up to my car. The passenger side window rolled down. "Get in," Derrick said.

I locked my car and climbed up into the warm cab of the SUV. "Hi, Olivia. Hi, Hector. Thanks for doing this."

"It's all selfishness," Olivia Quincy said, putting the car in park and half-turning around in the driver's seat. "We think you have a good chance of getting him to stop complaining at us about how long he's got to stay in the hospital. He's nice to the staff, but he figures risking life and limb together exempts us from the niceness policy."

"I offered to sit on his head, but they wouldn't let me," Hector Canales said, his grizzled hair all that was visible of him in the darkness of the back seat next to me. An enormous gun with a bell-shaped muzzle lay across the seat between us. Hector was no magus, but a weapons expert whose passion in life was designing and improving semi-magical weapons for use against invaders.

"No point killing him before he's in a condition to fight back," Derrick said. "All right. Quincy?"

Olivia extended her hand to me. She held a gold chain from which dangled an enormous gold pendant decorated with filigree, at least two inches across and half an inch thick. She took the pendant in her other hand and squeezed, popping it open to reveal a hollow space inside. "Take this and put the chain around your neck. You'll wear the pendant under your clothes, next to your skin—no, not yet."

She brought out a little gray jewelry box, the kind engagement rings come in, and snapped it open. Inside lay a pink and green origami butterfly, made of dozens of intricate folds with two tiny curled antennae topping its head. Olivia picked it up with a pair of tweezers and gently dropped it into the locket. It twitched its wings once. The antennae quivered. Then it lay still again. Olivia shut the locket and handed it to me.

"This will give you two hours of invisibility," she said. "It refracts the light around you so you'll seem like a heat shimmer. You're not immaterial, of course, and if someone bumps into you there's a chance they'll see through the illusion. Which is why we're doing this at night. That, and some Campbell or other is almost always at his bedside during the day."

"Which explains some of his irritability," Hector said. "Madeleine Campbell is enough to give me indigestion, and she's not even related to me."

I put the chain around my neck and dropped the locket into my shirt, where it nestled inside my bra and made a cool spot. "Two hours as of a few seconds ago?"

"Yes," Derrick said. "But Canales rigged the locket to start feeling cold about twenty minutes before the illusion is up, so you won't have to stare at the clock."

I realized Derrick's eyes were fixed firmly on a spot between my eye and my left ear. I glanced down at my hands. "Am I invisible now? Is seeing myself part of the illusion, or is it just my ability?"

"Your ability," Olivia said. "It also gives off a slight don't-look-here energy that will gently direct people's attention elsewhere. It *should* keep the nurses from coming in to check on Campbell while you're there, but don't be too dependent on it."

"I'll be careful."

"Oh, and one other thing," Derrick said as I was about to exit the car. "The door's sensors won't perceive you easily. One of us will trigger the doors for you on the way in, but you're on your own getting out."

"I hadn't thought of that. What do you mean, not easily?"

"The heat shimmer will set them off, but it's not very strong and you may have to walk back and forth in front of the doors a few times to trigger them. It's a design flaw, but it can't be helped."

I was too impatient to care. "I'll deal with it when the time comes. Shouldn't I go now?"

"Unless you have any other questions."

"I don't think so."

Derrick held out a small piece of note paper. "The room number, and how to get to it," he said. I took it from him, and he twitched, making me wonder how the exchange had looked to him. Had the paper vanished immediately, or had it faded out? Either way, it had to look startling.

We drove down in front of the doors, and Derrick got out and walked quickly toward the doors, outpacing me. I had to hurry to catch up. The first set of doors slid open smoothly, then the second. "Good luck," Derrick whispered, and turned around and left.

I stood for a moment in the reception area to get my bearings. It didn't smell of anything in particular and looked more like a hotel lobby than a hospital, with a sunken area just ahead of me filled with couches and chairs and a big square planter in the middle. To my right was the door to the chapel, flanked by a statue of Our Lady of Providence. The reception desk—was that what it was called in a hospital?—was to the left, and it was empty. So far, so good.

I followed Derrick's directions to the stairs, bypassing the elevators, which were all colored, blue or gray or yellow or green. I pictured them winding their way through the hospital like lines on a subway map. Though I was sure they didn't run sideways or diagonally the way the ones at the tribunal building down by the Morrison Bridge did.

At the far end of the hall, someone clad in black from head to toe appeared, heading my way. A nun, wandering the halls—I'd never seen a habit like hers, not that I knew anything about nuns except from movies like *Black Narcissus*, and probably most of that was wrong.

I walked a little faster, hoping to reach the stairs before she did. I had my hand on the door handle before I realized I couldn't open the door with her practically on top of me. I pressed myself into the recess and waited for her to pass. She was so close to the wall I was sure she'd brush up against me. She was looking straight ahead, not at me or my heat shimmer or whatever she might see of me, and I sucked in a breath and flattened myself as best I could.

As she drew even with where I stood, her steps slowed, until finally she stood in front of the door, inches from me. I watched her hand, tucked into her habit. If she decided to use the stairs...I'd just have to move quickly, and pray for concealment. Though it was unlikely God would grant a prayer said to counter one of His servants.

With a little shake of the head, the nun moved on, but I didn't let out my breath until I grew dizzy. Then I eased open the door and backed into the chilly stairwell, letting the door close slowly and silently in front of me. My footsteps echoed quietly as I ran up the steps, hoping nobody else was using them at this hour. I felt my precious minutes slipping away. I checked the time: just 9:37. It had only felt like an hour.

The second floor was as empty and still as the first, though the air smelled cleaner, with a hint of antiseptic. I passed a couple of nurses, male and female, having a quiet conversation, then the nursing station, where another nurse sat typing at a computer, but no one noticed my passing.

I looked at the paper Derrick had given me and began checking room numbers, my heart beating faster with excitement. This one... no, the next. I put my hand on the door's handle, glanced around to see if I was being observed, then opened it a crack and let myself in.

The room was dimly lit, the window blinds closed, but it didn't matter because I had eyes only for the bed in the middle of the room and its occupant. Malcolm lay sleeping, his dark hair tousled against the white pillow, and I stood for a moment, drinking him in. His right arm was encased to above the elbow in a cast that was propped up on a pillow, his face was scratched, and there was a bruise extending from his right temple down his cheek. The hospital gown, what I could see of it, looked comical on his powerful form. Tubes and wires extended from his left arm toward a couple of machines. He looked awful. He looked wonderful. I felt tears come to my eyes and scrubbed them away harshly. Crying was idiotic. And I was running out of time.

I took a few steps toward the bed and leaned over, gently shaking him and then snatching my hand away, remembering what had happened the last time I'd woken him unexpectedly. "Malcolm. Wake up."

Malcolm jerked awake, his right arm moving toward me, and he gasped in pain. "Helena?" he said. He cast his eyes about the room.

"I'm here," I said.

He swiftly turned his head and reached toward me with his left hand. "I meant to be awake when you arrived, but they give me pain medication just before bedtime."

"That's all right. I'm sorry about disturbing your rest."

"I'd rather have you than sleep. Quincy said you'd be invisible, but I somehow thought I'd be able to see you."

"I'd take off the pendant, but I'm afraid that would destroy the magic. I'm sorry."

His groping fingers found my elbow, then slid upward along my arm to my shoulder and then to my face. "So long as you are here, I don't care if I can see you," he said. "You're well? Tinsley said you were healed from the accident—Helena, I am so sorry—"

"Close your eyes," I said, and leaned in to kiss him. He smelled of soap and antiseptic, not at all like himself, but his kiss was the same, his lips parting for mine in a way that made me want more. He slid his free hand around my waist and pulled me closer until I overbalanced and had to put my hand out to support myself on the pillow beside his head.

"Come on up here," he whispered, shifting over awkwardly. He found the bed controls and the head of the bed began rising.

"You're sure it won't hurt you?" His face was creased with pain, and he closed his eyes once as if even that motion hurt him.

"Just don't lean on my chest or right arm—there."

I sat on the edge of his bed and scooted around until I lay in the curve of his left arm, my head tucked up against his neck. I put my arm across his waist and sighed with happiness. "I missed you. I was so worried."

"Not as worried as I was when I woke up after surgery and had no idea what had happened to you, and no way to find out. I spent—it was only a couple of hours, but it felt like forever before I saw Tinsley and he told me you were safe and unharmed. I'm so sorry, love. I should—"

"You'd better not be about to say something about how you should have driven us to safety. There wasn't anywhere to go on that freeway, Malcolm. You did your best to protect me while you were having a heart attack, or whatever it was. I don't blame you for anything."

Malcolm's arm tightened on me. "I'm grateful to be alive. I should be dead. Those surgeons worked a miracle."

"I wish I could thank them."

"I know."

He fell silent for a moment. I lay still, breathing him in as I'd done so many nights before. "How many died?" he finally said. "Tinsley wouldn't say."

"Seventy-six. Over a hundred more had attacks, but mild ones."

"So strange. All those aegises failing all at once. I've never known an electromagical pulse to have that kind of effect. It's frightening, to think it might happen again without warning."

I didn't say anything. I was struggling with myself. I'd thought about this all the way to the hospital, what I was going to say, and I still hadn't come to a decision. Lucia hadn't said I could tell Malcolm the truth, but she'd acknowledged he wasn't a traitor and she hadn't said I *couldn't* tell him. I just wasn't sure if it was a good idea to give him something else to fret about while he was trapped here. And maybe telling him was just selfishness on my part, wanting someone I could share the burden with.

On the other hand...Malcolm was smart, and ruthless, and if anyone was equipped to fight an enemy within the Wardens, he was. "It wasn't an electromagical pulse," I said. "Or, maybe it was, but it didn't occur naturally."

"What do you mean?"

I took a deep breath. "Remember Christmas? The Conference of Neutralities?"

"Of course."

"Well, Christmas Eve day, I had a visitor..."

I told him everything. About how an intelligent invader had entered the store in human guise, wanting me to work for him. About the secret group within the Wardens that was allied with the invaders. The marker that distinguished the enemy—sort of. Lucia's work to ferret out friend from foe. "She's convinced the event that struck down the steel magi was an attack by the shadow cabal—that's what Ms. Stirlaugson calls them. Whatever it was, it was the most complex magic anyone's ever worked. I'm sure Lucia is trying to find a way to defend against it, if they try again."

Malcolm was silent, his fingers stroking my arm idly. "Ewan wasn't affected," he said.

"No. Neither was Ryan Parish."

"There'll be hell to pay if either of them is a traitor. And I'm stuck to this damned bed, unable to do anything about it."

"Malcolm, *please* don't get worked up over this. I don't want to regret telling you."

"You did the right thing. This is something I need to know."

"Yes, but you're going to be in the hospital for at least another week, and I don't want you chafing at your limitations. Isn't there some more...intellectual way you can fight this battle?"

He laughed quietly. "Tinsley's been telling tales."

"He says you're a crappy patient. They sent me in here to calm you down. Possibly as a sacrificial lamb."

He laughed a little more loudly, then coughed, grimacing with pain. "Don't worry," he said, when I moved away from him in alarm, and tightened his grip around me. "My sternum is broken, and Tinsley can't heal it without causing notice. It hurts like hell when I cough, but otherwise it's just a constant sharp ache."

"I can't wait for you to be out of here so you can be restored to normal."

"Neither can I." He sighed, his warm breath brushing my forehead. "All right. I can be patient. But I need Lucia to clear the rest of my team. This marker, it only shows up in magi?"

"No, in everyone. Lucia says I have it, but I've already proved where my loyalties lie."

"Get her to clear the others. Then I can start cleaning house at Campbell Security. And if she can prove Ewan isn't a traitor...let's hope she can. If he is, tell her I'll deal with him myself."

He sounded grim, his voice flat and expressionless, and I shivered. "Cold?" Malcolm said.

"No. I love being next to you. I love you."

Malcolm kissed my forehead. "I love you. I wish I could declare my love openly. Though it would open you up to some unpleasant influences, namely, my mother."

"She can't be that bad."

"She's passive-aggressive and wants to run my life. Also, she thinks Andria would be the perfect daughter-in-law. You, a nobody from nowhere as far as Warden aristocracy goes—"

"There's an aristocracy? Malcolm, are you a prince? Tell me you're a prince. Though I'm not sure what that would make me. Cinderella, maybe. I've never liked that story."

Malcolm chuckled. "It's not that kind of aristocracy. It would be more accurate to say that certain families have lineages that reach all the way back to the founding days of magery. The Campbells have been steel magi for generations, and my mother is excessively proud of that fact, despite not being a Campbell by birth. Andria's family—Andria isn't a magus, mind—have been wood and bone magi nearly as long as the Campbells. That makes her a suitable match for a Campbell, i.e., me."

That irritated me, the idea that anyone might consider Malcolm a pawn in some genetic breeding game. "Why doesn't your mother marry her off to Ewan, if she's so hot on the idea?"

"She has someone else picked out for Ewan. He's dutifully courting the woman. I have no idea how he really feels about her, though he might actually be in love. But Mother likes her, so Ewan tells himself he likes her too. She—Mother—has been behaving as if they're already married. Poor Cathy is so awestruck she lets Mother boss her around even though you'd think, owning her own business, she'd be immune to that kind of behavior."

"I take it back. She sounds every bit as bad as you implied. How did you turn out so well?"

"My father."

His voice was even quieter than it had been, and I felt uncomfortable. "I know you don't like to talk about him—"

He shook his head. "Some of my memories are painful. Mostly I just miss him, as much today as I did the day he died. It was a horrible debacle—he was hunting an invader, and his team ran into a Nicollien team on the same trail. The Nicolliens had two familiars and gave them conflicting instructions that put one of my father's teammates directly in the path of the invader. My father stepped up to intervene, and the thing got in a lucky blow to his throat. It killed him almost instantly. The Nicolliens never admitted to any culpability in that disaster. I hated them for so long, them and their familiars."

"You seem mostly even-handed in your treatment of them now."

"I realized I shouldn't hold the entire faction to blame for the actions of a few people. But Brittany Spinelli—" He drew in a deep breath and let it out slowly. "We dueled, unsatisfactorily, and even now if I came upon her wounded unto death, I'm not sure I'd reach out a hand to save her."

"I understand that."

He shot me a keen-eyed glance. "Do you? I would think you'd disapprove."

I took a moment to think before responding. "I believe hatred hurts you even if the other person deserves it. But I'm not going to tell you how you should feel. I only want you to find peace, however you do it."

"You are remarkably wise. I love you, Helena. You see to the heart of things so clearly."

"Only for other people. In my own life, I sort of muddle along."

We lay together in silence for a while longer, until the locket lying next to my heart turned chilly. I kissed Malcolm, which was a mistake because one kiss turned into a dozen warm, passionate kisses, and every kiss felt like saying goodbye. Finally, I extricated myself from his embrace. "I'll try to come again," I said, unable to look away from his dark eyes.

"I hope you can," he said. "But I would rather you stayed free from detection. I'll be well soon enough, and then...."

I touched his cheek. "Good night. I love you."

"I love you, Helena. Be safe."

There were more nurses in the hall, and it took time to find a break in their pattern I could slip through. The locket was burning cold by the time I left the stairwell to hurry down the hall to the front lobby. This time, someone sat at the reception desk, though I couldn't imagine why anyone would need to at nearly midnight. Whoever it was had their head down over a tablet, but I was sure if I became visible, they'd notice.

I headed for the sliding doors and came up short when they wouldn't open. I couldn't see the sensor that would register my presence, so I ran back and forth in front of the door, hopping and waving like a lunatic. Still nothing. I tried pressing my hand flat against the glass, tried backing up and walking at the door slowly. No response. The locket was painfully cold against my skin. I rubbed it and felt a jolt run through me. My time was almost up.

I leaned with my head pressed against the glass. I was mostly out of sight of the reception desk; maybe I could run through when I became visible. Besides, what was the harm, really, if I were seen? My eyes focused on a bar that ran the length of the door at about waist height. FOR EMERGENCY USE, it read in black letters against a yellow background. Well, if this wasn't an emergency, I wasn't sure what one was. I put my hands against the bar and pushed.

Groaning, the door inched open, and I squeezed through the crack. I didn't stop to look behind me to see if the person noticed—I took a few quick steps and pushed on the second door, which eased open even more slowly. Free of the door, I ran for my car. Behind me, I heard the door shut, but no cries of alarm or warning. The cold feeling vanished just as I had my hand on my car door handle. I breathed out relief and threw myself into the Civic's front seat. Nobody had followed me.

My heart beating rapidly, I started the car and headed for home. I felt better than I had all week. I hated having to leave Malcolm, but things were what they were, and there was no sense pining over what I couldn't have. And maybe my visit had done him some good. If he could put his mind to solving the problem of identifying our traitor Wardens, it might keep him from fretting at his physical limitations. *I hope Lucia doesn't kill me for telling him.* But I had a feeling she'd be happy to have one more ally, particularly this one.

7

Rain fell steadily the next two days, a dull, chilly rain that seeped into everything I owned. The store stayed dry and warm thanks to its semi-magical climate control system, but that system didn't extend to the second floor. Saturday morning I stood at my upstairs window and watched the cars creep past and shivered. It was one of those days where it was hard to imagine ever being warm again.

A flicker of light across the street caught my eye, but when I looked for it, I couldn't see anything out of the ordinary. There were a couple of stores opposite me, two of them, like Abernathy's, with second stories used for storage or extra floor space. I didn't think anyone else in our neighborhood lived above their store.

There it was again—a gray flicker, like a piece of glass catching what little sunlight there was. It had come from a second story window two stores down from mine, a cute little consignment store owned by a couple of women I knew by sight but not name. I leaned on my windowsill, thought better of it when my arms came away damp, and pressed my face to the glass. The window in question was dark, and I couldn't see anyone there, but—there it was again. A lens, like a telescope or a camera, changing its angle and flashing light back into the street. Someone was taking pictures of my street.

I wasn't sure why that made me uneasy. There were lots of reasons someone might want pictures of the stores along this street. They were picturesque, for one, and then there were the people, who tended to be trendy and interesting-looking. But how good a picture could you get from behind window glass? It was odd, and I didn't like odd things. They rarely led to anything good.

I busied myself with cleaning until the store opened. Judy had arrived at 9:25 and grabbed the deposit bag for a quick run to the bank, with its shorter Saturday hours, and I swept the floor and dusted the cash register, my mind on Malcolm. When could I see him again? I didn't want to wait until he was out of the hospital; that could take up to another week, and then there was however long it would take Derrick to heal him fully. Maybe I could buy another of those butterfly illusions at the Beaverton market, where magi sold and traded their wares—sometimes even illegally, though Lucia's enforcers cracked down on that when they found out about it.

The door slammed open, startling me. "I'll be in the office," Judy snarled. "I have to make a call." She stomped away, furiously unbuttoning her coat and snatching off her tam, disordering her short black hair.

"What's wrong?" I ran after her.

"Those detectives are what's wrong. Father?" She threw herself into the office chair, her phone held to her ear. "I need you to do something about Acosta and Green. No, the detectives. They had the nerve to accost me on the street and—no, it's not like that, I'm not hurt, I'm just furious."

"Judy!"

She held up a hand for my silence. "They think you're some kind of Mob boss and I'm a courier, taking the store's profits to the bank for money laundering. They offered me a deal—well, it's not like there's anything to tell them. I just want them off my back. I know they've harassed Helena as well. And I'm tired of waiting for the Board to handle it."

I sat on the edge of the desk and crossed my arms over my chest. I felt as angry as Judy clearly was. Harassment was exactly what it was. Acosta, not able to prove his case any other way, was going after Judy and me. What would he do next—follow our customers, try to get them to confess to nonexistent crimes?

Judy sat silently listening to Rasmussen, whose voice I could hear as an indistinct murmur. Finally, she said, "We'll do that. Thank you," and hung up. She leaned back in the chair, which tilted alarmingly. "There. Let's see what happens when Father gets through with them."

"What will he do?"

"I don't know, but he has influence everywhere. I hope he gets them pulled off the case, or disbarred—no, that's lawyers. Anyway, he can cause serious trouble for them."

"Did Acosta and Green really stop you on the street?"

"Green did. At the corner where I was coming around from the parking lot. I'm sure his partner was lurking somewhere nearby. He knew I'd been to the bank and had all sorts of questions about our business—why we went to the bank so often, how did a bookstore do so much business in cash, that sort of thing. It would have been frightening if I hadn't been so angry, because he knew a *lot* about our revenue stream and far too much about me. I told him to get out of my face and came straight here."

I thought of the lens flash, and anger swelled inside me. I ran back to the front of the store and opened the front door, looking down the street at the consignment store. It wasn't open yet, and I didn't see anything incriminating, like Acosta or Green going through its door. The window where I'd seen the flash of light was dark. Even so, I felt certain we were being watched.

I shut the door, but left it unlocked, and turned the sign to OPEN. "I hope Mr. Rasmussen punches them in their smug faces," I said. "Metaphorically."

"He's got men and women who'd do it literally if necessary," Judy said. "But it's almost more satisfying to picture them called up in front of their captain and yelled at for persecuting innocent young women."

"That's an image that will keep me warm tonight. I almost want to tell Acosta the truth just to see his eyes bug out of his head."

Judy laughed. "Lucia would kill us both. It might be worth it."

THE RAIN finally stopped around two, just when the Ambrosites were lining up outside, and watery sunlight filtered through the remaining clouds. I kept an eye on that upper window, and occasionally saw a flash of light, but neither Acosta nor Green appeared. I wondered what they'd told the women who owned the shop—that they were staking out a Mob front, probably. I thought about going over there just to yank Acosta's chain, but I wasn't sure if that constituted interfering in an ongoing police investigation, and I didn't want to give the detectives actual cause to arrest me. So I watched, and fumed.

Derrick called just after closing. "I've been meaning to call you," he said. "Whatever you did, it worked. He hasn't bitched nearly so much about being trapped as he did earlier this week. Thanks."

"Can I see him again? Or is that too dangerous?"

"It's not really dangerous if you go after hours, except for the issue of getting past the doors. Just expensive. The illusion costs about a thousand dollars."

I gasped. "Derrick, how could you let me use your money like that!"

"It was Campbell's money, and I'm fairly certain he'd have spent ten times that without complaint. I was also thinking of the time cost. By the time Quincy gets another one ready, he might be out of the hospital."

"What about if I went to Beaverton?"

"You could do that, sure. Probably won't find one that lasts as long as Quincy's, but you could get an hour's worth of invisibility. And tomorrow's not a bad day to go. His family doesn't spend as much time at the hospital on Sundays. Madeleine's a churchgoer."

"How late is the market open?"

"Until ten. Look, just be careful, all right? Take Judy with you or something."

Wary, I said, "I didn't think the market was dangerous."

"The market isn't, but some of the sellers are shady, and they get nervous if they think someone's poking around in their business. Weird, since people have to poke around for them to sell their stuff, but there it is. Anyway, just don't go alone. Judy will know what parts to stay away from."

"Thanks, Derrick."

"Don't thank me. I'm acting from purely selfish motives."

I put my phone away. "Judy!"

"I'm right here," Judy said, emerging from the break room. "What?"

"Want to go to Beaverton with me?"

"To the market? Why?" Her eyebrows went up.

"I want to buy an origami illusion so I can visit my boyfriend illicitly in the hospital."

Judy rolled her eyes. "The things I do for my friends."

"We can pick up Viv and hang out afterward. Please?"

"All right. But I'm driving. You drive like a granny on sedatives when you're on the freeway."

"I do not." I wasn't about to admit that I was nervous about freeway driving after the accident. I sometimes woke from nightmares of slewing across ten lanes of traffic, pulling myself out of sleep just as a mile-high wall of concrete loomed in front of me. "But you can drive if you want."

I called Viv as Judy headed for the freeway. "Do you have a date tonight?"

"I don't. Jeremiah is hunting tonight. Why? Do you have some exciting adventure planned, counter to everything I know and love about you?"

"Are you saying I'm boring?" I said, pretending to be insulted.

"I'm saying you're conservative."

"Which is a longer way of saying boring. Well, I intend to buy an expensive piece of magical folded paper so I can sneak into a hospital and see the boyfriend I'm not supposed to be dating, how's that for exciting?"

Viv squealed. "Can I come? Are we going to that place in Beaverton you keep talking about? You'd better let me come or I'll never speak to you again."

"That would last until Monday. You have trouble holding grudges."

"That's true. Okay, come pick me up."

Viv was standing on the corner in front of her apartment complex waiting for us when Judy pulled up to the curb. In her turquoise peasant skirt that winked with dozens of round mirrored eyes, full-sleeved poet's shirt, and orange quilted vest, she looked like Hollywood's idea of a Romany, a gypsy straight out of a '50s Technicolor extravaganza. "I brought money," she said. "I'm allowed to buy things there, right?"

"It's like Abernathy's," Judy said. "If you know enough to get in, you know enough to buy the merchandise. Though I'm not sure what you'd want, where we're going. That part of the market sells mostly illusions."

Viv settled into the back seat. "I'll just browse, then. You never know what you'll find. I picture it as some kind of Arabian Nights market with all these booths and stuff. And one booth that sells nothing but pots and pans. There's always one of those in the movies."

Judy shrugged. "It's really just a strip mall. It has to look boring to keep the mundanes from interfering. But getting in is complicated."

Traffic was unexpectedly heavy on the way into Beaverton. It was a little after seven before we got off the freeway and headed west. "The market occupies a complicated patch of space," Judy said. "It changes depending on where you go in, so stores overlap with each other in multiple dimensions, I guess you could say."

"And we're going to the dimension where they sell illusions," I said.

Judy nodded and made a right turn. "This is where it gets complicated."

Off to the left, I saw a dispirited-looking strip mall with a wide parking lot about two-thirds full of cars. Viv pressed her nose against the glass. "Wow, is that it?" she said. "It looks empty. There's practically no stores there."

"That's what I see," I said. "There's nothing there that looks interesting. Isn't there an illusion?"

"Not the magical kind," Judy said, and made a left turn. "We have to go in on the far side."

The far side turned out to be another row of dull shops with one big dollar store for an anchor. Judy passed the first parking lot entrance and slowly nosed her car over the curb between that one and the next. She pulled into a spot between a little blue Ford Focus and an ancient pickup truck that had once been white and orange. "Follow me," she said.

The parking lot was in need of resurfacing, its pavement cracked in long zig-zagging lines with fat-leaved green weeds growing in them. Half the store fronts were empty, and the others contained merchandise that already looked picked over. There was a barber shop with an old-fashioned striped pole attached to the wall by its door, but it had a CLOSED sign in the window. I glanced behind me at the street, and the houses on the far side of the street. They weren't more than cracker boxes, painted a variety of colors according to the whims of their owners, but I saw a kid's bike on one lawn and the glow of a television set through one of the windows, and it reassured me. I'd begun to feel the zombie apocalypse had come and no one had bothered to tell me.

Judy headed for the dollar store, which was brightly lit and had posters in its windows declaring the day's bargains. I almost protested that I didn't need anything there, thanks, but remembered in time that it was a front for something else. The illusion—man-made, not magical—was so convincing I'd forgotten for the moment why I was there.

Inside, it still just looked like a dollar store. The bright fluorescent lighting cast a glow over the store's aisles, filled with cheap merchandise. Viv walked away from us toward the craft aisle. "I could really use—"

"This is just the front, remember?" Judy said. "Back this way."

We followed her to a door marked EMPLOYEES ONLY and pushed through it. Instead of the storage area I'd expected, full of overstocked items, there was a short hallway extending right and left. I caught a whiff of rubber, like we'd entered a tire store, but the hall was completely empty. "I don't know where to go from here," Judy said, "so I was thinking we could just ask around."

"Ask who? There's no one here," I said.

Judy pointed to the left. "This is how we reach the stores," she said, and pushed through a pair of glass doors that squeaked as they opened.

The hallway beyond was much wider, as broad as a two-lane road and paved with speckled vinyl tile. Above, the roof curved in a great arc set with skylights that had certainly not been visible from the outside. It looked like a regular mall—a boring mall with only one level and no bright lights or canned music. Storefronts opened on the hallway, and I saw a couple of people far down the hall exit one of the stores and come toward us. They walked past without acknowledging us and went through the glass doors, which squeaked again.

"So this is like the back side of all those stores?" Viv said. "And there's illusions that make them look empty?"

"Not illusions. The fronts of those stores are exactly what they appear to be."

"Right, because otherwise I'd see through them," I said. "Why not illusions, then?"

"Too expensive to maintain. It would be like covering the whole front of the store with hundred-watt bulbs and letting them burn 24/7." Judy started walking down the hallway. "Let's see what's here."

Once again I felt I'd stumbled into some weird post-apocalyptic world. The "mall" was brightly lit above, but each store had its own lighting as well, and sometimes the two clashed. I'd never realized there were different shades of white light. The place smelled clean, not fresh exactly, but not musty either—more like a room that's been shut up for a few days after a good scrubbing. It wasn't unpleasant, but I felt uncomfortable, out of place and awkward, like I'd entered an unfamiliar church and it was just a matter of time before the minister threw me out.

Judy passed the first store, which reminded me of Abernathy's, it was packed so full of books. I trailed behind a little to look at them and discovered none of the books had titles printed on their spines. They were organized in a rainbow swath of color, subtle shades blending into other shades, and I was so fascinated I didn't realize at first that Judy and Viv had walked on.

"You in the market for a prefab magnifica?" A young man emerged from between the shelves, dressed casually in jeans and a faded blue T-shirt with a Captain America shield on it. His lank blond hair hung around his face, which was long and had a prominent chin.

"Um...no. I was just looking."

He shrugged. "Don't wait too long. The best ones sell out quickly."

"Helena, come on," Judy said, startling me. She grabbed my elbow and tugged me along. "Those places don't have reputable sources for their illusions," she whispered. "I'm not saying they're illegal, but I wouldn't want to take the chance. Besides, that's not what you need."

We caught up to Viv, who was staring raptly at a display of dangling silver balls the size of large apples. "These are incredible," she murmured. "I want one."

"They don't last long. No more than a couple of days. Probably way overpriced, too," Judy said.

"What is it?" I asked.

"Look at—oh, right," Viv said. "They're like Christmas balls, only with little scenes inside. Like looking into a tiny house. You can watch the people making dinner, or playing games, or there's one with a young man dancing...they're so pretty."

"Let's ask here," Judy said, so I followed her into the store, which to me looked bare and empty except for some stacked shoeboxes and a wall filled with smaller ones. "Excuse me?"

"Yes?" said the shopkeeper. She was a middle-aged woman with glasses hung round her neck on a beaded chain that glittered in the low light of the store.

"We're looking for origami butterflies," Judy said. "I know you don't sell them, but I was hoping you'd know who would."

The woman smiled. "I might." She inclined her head toward a stack of boxes with a SALE sign atop it.

Judy rolled her eyes. "Thanks for your time." She turned and headed out of the store.

"Wait!" the woman said. "Hey, you can't blame me for trying, right? I have a business to run."

"It's smarter for you to generate good will by helping us so we'll come to you first when we need a delica illusion."

"*I* need a delica illusion," Viv called out. "Can I get the one with the ballet dancer? He's amazing. It's not too expensive, is it?"

"Fifty dollars," the woman said.

Viv whistled. "I have no idea whether that's too much or too little. Judy?"

"It's reasonable."

"Then I'll take it."

The shopkeeper, smiling more broadly, climbed a short stepladder to reach a box high on the wall. It was pink and looked the right size to hold a pair of My Little Pony sneakers for a six-year-old. She took Viv's money and gave her a receipt. "Activation instructions are on the box lid," she said. "And you can find origami butterflies at Mirage or Fata Morgana. Stores 843 and 821 respectively. Thank you for your purchase, and have a wonderful evening."

Judy scowled, but thanked the woman. Viv danced out of the store, clutching her box to her chest and twirling like the ballet dancer in her delica ball. "I love this place. Let's always come here."

"I don't think my bank account can take it," I said. "Derrick said the butterfly illusion costs a thousand dollars."

"I'm glad you know that, because some of these places may try to cheat us," Judy said. "I think that's Fata Morgana up ahead. Let me do the talking."

Fata Morgana, as I might have guessed, had an Arabian Nights feel to it. It was dimly lit and the air was filled with spices, cinnamon and cloves and something sweet I couldn't identify. It also looked tacky, with a couple of fake palm trees outlined with neon in tubs flanking the door. A woman dressed like Jasmine from Disney's *Aladdin* came to greet us, putting both palms together and bowing. "*As-salaam-alaikum*," she said in a bored voice. "How can I help you?"

"We're looking for an origami butterfly," Judy said.

"Come this way," the woman said. I'd expected her to sound like the character from the movie, but her voice was flat and a little nasal. It was disconcerting.

There was origami of all shapes displayed throughout the store, and by the sound of Viv's exhalations, the illusions they produced were on display as well. I found it interesting that a shop with a Middle Eastern theme to it sold Asian magic, but then Olivia Quincy wasn't Asian and she was a master of the art, so probably there weren't rules or restrictions saying you had to be Asian to do origami illusions.

Jasmine stopped in front of a display cabinet with mirrored doors and picked up something small from the counter. "Is this what you were thinking?"

It was a butterfly identical to Olivia's, though in purple polka-dot paper, and it sat in the woman's hand as if trembling to take flight. "How long will it last?" Judy said, sounding bored.

"Half an hour."

"We need something longer than that. An hour, maybe two."

"Those are way expensive."

"So you don't have them."

"I didn't say that." Jasmine put the butterfly down and picked up a different one. It was slightly larger and the paper shimmered in the light. "This one's guaranteed for ninety minutes."

"That's more like it. How much?"

"For you, $1500."

Judy glanced at me. I shook my head. "Too expensive," Judy said.

"I don't set the prices."

"Too bad. I guess we'll try our luck at Mirage."

"Mirage's quality isn't nearly as good as ours. They don't guarantee theirs like we do, either."

"But the price is better."

Jasmine let out a put-upon sigh. "I can let you have it for twelve. That's my lowest price."

Judy once again looked at me. I thought about it briefly, then nodded. Jasmine put the butterfly down and opened the mirrored cabinet, removing a ring box and popping it open to reveal a butterfly that was the twin of the one she'd showed us. "You know how to activate it?"

"Yes."

"Don't touch it with your hand or the magic is null. We don't do refunds if you void the warranty." She snapped the box closed and handed it to Judy. "We take cash or card."

I paid for my little treasure, and we left the store. "What other stores are there?" I asked as we headed back toward the entrance. "I mean sets of stores, I guess. Other than illusions."

"There's weaponry," Judy said. "Security items like alarms and things. Body-altering magic."

"What, like plastic surgery you do on yourself? Ew," Viv said.

"Nothing so coarse. A lot of it is first aid, but there's diet supplements, cleanses. A lot of that stuff is sketchy. And then there's the flea market. Magi bring stuff, non-magical stuff, to sell to other magi. That's...there are some magi who would prefer never to deal with non-Wardens, ever, and here's where they contract with other Wardens for services. It's a busy place."

I nodded. "Why isn't it a Neutrality?"

"It's not on a node."

"And yet Nicolliens and Ambrosites probably do business with each other here all the time." The thought irritated me. "Why didn't the Board use this as a model?"

"Who knows how they think?" Judy tapped the box I held in both hands as if I feared it might leap away from me. "When do you plan to use this?"

"Tomorrow night. Derrick said Sundays were quieter."

"Then let's hit the mall and do some real shopping," Viv said, "and get pedicures."

"You're sort of obsessed with pedicures," Judy said.

Viv hooked her arms through both of ours. "When will both of you learn," she said, "that pedicures are the solution to all of life's problems?"

"They are sort of relaxing," I said to Judy.

Judy sighed. "The things I do for friends."

8

I picked up the shimmering origami butterfly with my tweezers and gingerly dropped it into the locket. It twitched, then lay still, and I closed the locket and settled it under my shirt, between my breasts. I'd watched the hospital for about half an hour until I was certain it wasn't busy, and now I was ready to make my move.

I locked my car and trotted down the incline to the front doors. They didn't open for me, and I realized to my dismay that the emergency bars were on the inside. It made sense—they didn't want people to be trapped inside, not to have free access from the outside —but at the moment it was just frustrating. I walked back and forth in front of the door, waving my hands and occasionally jumping, but the doors stayed shut.

I let out a deep breath, then froze, because the air was cold enough for my breath to show in a thin stream of condensation. I breathed more shallowly and slowly, grateful no one was nearby to see my little mistake. The average person wouldn't think a little cloud of steam meant an invisible person was nearby, but I didn't want to take any chances.

I looked through the doors across the lobby and saw a couple of women headed my way. I backed up and to the side to stay out of their way—then an idea struck. I stepped back in front of the doors, bouncing on the balls of my feet, readying myself. The inner door slid open, then the outer door, and I raced past the two women, one older, one about my age, and slid through the inner door just as it was closing. My heart pounding, I stopped for a moment to catch my breath. Then I strolled off toward the stairs, feeling very proud of my cleverness.

The second floor was as quiet as before. I slipped down the hall and into Malcolm's room. This time, the door was slightly ajar. Malcolm was awake and sitting on the edge of his bed. "You look so much better!" I said.

"Helena?" Malcolm looked up. Astonishment swiftly turned to fear. "Get out of here, *now*."

"What—why?"

"Can't explain. Just get out!"

I turned to go. The door burst open fully and a couple of men in black fatigues came running in. I had to flatten myself against the wall by the door to avoid being run over. "Sir, the alarm," one of them said, but I didn't hear any more because as soon as the door was clear, I was out and running. I didn't get very far. More men and a woman, all dressed in black fatigues, came trotting down the hall toward me. I pressed myself flat against the nearest door, which opened slightly behind me, so I slipped inside, leaving the door ajar so I could hear and see a little.

The room I'd entered was empty, the lights off, and it felt safe—a false feeling, I was sure, if those men decided to search the floor for the intruder who'd set off whatever alarm was in Malcolm's room. They had to be Campbell Security. Why had they set an alarm, anyway? Not for me specifically, because there was no way they could know of my existence. But if there had been some sort of threat to Malcolm...

I peeked out again. The men and woman were gone, probably crowded into Malcolm's room like so many sardines in a can. If I was going to go, now was the best time.

I slid through the narrow opening and headed down the hall toward the elevator, moving slowly though I wanted to run. I still had to worry about being detected by ordinary people, of whom there were suddenly dozens, it seemed. Campbell Security had seriously disrupted the second floor. It took me nearly five minutes to get to the stairs, where I had another setback: someone dressed in the black fatigues of Campbell Security stood in front of them. She wasn't armed, at least as far as I could see, but she had the look of someone who could kill me with her pinky finger.

I turned around and headed for the green elevator, where I mashed the down button with relief at finding a way out. *Well, that was a waste of twelve hundred dollars.*

The elevator finally arrived, and for a miracle no one was around to wonder why it stopped for no one on the second floor. I stood off to one side and leaned against the wall. I'd have to ask Derrick why there was so much security around Malcolm—though he couldn't have known about it, or he would have warned me. I'd just have to be patient a while longer, and wait for Malcolm to be out of the hospital and fully healed. I hated being patient.

The elevator came to a stop, and the door slid open. I pushed myself off the wall, took a step, and had to fling myself backward to avoid the two women who got on. "—too far away," the older woman said.

"It's still inconvenient," the younger woman said. I edged around her, trying to get past, but she and her companion stood too far apart and too close to the door. They were perfectly configured to make it impossible for me to pass. Odd—it was the two women who'd allowed me to enter the hospital a few minutes ago. I stepped back into the corner as the door shut. I'd just have to ride the elevator until they got off. Fortunately, I had about seventy-five minutes of invisibility left. This whole evening was seriously annoying.

"I hardly consider his safety an inconvenience," the older woman said. "If they have caught someone, that makes it worth the time and money." She had a slight French accent and was dressed expensively in a fur coat, pantsuit, and pearls, and her black hair, which based on her age was probably dyed, was piled high on her head.

"Caught who?" the younger woman said. She was beautiful, with long dark hair caught back from her face with a diamond-studded clasp. "Thinking the episode was an attack verges on paranoia."

"All the steel magi, all at once," the older woman said, sounding weary, as if she'd had this argument before, and I had to control an astonished intake of breath. "I am not willing to take chances with my son's life."

"I care about his health as much as you do. I'm just saying it's unlikely anyone's going to attack him here."

The elevator door slid open, and the two women got off. Without even thinking twice, I followed them. It was stupid, walking back into that commotion, but I had no doubt the older woman was Madeleine Campbell, Malcolm's mother, and the younger woman was probably the lovely Andria. It was risky, but I wanted to hear more.

The two continued their conversation as they went down the hall toward Malcolm's room. I followed closely, staying in their wake so I could avoid the nurses and doctors in the hall. There was a knot of people around Malcolm's door, mostly Campbell Security, but a couple of people in scrubs as well. They parted for Madeleine and Andria, but I stayed outside. The alarm might still be active, and I didn't want it detecting me again. Besides, the room was crowded enough without adding me to it.

"—these people leave!" I couldn't see the speaker, but she sounded tired as well as authoritative. Probably one of the medical staff.

"They are here for my son's safety," Madeleine said. "He has been attacked once already and I want him safe."

"Mother, be reasonable," Malcolm said. My heart leaped at the sound of his voice.

"No weapons are allowed in the hospital. There's no way anyone can harm him," the same voice said. I could practically see the smile on Malcolm's face, knowing he didn't need a weapon to—but he couldn't anymore, could he? He wasn't a magus. Suddenly it wasn't so funny.

"Nevertheless."

"Surely we don't need *all* these people, *Tante* Madeleine," Andria said. She sounded so reasonable even I was nodding along with her. "This was a false alarm."

"I insist we post guards," Madeleine said.

"And I'm telling you what I told you the last three times you insisted on that," the tired voice said. "Mr. Campbell is not the only patient on this floor, and he cannot be allowed to disrupt the others. I was required to give you a room for your...men...and frankly I don't know what they were responding to, since the floor's been quiet all evening. But I won't let you treat this ward like your personal fief."

Silently, I cheered the tired woman. Standing up to Madeleine Campbell had to be difficult.

"I don't need guards, Mother," Malcolm said. "I would like to sleep, if that's all right with you." Dry sarcasm filled the air.

"You are not capable of defending yourself right now, Malcolm," Madeleine said. "Humor me."

Malcolm sighed. "Dr. Winston, thank you for your patience," he said. "Can we compromise on two men remaining? If they stay in the room you've provided?"

"I'd rather none, but it's been made clear to me my opinion isn't important."

"I think your opinion is very important. Thank you for your understanding."

The people nearest the doorway moved, and Dr. Winston emerged. She was a short woman with light brown skin and thick, curly dark hair who walked as if she were bearing a great weight on her shoulders. Was she Malcolm's surgeon? No, surely a surgeon wouldn't be doing rounds this late at night. But she was someone responsible for his care. I wished I could thank her for everything she'd done, but even if I'd been visible, she was walking away in the direction opposite the elevator, and soon she turned a corner and was out of sight.

"Caprelese and Johnson, you can stay," Malcolm said. "The rest of you escort my mother and Ms. Lemaire to their car. Thank you for responding so promptly to the alarm."

"Malcolm, are you sure you're all right?" Andria said. I didn't like her voice. It was too smooth, too cultured, too…and I was succumbing to jealousy like an idiot. Malcolm didn't care anything for her, and it was beneath me to think such negative thoughts about a woman who'd never done me any harm.

"I am tired, and I would like to sleep," Malcolm said. "Unless you'd like to sit around chatting some more?"

"Temper, temper, sweetness," Andria said, and despite myself I grew irritated again. Calling him "sweetness" like he was her property, and a child at that.

"Good night, Mother, Andria," Malcolm said. "Caprelese and Johnson, a word?"

I stepped back as Andria and Madeleine emerged from the room, flanked by men in black fatigues. Madeleine looked annoyed. Andria looked smug, like she'd won a prize. Curious about what Malcolm was telling his men, I sneaked over to his door to listen.

"—turn it off," he said.

"Sir," said the woman, "Mrs. Campbell was very specific—"

"I'm sure she was," Malcolm said, his voice low and steely. "Mrs. Campbell is always very specific. I, on the other hand, am the one who pays your salary. Until we can be sure there will be no more false alarms, I want it turned off. I don't want to be woken in the night by a room full of bodyguards looking for nonexistent intruders. I need my rest. Is that clear?"

"Yes, sir," the woman said. "But what if—"

"No more objections, Johnson. You and Caprelese turn off the alarm and take yourselves off to the room Dr. Winston so obligingly provided for you. It's within sight of this room and you'll hear me if I scream for help."

The two guards chuckled. "Yes, sir," Caprelese said. "Sorry about all this."

"Your response time was excellent. I'm adding a commendation to your records, all of you. Now—out."

I stepped to one side and waited. About a minute later, Caprelese and Johnson exited the room and went down the hall a short distance to another door, which they entered. I waited again. The hall was quiet, the nurses at their station busy with their own tasks. I eased the door open and stuck my hand inside, then eased the rest of my body in. No shouts, no pounding feet.

Malcolm lay propped up in the bed, eyes fixed on the gap in the doorway. "I hoped you were still here somewhere," he said quietly.

I shut the door behind me. "That was exciting."

"If they'd found you..." Malcolm ran his left hand through his hair. "Let's just be grateful they didn't find you."

I dragged a chair next to the bed and sat, taking his hand. "What's up with the alarm? Were you attacked here?"

"It's set to detect active magic," Malcolm said. "My mother has decided the failure of the steel aegises was intended to conceal an attack on me, and that whoever it was will return to finish the job."

My mouth fell open. "But—she thinks someone attacked over two hundred magi as a *blind*? No—*thousands* worldwide?"

"Mother has an inflated opinion of the worth of a Campbell soul," Malcolm said drily. "I am rather more concerned with the fact that she's intuited this was an attack and not an accident of electromagical energy."

"That's true. But if she thinks it was directed at you...who does she think did it?"

"Some Nicollien or other. We've made plenty of enemies over the years." Malcolm sighed and squeezed my hand. "Mother won't think past the general threat. Andria is more likely to reason to the correct conclusion. Fortunately, she doesn't care."

"She seems...nice?"

Malcolm chuckled. "You don't think that."

"No, I don't. But I'm trying not to be jealous of your ex-girlfriend. She actually sounds kind of self-centered."

"I love how perceptive you are." He raised my hand to his lips and kissed it. "Andria is rapacious and wholly self-absorbed, but she's also clever and committed to winning the Long War despite not being a magus. She's an excellent administrator and will make some man a terrible wife one day. Fortunately for me, I won't be that man."

Tension went out of me I hadn't realized I was bearing. "Your mother seems committed to keeping you safe."

"That sounds like a leading question."

"I guess it sort of is. Does she care about you, or about the business?"

"Insightful, Helena. I'm sure my mother loves me, insofar as she's capable of loving anyone, but she fears change and I think she knows, despite her affection for Ewan, that he's not as qualified to run this business as I am. But it's impossible to tell her, if he's not capable, it's because she's kept him under her thumb all these years."

"I'm starting to understand what you meant about how lucky I am in my family. I'm sorry."

"I have you, love. I feel like the luckiest man alive."

I shifted closer so I could lay my hand along his cheek. "You really are," I said, and kissed him.

We kissed, and talked, and kissed some more, for about an hour, then I hugged him one last time and made my slow, creeping way along the hall and down to the lobby. This time, I didn't bother with dancing in front of the doors; the reception desk was empty, so I just removed the locket and went out as quickly as possible.

Safely in my car, I stowed the locket away and waited for the car to warm up. So. That was Madeleine and Andria. Despite what I'd told Malcolm, I'd drawn some conclusions about the women, none of them flattering. Maybe it was just my loyalty to Malcolm, but it certainly seemed that neither Madeleine nor Andria really cared much about him. Since I cared about Malcolm very much, I felt inclined to resent them. Malcolm was no longer a magus, and he was going to need a lot of support when he left the hospital. Not because of his physical condition—I was sure Derrick could have him back to normal in no time—but because so much of who Malcolm was was tied up in his identity as a magus—an identity he no longer had.

Now that Malcolm wasn't going to die, I could direct my worries elsewhere, like wondering how Malcolm would cope with losing something so essential to him. Maybe I should get him to talk to Harry Keller. Harry had been badly injured by his familiar a few months back, badly enough that his aegis had stopped working and he'd lost his magic. But Harry seemed to be coping with life as a non-magus well...of course, he had his wife Harriet's support. Maybe *I* needed to talk to *Harriet*. Nothing direct, since Harry and Harriet didn't know Malcolm and I were together, but I could use Harriet's experience to guide me in helping Malcolm.

I put the car in gear and headed home. Or maybe this was all premature, and Malcolm would adapt to his new life with no difficulties. He wasn't even out of the hospital yet. He was strong, and capable...but I'd make plans anyway. It might not benefit Malcolm, but it would keep me from going crazy.

9

Wednesday morning, Derrick called as I was brushing my teeth. "He's coming home Friday," he said. "Then the real healing can begin."

"Will you be able to? I mean, won't people be suspicious if he comes home with his arm in a cast and then it's off the next day?"

"The cast has to stay on for a few weeks, unfortunately, because he'll be seeing his doctors for follow-up treatment. But I'll heal the arm so the cast won't be more than an annoyance. A serious annoyance, knowing Campbell."

"But he'll be well otherwise. His sternum, and all that."

"Better than new."

"I'm so glad. Thank you."

"He's put his life on the line for my sake too many times for me to begrudge him a little healing now."

"Derrick." I wasn't sure how to ask this. "He's not a magus anymore."

"No. And no, I don't know how he's taking it. He won't talk about it—steers the conversation elsewhere, or pretends to be tired so we won't bug him. I want you to see if you can get it out of him. It's a huge adjustment, losing your magic, and a lot of people...don't make it."

"What do you mean?" But I knew what he meant, and it chilled me. "You don't think he'd...take his own life? Just because he's not a magus anymore?"

"I hope not. I just want him to remember he's got a lot to live for, and that there are other ways of fighting the Long War. And I'm going to put much of that burden on you."

"That's not a burden. I've been thinking about the problem and I have some ideas. Mainly I want him to talk to Harry Keller."

"A Nicollien? Seriously?"

"Everyone likes the Kellers, Derrick. And he and Malcolm are friends. I think Harry might be helpful."

"All right." Derrick still sounded dubious. "It makes sense, I guess." He sighed. "I don't know how soon he'll be able to come to see you, but sometime after Saturday. He won't be able to sneak around the way he used to—can't make any more quick and dirty illusions—but I'm sure he'll think of something. Do what you can to get him to talk about it, all right? And call me if you're at all concerned about his mental health."

"I will."

I rinsed my toothbrush for a long time after Derrick hung up. I didn't think Malcolm would commit suicide just because he'd lost his magic, but I wasn't totally confident of this. I had no idea what other magi in his position had done, except for Harry, and Harry hadn't been on the front lines fighting invaders. I knew little about the details of what a hunting team did, so I didn't know if Malcolm could still fight without his magic. He was ex-military, trained in combat, but his steel aegis had given him immunity to the invaders' ability to drain a human of his magic, which meant he was now as vulnerable as anyone. He might be a liability to his team now. And there was a part of me that didn't want him to go back to the fight under those conditions, no matter what he wanted.

I got dressed in a knee-length skirt and black sweater over a white button-down shirt, brushed my hair, and went downstairs. For now, I'd just be grateful he was well and about to get better.

It was one of those days where I resented having to stay inside. The sky was cloudless blue, the sun shone brightly through the windows, warming me, and it felt like spring rather than winter. I walked to the corner market for lunch for me and Judy and left my jacket at home. The air smelled clean and fresh and made me think of white sheets hanging on a line, soaking up the sunlight.

Everyone else seemed to feel it, too, because we had very few customers, and the ones who did come in were cheerful and inclined to gossip. I waved goodbye to the latest Ambrosite to enter the store and took a few steps toward the cash register. My phone rang. "Hi, Lucia, what's up?"

"Armageddon," Lucia said. "The Board is going to strike at the shadow cabal at midnight Greenwich mean time. That's five p.m. our time, in case you were wondering. They've instructed me to round up all the traitors I've tagged at that exact moment."

Less than an hour away. A chill touched my heart. "Why are you telling me?"

"So you'll be prepared. I've got people trailing our traitors and there's a chance they might have to apprehend someone in Abernathy's."

"Apprehend, or kill?"

There was a pause. "I'm under orders to take as many cabal members alive as possible, for interrogation. But if it's a choice between letting them escape and killing them to prevent escape, I'm authorized to kill."

"This is terrifying. What if you're wrong about a traitor? What if it's just an innocent with the marker?"

"Another reason to apprehend. Don't worry about it, Davies. It's the ones we haven't had time to clear yet that are a problem. But the Board wouldn't give me any more time, so I'm having to bring in everyone with the marker we've identified. And there are a lot of magi I haven't tested yet. God only knows how many traitors we don't even suspect."

"Are you sure there's nothing I can do?"

"Bless you for asking, Davies, but no, just let me worry about it." She hung up.

I sank onto the stool behind the cash register and stared blindly at its worn keys. Ryan Parish. Ewan Campbell. How many other potential traitors did I know? How many of them did I call friend? I hoped desperately they wouldn't have to capture someone within Abernathy's walls.

Time wore on. Judy left early on some errand or other for her father. I checked my watch every few minutes, wondering what Lucia was doing. Whether the secret was out yet, leaked by some traitor within Lucia's organization she'd overlooked. A customer came in, and I accepted his augury slip, wondering *Is this someone I should fear?* He gave me a pleasant smile, but I hurried him out the door anyway, then went back to fiddling with the cash register, watching for five o'clock to hurry up and get here already.

4:47. The door swung open. "I bet you're happy with yourself right now, aren't you, Ms. Davies?" Acosta said. He looked rumpled, his eyes dark-circled like he hadn't slept in days, and his breath stank of stale French fries.

"I—excuse me, detective?" I took a step back, but he didn't follow me, just put his hands in his coat pockets and surveyed the store casually, as if he'd never been here before.

"Do you really expect me to believe you're not backed by the Mob, after this?"

Confused, I said, "I have no idea what you're talking about."

"You don't? I'm surprised. I've been ordered to drop this case just as I have proof about what's really going on here. Threatened with reprisal if I don't. I should probably thank you, actually."

"What?"

"Now I know this corruption has reached into the police force. Your boss William Rasmussen has a lot of pull, to be able to get my superiors to dance to his tune. Don't think this changes anything. I know the truth."

I took a step backward. "Um...what truth is that?" He sounded calm, but there was a manic light in his eyes, and he looked like a man on the edge. I should probably have been afraid, but I couldn't help wondering what he thought he'd learned. Rasmussen's people seemed to have been thorough in stopping his investigation, but they couldn't stop him leaping to conclusions.

Now he did walk toward me, just a few paces, but enough to make me even more nervous. "Don't act so innocent, Ms. Davies. You're not ignorant of what's happening here. Rasmussen has control of an entire criminal empire, and this bookstore is only one of his fronts. Selling trash for thousands of dollars, laundering the proceeds of his crimes—you're paid far too well for someone who's just a bookseller."

"I am—how do you know how much I'm paid?"

"I don't know why Rasmussen's daughter is just a courier. I'd have thought she'd be running this place instead of you."

"Detective Acosta, I think you should leave."

He smiled at me pleasantly, though his eyes were still hard and cold. "Why? I happen to be interested in buying a book. I'll just browse your shelves for a while, I think. If you're innocent, you shouldn't have any problem with that." He moved off toward the nearest bookcase, took a book down and began leafing through it.

The door swung open, and Georgina Eisen, breathtaking in her usual white furs, drifted through it and approached me. Her pale, frost-kissed lips parted in a silent O as she registered Acosta's presence. "I would like you to find this for me," she said. Acosta, for his part, seemed unimpressed by her elven beauty, glancing her over once and then returning to his "reading."

I took the augury slip from her gloved hand. "I'll be right back, Mrs. Eisen." I headed into the oracle. Maybe Acosta would be gone when I returned. I could always hope.

Eisen's augury was easy to find—a slim little book titled *Backgammon For Beginners*. I tucked it under my arm and exited the oracle. Two more magi had entered the store while I was gone. Unfortunately, Acosta was still there, too. What was he trying to do—intimidate me? It was sort of working. But there was only about an hour until closing, and I could wait him out.

"I'll be with you in a moment," I said to the new customers, then looked at them more closely. I knew them both by sight if not by name—they were two of Lucia's enforcers from the Gunther Node. Dread crept up my spine. It was nearly five o'clock. Were they anticipating an arrival...or was she already here?

Eisen, as usual, ignored everyone else in the store. Acosta had his eye on the new arrivals, possibly sensing kindred spirits of law enforcement. I had to admit, as wrong-headed as he was, he was good at his job, if he'd learned Judy's identity to link her to Rasmussen.

I glanced at the enforcers again. Both women were browsing the shelves, but one of them stood between Eisen and the door, casually, holding a book in her hands she was slowly leafing through. I made myself breathe naturally and smiled at Eisen. "That will be $1250."

Acosta coughed explosively.

"Something wrong, detective?" I asked.

Acosta waved a hand like brushing away smoke from his face. "That's a lot of money for such a small book."

Keeping my voice calm, I said, "I didn't know you were an expert antiquarian. This is a very old book and needs careful handling. Mrs. Eisen?"

Eisen, ignoring Acosta, had out her white checkbook and was writing a check. "How much is this book?" Acosta said, waving the one he was holding at me. "I wouldn't want to mishandle your merchandise."

That sounded ominous to me, or would if I cared at all about the condition of the books, which was irrelevant to the oracle. "More than you can afford. Thank you," I said to Eisen, trading her the book for the check. "Let me write you a receipt."

The enforcers had started to move toward Eisen, unnoticed either by her or by Acosta, who was intent on Eisen's transaction. They were going to arrest her right here in the store in front of Acosta, and then all hell would break loose. Unless they intended to do something to Acosta to silence him. I slapped the receipt book down on the counter and wished Judy was here. As if what this fiasco needed was more witnesses.

"Where are you going after this, Mrs. Eisen?" I said loudly, glaring at the enforcers. They stopped, glanced at Acosta, who was looming over an oblivious Eisen, and backed away toward the door.

Eisen looked startled, as if the cash register had come to life and spoken to her. "The jeweler's," she said. "The setting on my ring is loose."

"That's nice," I said, widening my eyes at the enforcers, willing them to hear my thoughts: *Pick her up on the way there, don't stop here!*

The woman on the right flicked a glance at Eisen, then at Acosta. She tapped her wrist and shook her head slightly. My heart sank. Why couldn't they wait even a few minutes? Acosta was going to see everything!

I paused in writing the receipt. "Detective, don't let me keep you," I said. "There's nothing interesting for you here."

"Could you hurry it up, Ms. Davies?" the woman on the right said. "We're on a deadline."

"I know, and I'm sorry." I finished writing the receipt and handed it to Eisen. "Have a nice day, Mrs. Eisen."

She turned away, tucking the receipt and book into her bag. Acosta turned to watch her go. The enforcers stepped to either side, and I breathed more easily. They'd take her on the street, throw up an illusion, and Acosta would remain clueless.

Eisen stopped. She looked at the enforcers, first one, then the other. She looked over her shoulder at me. For a moment, her usual vacant gaze was replaced by a malevolent snarl. Then she shoved both hands into her sleeves like a muff and ran.

Both the enforcers cried out and staggered backward. One of them pulled out a gun and pointed it roughly in Eisen's direction. "What the hell?" Acosta shouted, drawing his gun. "Police! Drop your weapon!"

The enforcer ignored him and took a shot. The bullet struck the plate glass window and shattered it. "She's heading for the door!" I shouted, guessing by the way they moved that Eisen had gone invisible.

I had no trouble seeing through the illusion and threw the receipt book after her. The book hit her on the back of the head and made her stagger long enough for me to take a couple of running steps and throw myself at her legs, bringing her down. Two more shots went off, explosively loud, and I heard someone cry out in pain. "Somebody help me!" I shouted.

Eisen fought me like a crazed tiger, thrashing her legs, but I clung tightly to her. I heard another shot, but saw nothing—my face was buried in the back of her fur coat, and my eyes and nose itched. Then something exploded near my face, something louder than the other gunshots, and Eisen went limp. I released Eisen and stood upright, swaying and dizzy. Through the broken window I saw pedestrians scattering in all directions. So much for a quiet apprehension.

One of the enforcers lay on the floor with her partner kneeling over her, pulling her sweater off over her head and wrapping it tightly around the woman's arm. "Ms. Davies, call the node," the partner said, and I scrabbled for my phone. I glanced over my shoulder. Half a dozen people had their phones out and I could just imagine them talking to emergency dispatchers about this fiasco. Damn.

Acosta sat sprawled next to the counter, half-propped against its base, staring at nothing. His gun lay a few paces from him, disregarded. I called, not Lucia, who always let her calls go to voice mail and who would probably be too busy to answer anyway, but her assistant Dave Henry. "Dave," I said breathlessly, not giving him a chance to speak, "I need enforcers at Abernathy's immediately. They tried to arrest Georgina Eisen and, I don't know, somehow she knew what they were after and fought back—someone was shot—"

"Slow down, Helena," Dave said. "Did anyone see?"

I looked out on the street again. "Someone called 911. Maybe a lot of people."

Dave swore at length. "There's no one to send," he said. "The node is in an uproar. You'll just have to brazen it out. Who was shot?"

"I don't know her name—let me let you talk to her partner." I held the phone to the woman's ear and let my attention go briefly back to Acosta. He looked utterly stunned, like someone had bludgeoned him. I really didn't have time for him now.

"Ms. Davies? Mr. Henry wants to speak with you," the woman said.

"Tell me if Georgina Eisen is still alive," Dave said.

I knelt beside her and checked for a pulse, then laid my cheek against her lips to feel if there was breath. "I think she's dead," I said, "but there's no marks."

"Thank God," Dave said. "Martinez said she was pretty sure she'd hit her with the jolter." I remembered the explosion, practically in my ear, and my hands began shaking. Inches lower, and that blast would have caught me. "All right. Is anyone watching?"

"Hey! Are you all right?" Some foolhardy soul stood at the window, peeking in around its edge. He was either brave or stupid, since for all he knew there was an armed gunman in here, ready to shoot the next person who showed his face.

"Call 911," I told him, then to Dave, "Yes, there's someone right here."

"Distract them for a couple of seconds. That's all Martinez needs. Then the story is—Eisen shot Carlson, and you don't know why Eisen snapped or how she was killed. We'll get a bone magus in there at some point to fake a convincing cause of death. Understand?"

"What about Acosta?"

"Who?"

"The detective. He saw everything."

Dave swore again, even more eloquently. "We'll have to deal with him later. Just distract now, and everything will be all right." He hung up.

I turned around and went to the window. "We heard gunshots. Are you all right?" said the man.

"I don't know. I can't remember. Look, is that the ambulance?" I pointed through the window, up the street. Sure enough, the man turned away to look. I hoped it was long enough for Martinez to do whatever she had in mind. "No, it's not—I have to help this woman —*no*, please stay outside, I'm sure the police don't want anyone messing up their crime scene."

I stepped over Eisen's body and knelt beside the fallen enforcer—

Carlson, Dave had said her name was. She was cursing steadily under her breath and had her hand pressed to her arm, wrapped in the bloody sweater. “That was stupid,” she said. “Lucia’s going to tear us apart for failing like that.”

“Mrs. Eisen didn’t escape,” I said.

“We were supposed to take her alive,” Martinez said. “And that man saw everything. A police officer, no less. We are so screwed.”

I couldn’t think of anything to say to that. “Did Mrs. Eisen shoot you?”

“No, that idiot officer did. I hope I made it look like Eisen did instead. Right now I’m not sure of anything.” Carlson pushed herself into a sitting position. “We should—aaah!—talk to the officer. I hit him with the jolter on its lowest setting, but it didn’t knock him out—”

“Let me. I’ve dealt with him before.”

I walked across the room to where Acosta sat and squatted next to him. “You’re lucky you didn’t kill Ms. Carlson,” I said.

“I saw a gun. She was going to shoot that woman,” Acosta said. His pupils were wide and dilated. “And the bear—where did the bear come from?”

“You’ve been under a lot of stress, detective,” I said. “I didn’t see a bear.” Totally true.

“A polar bear in a bookstore.” Acosta reached out to pick up his gun. “What the hell is going on here?”

“I don’t know what you’re talking about. Maybe you hit your head.” I felt myself beginning to panic and shut my mouth.

“It wasn’t just the gun. She had another weapon. That weapon, whatever it is, hit the woman.” Acosta stood and swayed for a moment, then holstered his gun. “And that woman—the bear vanished, and the woman appeared. Is she dead?”

“Yes.”

“I didn’t shoot her. I shot the woman with the gun.”

“No, Mrs. Eisen shot her. You must have missed.” I hoped I wasn’t muddying the story entirely in my growing confusion. Acosta’s gun, Carlson’s gun, two jolters...the place had turned into an arsenal.

Acosta knelt beside Eisen and felt for a pulse. "There's no blood. And she didn't have a gun."

In the distance, I heard sirens. "I don't know anything about that." I noticed for the first time that a gun lay next to Eisen's right hand. Whose gun was that? I was positive Eisen hadn't been armed. I shook the cobwebs out of my brain. There was too much about this I was never going to understand. I hoped Martinez was capable of dusting Eisen's hand with gunpowder residue, or whatever it was they always tested people for on shows like *C.S.I.*

"There was a bear. Then there was a woman. She's dead with no marks on her." He sounded like he was making a shopping list. "And I know I shot that woman over there."

I gave up. I'd have to turn the problem over to Lucia and hope, in the meantime, that Acosta would sound crazy enough that no one would listen to him. I went back to the enforcers and squatted beside Carlson. "What is this bear he keeps talking about?"

"Eisen's a paper magus. She made herself look like a bear. You didn't see it?"

I didn't bother to explain my ability, either natural or granted by Abernathy's, I wasn't sure, to see through illusions. "Where did the gun come from?"

"It was mine," Martinez said. "What did you tell that officer?"

"He's a detective. And I told him he was delusional. I hope he believes it."

I watched Acosta climb out through the shattered window as the ambulance, sirens blaring, came into view. I retreated to my stool and wound my hands into my skirt to keep them from shaking. Acosta had seen everything, but it sounded like he didn't believe the evidence of his eyes. It didn't matter. Lucia would find a way to keep him from talking. At the moment, I didn't care if it involved vigilante justice.

The police came shortly after the ambulance, completing the impression of a three-ring circus complete with clowns, the clown in question being Detective Acosta. I stayed far away from him while the police took my statement—I hadn't seen much, but I knew Eisen was armed, Carlson wasn't, and Eisen had shot Carlson. I hoped that would be enough.

Eventually, the ambulances—the police called for a second one when it was clear Eisen was dead—took the body and Carlson away, the police finished their investigation, and somebody found boards to cover the window. They even swept up the glass on the sidewalk, which I thought was nice as I was exhausted from the ordeal. I called Campbell Security while they were doing this and got a very helpful man who assured me the alarm wouldn't be affected by the missing window. Then I dragged myself upstairs and got into bed, too weary to eat despite my hunger.

I tried calling Lucia, thinking I should update her, even though she probably already knew more details than I did about Eisen's death. To my surprise, she picked up on the third ring. "What do you want, Davies?" Her voice was hoarse, as if she'd been crying.

"Um—did Martinez tell you—"

"I've been briefed, yes. Unless you feel the need to bore me with more details."

"Lucia, are you all right?"

"I'm fine." She cleared her throat. "Sorry. It's been an overwhelming couple of hours."

"You don't sound fine."

"Don't worry about me."

It was sharp enough I decided not to push. "So...how did everything go?" I asked instead.

"As well as could be expected, given that there are almost certainly dozens, maybe hundreds of Wardens we didn't know to pick up. For a miracle, we managed to keep the secret until zero hour and took most of our suspects by surprise. Yours was the most explosive of the arrests. A few potential traitors eluded us and are being hunted. Ryan Parish is still on the loose. Very few...few deaths, surprisingly. Or, I should say, very few deaths during apprehension. The executions began half an hour ago."

I shuddered. "Don't. I know it's necessary, but...I just don't want to know about it."

"You wouldn't," Lucia said. "Thank God you're not in charge. You're not hard enough to kill someone who deserves it."

I'd never heard Lucia sound so derisive, so dismissive of me, and it hurt. "Not like you," I shot back without thinking. "I'm surprised you bothered to take this call, since you're probably eager to get back to those executions you're so proud of."

Lucia sighed. "I shouldn't have said that. I apologize."

Lucia never apologized. It stunned me into saying, "No, I'm sorry. You're under a lot of stress."

"You have no idea." Now her voice sounded choked, like the words hurt her. "This war is brutal and cold, but you'd better not think I enjoy it."

"I don't." I'd sort of wondered if she did—not the executions, but the harsher parts of her job—but I would never admit that to her. "How do you cover something like that up? All those deaths, I mean."

"It's execution by draining the person's magic. I'm sure you remember how that looks. Natural causes, and it doesn't cause any pain. But we can't afford to lock up traitors who might escape."

"Do you really think Mr. Parish is a traitor?"

"I don't, actually. He's got strong opinions about individual rights, and when he was asked to come down and prove he wasn't a traitor, he got angry about the insinuation that he might be. But he didn't kill anyone when he made his escape, and I'm sure you know he's willing to kill to defend himself. So I have hopes."

"What about Ewan Campbell?"

"In custody, waiting for testing. I have no guesses one way or the other about him. Harriet Keller is in custody, too."

I caught my breath. "No. Not Harriet."

"Don't get your panties in a wad, Davies. The odds are in her favor."

"Even so—"

"I know. But, honestly, with the kind of marriage she has, I find it difficult to believe she could have kept the secret from Harry all these years, and he's unmarked. So, again, I have hopes."

"You're just saying that to make me feel better."

"You've figured me out. My whole life is about cosseting people's feelings." Lucia snorted. That had sounded more like the woman I knew. "Get some sleep. You're probably due."

"So are you."

"Ah, but unlike you, I'm still at work and will be until the wee hours. You'll have to sleep for both of us."

She hung up, and I plugged my phone in and set it on the nightstand. If Ewan Campbell was a traitor...that was bad news for Campbell Security, and bad news for the Campbell family. Malcolm didn't need that stress on top of everything else.

I realized I'd forgotten to ask Lucia about Detective Acosta—what was she going to do about him? Probably he was low on her list of priorities, but I really wanted to know what his fate would be. I fell asleep and dreamed of Georgina Eisen shifting from woman to bear to woman again, straining my eyes to see through the illusion.

10

Nobody came into the store on Thursday morning except a couple of enforcers, who lurked by the broken window as if hoping someone might try breaking in. I filled mail-in augury requests and tried not to think about the ongoing arrests and the executions that came afterward.

Judy burst through the door at quarter after ten, startling the enforcers into drawing their guns on her. She ignored them. "Did you hear about Martin Maxwell?"

"No. Is he all right?"

"He's dead. Turns out he was a traitor. He fought back when they came for him and Lucia killed him herself."

I sucked in a horrified breath. "That's impossible. She didn't say anything about it to me."

"No one's talking about it where she can hear. I only know because Father asked me to contact the node early this morning and Pringle, the woman on the switchboard, told me. I thought they were lovers!"

"They were." No wonder Lucia had sounded strange. *And I as much as accused her of being happy about the deaths.* "She must be devastated."

"To hear Pringle talk, she just carried on like the cast-iron bitch she is."

"That is *not* true. And it's cruel. Can you imagine having to kill someone you loved in the name of the Long War? And she must have known about him for months. Just because she's good at hiding—"

"Calm down, Helena, I was just repeating Pringle's words. I don't like Lucia, but I know she's not vicious or cold, though she gives a good impression of it. Just don't say anything to her, all right? If she's not talking about it, she doesn't want to be reminded about it."

"I...you're right." Even so, I couldn't imagine carrying on after that. Lucia was far stronger than I'd ever be. At least she had Dave Henry, the other member of their unorthodox romantic relationship. I hoped it was enough.

Still, no one came. Lucia didn't call with new information, and Judy was nearly as much out of the loop as I was. Around lunchtime, she got a text, a lengthy one, and I waited in silence for her to read it. Finally, she looked up and said, "Someone just tried to kill my father. The assassin hadn't been tested yet and no one even knew she had the marker, let alone that she was a traitor. He'll be fine after the bone magi finish treating him."

"It's all the secret ones that scare me. Not to mention the ones who might be invaders in disguise."

"There has to be something we can do. I feel so helpless."

"Like what? We're not magi—we're not even trained fighters!"

Judy threw her apple core at the trash can. It hit the bottom with a loud *thunk*. "I don't know, but *something*."

I heard the door open. Judy and I looked at each other. "The enforcers will take care of it," Judy said.

"It's probably a customer," I said, though my heart quailed at the idea of going out there and facing someone who might be a traitor, armed and ready to kill us. It was stupid, but not knowing what was going on had me on edge.

But when Judy and I returned to the front of the store, we found it full of Wardens. Most of them were engaged in replacing the plate glass window, but a few had taken the front door off its hinges and were taking measurements of the door and frame. "Ms. Davies," said a man dressed not in work clothes, but in the kind of suit Malcolm always wore. He extended his hand for me to shake. "Sam Humphreys. We're here to install your new security system."

"We need a new system?"

Humphreys handed me an envelope. "This explains how it works, but the short version is, it's to provide a second layer of protection against unwanted...invaders." He glanced quickly to both sides, looking exactly like an informant handing over confidential files to a spy, i.e., me. I accepted the envelope and opened it, turning away from him to read it in private.

The first page was a schematic of Abernathy's front door, or rather the frame around the door. I didn't understand half of it, though I could tell the new security system involved embedding bits of metal or glass or something into the lintel and frame. The second page was a list of security features, which I read with interest. The new system would prevent an invader, even one encased in human form, from entering the store at all. The door frame would screen out non-humans, no matter what their appearance, and make an invader bounce off, like running into a clear glass door, though one that couldn't break.

The new doorknob—I glanced over at where the door lay against the wall and saw a couple of women unscrewing the old knob—would deliver a directed burst of magical force that would paralyze the human form and prevent the invader from leaving it immediately. I wasn't sure that was a great idea. If the invader couldn't pass through the door, it would have to lie paralyzed on the street, where anyone would assume it was an injured person in need of help, and that struck me as potentially fatal for the helper. But invaders not getting into Abernathy's—that was something I approved of.

I turned back to speak to Humphreys and found he'd moved on. I handed the papers to Judy and said, "This day just got better."

Judy scanned the papers. "This is something, anyway. Do you suppose this means Ewan Campbell was cleared?"

"It's more likely Malcolm finally got fed up with being sidelined and set all this in motion. But I hope..." I fingered my phone in my pocket, but there was no one I could call who would know about Ewan. My impatience to see Malcolm again grew.

We watched the construction until it got noisy, when we retreated to the break room. Judy texted friends in the hope that someone would know what was happening. I played solitaire. It didn't help. Finally, I called Derrick. "Did Malcolm send security people to Abernathy's?"

"Hang on a sec," Derrick said.

After a moment, Malcolm said, "I take it they arrived."

The sound of his voice left me momentarily breathless. "They did. They're fixing the window and putting in a new door."

"You're well?" He didn't elaborate, which told me there were listeners who weren't in on the secret of our relationship.

"I'm fine. Thanks. This new system eases my mind considerably."

"Keeping Abernathy's safe is one of our top priorities. The new window glass should be more damage-proof, too."

"I hope we won't need that, but I appreciate it. Are you leaving the hospital tomorrow as planned?"

"Yes. I wish I could have left today. It will take Tinsley another three days to finish healing me and I would like that to start as soon as possible."

"That seems like a long time for a healing."

"It has to be slow so as not to reinjure me. It's frustrating, but I can endure."

"I know, you're a master of patience."

Malcolm laughed. "With Canales threatening to sit on my head, how could I be otherwise?"

"You sound good. I look forward to seeing you again." I wanted to say *I love you, I miss you, I need you,* but it occurred to me that my words might be audible to whoever was listening in. I also wanted to ask him how he felt about not being a magus any longer, but that wasn't a conversation for the telephone.

"I'll come by to assess the new system on Monday. If you have any other questions, we can discuss them at that time."

I hoped that was code for *I need to be alone with you* and said, “Of course. Thanks again, Malcolm.”

“My pleasure, Helena. I’ll see you on Monday.”

I set my phone down and stared at it, wishing today were Sunday. “Was that Campbell?” Judy said, as if she hadn’t been listening.

“He sent the security people. He’ll come to check their work Monday, after he’s out of the hospital and fully healed.”

“That’s nice.” Judy sounded distracted, so I left her to her texting and went to the office, hoping to find some overlooked augury request, anything to keep me busy and stop me thinking about how long it was until Monday.

The workers left around five, all except one wizened little man who stood on a stepladder painting ABERNATHY’S on the new window. I watched him, mesmerized. He was painting it backwards and without a stencil—was it magic? Or maybe he was just that skilled after a lifetime of window painting. I held my tongue, not wanting to distract him, but when he was finished I said, “That’s remarkable.”

“Just practice, Ms. Davies,” he said, stepping down from the ladder. “Is there anything else I can do for you?”

“No, thanks. I appreciate your work. Can I help you clean up?”

“That’s part of the job. But thanks for the offer.”

I showed him the basement, where he cleaned up his brushes in the big, dirty sink in the corner, then watched him bundle his paint cloth and ladder out to a truck parked in Abernathy’s magically reserved spot. I waited for him to drive away before I got out a cloth and some solvent and mopped up a few drops of paint he’d let fall. I didn’t want to hurt his feelings by implying he’d done less than his best.

A shadow loomed up outside the window. I looked up and stepped back, startled at the sudden appearance of Acosta just inches from me. He had both hands jammed into the pockets of his overcoat and was regarding me dispassionately. He looked better than he had the day before, less tired and unkempt, but that manic light was still in his eyes. At a loss, I waved at him. He smiled, the corners of his mouth just barely going up, and pointed at the door as if asking permission to enter. I nodded and capped off the bottle of solvent. I'd see what he wanted, then call Lucia and insist she sic someone on him immediately. I didn't need harassment on top of everything else.

"Ms. Davies. That was fast. You'd almost think there'd never been an attack here." Acosta shut the door behind him.

"We couldn't leave the window broken, not with as big as it is. How's your partner? *Where's* your partner, I should ask?"

"We're off duty. I'm here as a private citizen."

"Are police ever really off duty, though? I mean, I've heard where off-duty cops stopped robberies and things like that."

"You're thinking I'm still on the case. I told you I've been instructed to let it go."

I didn't want to say *Like I believe you'd do that*. Acosta was being polite and even-tempered, and I didn't want to change that. "There's really nothing here, detective."

"She's telling the truth," Judy said, emerging from the back of the store. "And this could constitute harassment."

"I told you, I'm here as a private citizen," Acosta said, smiling at Judy. "I'm just having trouble wrapping my head around what happened here yesterday. I was hoping you'd be willing to walk me through it."

"Why?"

"Because something doesn't add up." Acosta patted his chest, where his gun was probably holstered. "I know I shot that woman. My gun shows evidence of having been fired. But the bullet they removed from her arm didn't match my weapon."

"Aren't you happy about that? Wouldn't it be a huge administrative hassle if you had? Not to mention feeling bad about wounding an innocent person."

"I'm not so sure she was innocent. She was armed, after all." Acosta paced over to where he'd been standing the day before and mimed drawing his weapon, then pointed his "gun" toward the shelves where Carlson had been standing. "It was her gun that shattered your window, wasn't it?"

"I wasn't paying attention," I said. "I was watching Mrs. Eisen."

"Yes. We'll get to her in a minute." Acosta sighted down his arm and finger and walked slowly toward the shelves. "I shot twice. The second one struck her arm, but the first..." He knelt and removed a pen from his pocket, then dug with it where one of the shelves met the bookcase side. Something small popped free. Acosta picked it up and displayed it—a flattened lump of metal. "The first is right here."

"You shouldn't handle that if you want it to be evidence," Judy said.

"I'm not looking for evidence that will hold up in court. Just something to prove I'm not crazy. Besides, someone's gone to a lot of trouble to make it look like the dead woman, not me, shot my victim. Why should I ruin all that work?"

Judy and I exchanged glances. I could see Judy had her hand in her pocket, likely holding her phone, but what good would that do either of us? And it wasn't as if Acosta was attacking anyone. "So what *do* you want, detective?" I said.

"Let's play a little game," Acosta said. "Reenact the crime. I want to be clear on what did happen. So. The woman, Carlson, right? She drew a gun on Mrs. Eisen, who was headed for the door. Why don't you be Ms. Carlson, and you, Ms. Rasmussen, you can be Mrs. Eisen."

"I'm not interested in playing your game, and neither is Helena," Judy said.

"Oh, come on. It won't hurt. And after this I promise to go away and leave you alone."

I looked at Judy, who rolled her eyes. "Fine," she said, and went to stand halfway between the counter and the door. "Is this right?"

"Perfect. Then you, Ms. Davies, stand over here."

I took my place near the bookshelves. "Ms. Carlson drew, I drew, and then the bear appeared, just where you're standing, Ms. Rasmussen."

"A bear?" Judy said. The scorn in her voice could have cut steel. "You're kidding, right?"

"I've spent most of the night going over this, and here's the thing," Acosta said. "Something hit me, and I fell backward into the counter and might have struck my head. But that definitely happened *after* the bear appeared. So however impossible it might be, I have to conclude I didn't imagine it. There was a bear that took the place of Mrs. Eisen—that she turned into—that disappeared when she was struck by the same thing that hit me."

"I didn't see a bear," I said. "And I think maybe you should leave, if you're going to talk nonsense."

"You tackled the bear, Ms. Davies." Acosta took a few steps forward until he stood right next to Judy. "Maybe something prevented you seeing the truth, but you *did* encounter it."

I was starting to feel nervous. "I really don't know what you're talking about."

"What I don't understand is where the other weapons came from. And why one of them was powerful enough to kill Mrs. Eisen, while the other just rattled me a bit."

I was wondering that myself. I wasn't so bloodthirsty as to wish Acosta dead, but I couldn't help thinking if the enforcers had done their job, I wouldn't be in this position right now. "I don't know. Why don't you ask Ms. Carlson?"

"I will, don't worry." *Too late, I'm worried.* "I was just hoping you'd be willing to be honest with me."

"Detective, you've harassed me and accused me of several different crimes. Why on earth would I do you any favors?"

"Fair enough." He smiled and spread his palms wide in a "your move" gesture. "But I believed you were the sort of woman who'd want to know the truth behind any strange events on her premises."

"If I thought there was anything strange about what happened yesterday, I'd investigate. But I think you're blowing it out of proportion. I really don't want to talk about it anymore. Mrs. Eisen was a long-time customer and—"

"So you knew her? Why do you think she snapped?"

"We don't have to answer your questions," Judy said.

"I don't know," I said at the same time. Judy glared at me.

"This is what I think," Acosta said. "I think Mrs. Eisen was involved in something...unusual. Something Ms. Carlson wanted stopped. Advanced technology, maybe. Or...that doesn't matter. What matters is I think I was wrong about your store, Ms. Davies. The Mob is far too mundane an explanation for what's going on here."

"And what's that?"

"I don't know yet. I don't suppose you'd be interested in telling me?"

I almost told him. I was tired, emotionally and physically; I'd been this close to having my head blown off by a jolter; Acosta was persistent and annoying and I had a feeling he'd learn the truth eventually, so why not tell him now? But I held my tongue. I didn't owe Acosta anything and I certainly wasn't responsible for satisfying his curiosity. Also, Lucia would roast me over a slow fire with an apple in my mouth if I did.

"We're an ordinary bookstore," I said. "Sometimes strange things happen here, true, but I doubt there's a business in Portland that hasn't had at least one weird thing happen on its premises. I think you should look elsewhere for your big break."

Acosta laughed. It was such a cheery sound coming from him that I was taken aback. "All right, Ms. Davies, I'll go. But I'll probably be back. This isn't about making a name for myself anymore. I don't like unsolved mysteries, and I'll do whatever it takes to solve this one." He turned and left before I could say anything else.

"What in the hell was that about?" Judy pulled out her phone, but hesitated before dialing. "I don't know who to call first."

"You call your father, and I'll call Lucia," I said. "I don't know if Acosta's change of heart makes him more dangerous, or less, but either way I think the two of them need to know he's on our trail."

"He's far too observant," Judy said. "Most people, when they see an illusion like that one, dismiss it as overexcitement or something. And he knew the jolters were the same thing, even though they had different effects. I thought he was just a dumb detective."

"It makes me wonder what his partner thinks of all this. I can't imagine Acosta getting permission to investigate disappearing bears."

Judy nodded and put her phone to her ear. I listened to Lucia's phone ring with half my attention, the other half focused on Acosta and his conclusions. If he thought he was dealing with advanced technology, that was good. It was certainly more plausible than magic. On the other hand, if he kept prying, he'd eventually run into something technology couldn't explain. I left a message for Lucia, as concise as I could be under the circumstances, and hung up. It wasn't my problem.

"—otherwise," Judy was saying. "I just wanted you to—yes. All right. I'll see you in an hour or so." She hung up. "He actually sounded pleased. Like he was looking forward to running rings around Acosta. I think the assassination attempt has his blood up."

"I think—" My phone rang.

"So Acosta suspects Abernathy's of being central to some kind of spy operation," Lucia said.

"Um...I guess that could be what he's thinking. I don't know what to say to him."

"Don't worry about it."

"I thought you'd be more upset about this. Acosta's really close to figuring out the truth."

Lucia chuckled. "You're a movie lover. Ever see *The Matrix*?"

"It's not really my kind of movie, but yes. Why?"

"I'm not saying Acosta is The One, but he might prove useful. Like I said, don't worry about it. I have plans for the detective and maybe his partner, depending on how things play out. If Acosta comes back, answer his questions honestly. *All* his questions. If Green shows up alone, deny everything. Got it?"

"All right, but—"

"I don't have time to explain it to you. I have to worry about these disappearances."

She hung up unceremoniously. I lowered my phone and said, "Lucia can be really annoying at times, don't you think?"

"You know I do," Judy said.

"She said something about disappearances. Do you know anything about that?"

"Father said people have been vanishing. They think they might be undiscovered shadow cabal members, fleeing before they can be arrested. Or worse, they're being kidnapped by cabal members—almost all of them have had positions of authority."

"I'm just afraid of where they'll strike next. They tried to kill your father—Lucia could be next."

"If they can strike at her in the heart of the Gunther Node, nowhere is safe."

"Let's just hope they're not that powerful," I said, but I couldn't help thinking of seventy-six dead steel magi, of Malcolm's bloody face, and felt it might be a false hope.

11

I curled up in the corner of my couch and stroked its velvet upholstery. Its soft touch was soothing to my anxious spirits—anxious for no good reason. I'd spent the last two hours cleaning, not because I thought Malcolm would care, but because I needed something to do while I waited for him. He'd come home from the hospital three days ago, had spent those three days undergoing magical healing, and Derrick had called at five to let me know Malcolm would come to me at eight. I was as nervous as a girl going on her first date.

Derrick had also said, "Not that I want to tell you your business, but see if you can't get him to talk about losing his magic."

"He still hasn't said anything?"

"Not a word. And now it's just awkward. If he's going to talk to anyone, it'll be you."

That warmed me even as it gave me an uncomfortable feeling. "I'll do what I can, but wouldn't it be better coming from someone who understands about magic?"

"That's not nearly as important as it be someone who understands *him*. Just...follow your instincts, all right? And don't be shocked if he tries to do magic and fails. It takes time to adjust."

"I wouldn't do that." I hoped I was right about that. Mostly I just wanted Malcolm to be with me again, to hold him close and thank God he was alive and well. Magic wasn't everything he was.

It had been a long three days. More Wardens had disappeared, a few of the missing ones had turned up dead, and we'd received news of nodes, mostly small ones but a few Neutralities, erupting into violence. Abernathy's had been busy the whole time, with dozens of Wardens coming in and a stack of mail-in auguries each day. The new security system on the front door remained inert. It felt as if Portland was waiting for something, holding its breath and closing its eyes against some even worse threat.

My phone rang, startling me. I snatched it up. "Hello?"

"You'll need to let me in," Malcolm said. "The door can't be attuned to me anymore."

I flushed. I hadn't even seen him yet and already I'd made a mistake. "I'll be right down."

I ran down the stairs, took a deep breath, and opened the back door. Malcolm, dressed in his black fatigues, had his back turned to me and was scanning the parking lot. "All right," he said, stepping inside, and I closed the door so we stood together in the dimness that was my stairwell.

He looked at me, unsmiling, and for a moment he was a stranger. I stared at him, at a loss for words. Then he smiled and touched my cheek. "Helena," he said. "I've missed you so much."

"Malcolm," I said, and threw myself at him, putting my arms around his neck and holding him close. His arms went around me, lifting me up, those strong arms I loved—"Malcolm, what happened to your cast?"

"I made Tinsley remove it," he murmured. "I refuse to be injured, even make-believe, for one moment longer."

"But won't the doctors notice?"

His lips found mine, kissing me breathless. "They won't see me for another six weeks, at which point I could justify not needing it. I'm well and whole, love, and much as I enjoy kissing you, I think there are better places for it than this cold stairwell."

I nuzzled his earlobe, ran my fingers through his hair. "Do you?"

He swept me off my feet without even a wince of pain, making me laugh with delight. "I do," he said, "and I guarantee I have much more than kissing in mind."

WE ENDED up tangled naked together on my couch, warm and content. "Can you stay?" I asked, tracing the line of the new red scar along his breastbone. It was shiny and smooth to the touch.

"For a few hours only. I haven't yet worked out the details that will let me spend the night. We might need a hotel room for that."

"I see."

"You sound disapproving."

"It's just...that's what people in illicit love affairs do."

He laughed. "This is as illicit as it comes, love."

"I know, but...it's silly, I know. I just wish we didn't have to sneak around."

His arms tightened around me, and he dropped a kiss on my forehead. "Someday."

"Someday." I didn't want to think about it then, not while I was lying in his arms, surrounded by the woody smell of his aftershave and the warmth of his skin. "How did you manage it tonight?"

"Coming to see you? Nothing magical, just a car no one knows belongs to me and some careful misdirection while driving. And parking some ways away from the store. The greatest protection, of course, is that no one's looking for me. But we can't always assume that will be the case."

"I see." I took a breath. "How did you do it before?"

Malcolm was silent. Inside, I cringed. I'd thought I was being oblique. "I mean," I began.

"Tinsley told you to ask me, didn't he?" Malcolm's voice was quiet. He shifted his weight so he was holding me more comfortably.

"If you don't want to talk about it—"

"I don't. Which means I probably should." Malcolm sighed, and his warm breath stirred my hair. "I never realized how easy it all was. I've been—was a magus since I was seventeen. Almost fifteen years of wielding magic as easily as breathing. To answer your question, what I did before was generate a misdirection field, guiding people's attention away from me, and of course the door downstairs was like an old friend, welcoming me in. And I did all that without even thinking about it. Coming here tonight...I had to rely on other skills, and was in fear the entire way that I'd forgotten how."

"But you did it."

"That's not as comforting as you'd think. I was angry that it was even necessary. Anger has been my constant companion since I first tried to levitate something and it didn't respond. I didn't want to discuss it with my team—hah. If they're even still my team."

He sounded so bitter my heart went out to him. "Malcolm, you haven't stopped being a Warden," I said. "You're still a fighter. You didn't lose that with your aegis, did you?"

"Just the thing that made me valuable. My immunity to invaders."

"That's not what makes you valuable. Your ability to destroy half a dozen monsters without breaking a sweat is what makes you valuable. That, and how hot you look doing it."

Malcolm drew in a startled breath, then began to laugh. "Ah, Helena, what would I do without you?"

"Be miserable and lonely."

"That is God's own truth, right there." He turned me in his arms so he could look at me, though we were so close his eyes sort of blurred together and made a third one in the center of his forehead. "I won't lie to you," he said. "This will mean a great adjustment for me. So much of how I fight depended on magic—tactics, maneuvers. But I'm determined to make it work. If the team is behind me—"

"Of course they are."

"Then we'll find a way." He kissed me, first lightly, then with a warm passion that set me tingling all over. "And I will lean on *you*," he said between kisses, "for you are stronger than any aegis."

"I'm happy to be your strength," I said, and then we moved on to the kind of conversation that doesn't need words.

"MALCOLM?" I said in the darkness of my bedroom.

"Mmm?"

"What...happened to Ewan?"

Malcolm fumbled about until he could take my hand and raise it to his lips. "Ewan still hasn't been cleared. I understand Lucia is reluctant to use the more aggressive test on him, because of the risk of death. My mother is furious about the whole thing."

"Like, how could they possibly suspect a Campbell of treachery?"

"Exactly like that. Mother has sworn to see Lucia before a tribunal. Andria and I have been forced to make common cause to keep her from making a fool of herself. Though personally I think it might do her good to look ridiculous...but that would spill over onto me, and I have no interest in being a figure of fun among the magi, now that..." His voice trailed off.

I snuggled up close to him and kissed his cheek. "No one thinks less of you for having been attacked. If anything, they're in awe that you survived. You're one of the few who did, you know."

"There were over a hundred whose aegises became solid only for an instant, then reverted. They all survived."

"Yes, but of the ones whose aegises kept taking physical form like yours did, only four magi were in a position to have them surgically removed. That car accident saved your life."

"It put you in danger, so I'm not going to feel grateful to it. But I take your meaning."

"So what happens now?"

"You'll have to be more specific."

"I meant about hunting down the shadow cabal. Won't Campbell Security have something to do with it?"

"We are in the process of clearing, or not clearing, all the Wardens in our employ. Then we will assist Lucia in cleaning house for all of the Pacific Northwest. It will take months before we can be at all certain the traitors have been rooted out." He drew me closer, and I rested my head on his chest and listened to his heartbeat, deep and strong and reassuring. "Don't tell anyone, but I have my reservations about Lucia's technique for distinguishing traitors, and not just on Ewan's behalf. I have already spoken to her about it."

"You think she's too strict?"

"I think we can afford to err on the side of caution. But making a mistake...either we risk killing innocents, or we give traitors power over us. Either way could be disastrous."

"She always says this is a hard war."

"She is correct. A hard war, with hard choices. I've encouraged her to look for alternatives to her current technique, and offered her our services in developing such."

"Harriet Keller is still in custody."

"I hadn't heard that. I find it difficult to believe she's a traitor."

"Me too."

We both fell silent. I thought about Harry and Harriet. I'd been to their house so often—they were friends, close friends—how could *anyone* believe the invaders were right about *anything?* I remembered facing the thing that had worn a human being like a suit, how reasonable it had sounded. Not that I agreed with its philosophy, its attitude that a few humans could be sacrificed to the invaders so they could share our world. It had just been so clearly convinced of its rightness...maybe that was how the traitors could have believed the invaders. That sense of conviction. Or maybe the invaders promised them power in the new order. Either way, I just couldn't understand it.

Beside me, Malcolm shifted position and let out a gentle snore. It made my heart ache with love for him, that someone so proud and powerful was willing to let down his guard so completely with me. If only this didn't have to be for a few hours. If only he could stay with me forever.

I lay there, listening to him breathe, until nearly midnight. Then I gently woke him. He went from sleep to wakefulness instantly, his hand closing on my wrist firmly. "Helena—I didn't want to sleep, I wanted to be with you—"

"You were so tired, I couldn't bear to wake you. And I don't mind. There will be plenty of time to spend together."

"Even so...oh, love, I wish I didn't have to leave!"

I put my arms around his neck and kissed him deeply. "I know. I miss you already."

I turned on the light and we both dressed, me putting on my pajamas. "When can I see you again?" I asked.

"In a few days. I'm afraid my mother insists on knowing my every move now. I got away tonight by claiming to be on the hunt, and that's still a good excuse she won't challenge. The trouble is, I actually should be on the hunt some of those times. But I'll make time for you. I promise."

I scooped his shirt up from the floor and tossed it at him. "I know you will. And...be careful, all right?"

Malcolm paused in his dressing. "What's that supposed to mean?"

I blinked. "It means 'be careful.' Malcolm—"

"I'm sorry. I'm more sensitive about this than I thought. I don't want anyone treating me like I'm fragile."

"I didn't mean that at all."

"I know." He sighed and put his arms around me, holding me close. "I love you. I don't know what I would do without you."

"I feel the same." I buried my face in his chest. "I'm so glad you're alive."

We stood at the outside door, kissing—a little desperately, it felt to me—until finally Malcolm said, "I have to leave. I love you. I'll see you soon."

"Goodbye," I said, and with one final kiss he was gone. I locked the door and set the alarm and trudged upstairs to my bed. It still smelled like him, and I lay on my stomach, breathing him in, until I started to fall asleep. Then I rolled over and settled in for the night. Damn the Accords anyway. There had to be some way for me to be with Malcolm openly, no more of this sneaking around. But nothing I'd learned had given me that secret. The only thing I could see making a change would be for me to admit to the Board of Neutralities what we'd been doing, and that would lose me Abernathy's.

Malcolm feared it might cost me my life, but I didn't think that was likely. Probably. But losing Abernathy's...I loved the store almost as much as I loved Malcolm, and I hated that I was being forced to choose between them.

Eventually I drifted off to sleep, where I dreamed again of the giant polar bear, only this time it had Malcolm in its paws and raked a deep wound in his chest, exposing his heart. His heart was made of clockwork and pumped blue blood like an invader's, and when he opened his eyes they were inky black the way the disguised invader's had been. I tried to run, but he was faster, and just as he had me locked in his claws, I woke, sweating and terrified. It was 6:43. What a wonderful start to the day.

I took a long, hot soak, relishing how the water relaxed my muscles, then toweled off and put on my bathrobe. I had hours before I had to open the store, and I was going to take advantage of every one of them. I made coffee, toasted an English muffin, and drenched the latter in butter and honey that dribbled off the edges. It tasted like the nectar of the gods, hot and liquid, and I sipped and nibbled and felt the lingering effects of the dream fade. Malcolm was healed and I would see him again soon. Nothing else mattered.

My phone rang. I sucked honey off my finger and gingerly answered it. "Hi, Viv."

"Did Jeremiah come in for an augury recently?"

"Not terribly recently. Last Wednesday. Why?"

"I had a gig last night and he didn't come. And now he's not answering his phone."

"He's probably just on the hunt. Sometimes that can take a couple of days."

"He always tells me when he's leaving, though. I spoke to him Saturday afternoon, and he promised he'd be at the gig."

I swallowed my last bite of muffin. "Maybe something came up. I'm sure it's no big deal."

"Hel, I'm worried. Didn't you say there'd been disappearances?"

"It's only been, what, three days? That's not long enough to get worried." I hoped.

"But he said they wanted him to go in to be tested, and he didn't sound enthusiastic."

"It's not hugs and puppies, Viv. Why would he be enthusiastic?" But I was starting to worry, myself. "Look, I'll call the node and see if he went in for the test. I'm sure it's nothing."

"Thanks. I gotta go. You'll do it soon, right?"

"Viv, *calm down.*"

I decided I didn't want to wait on Lucia's call-returning schedule and called Dave Henry. "Is everything all right?" he asked.

"What? Oh, no, Abernathy's is fine. This is more of a personal call. Did Jeremiah Washburn come in to be tested?"

There was a pause. "You should talk to Lucia," Dave said.

"But I—"

"Why are you asking about Washburn?" Lucia demanded. Her voice sounded hoarse again, like she was coming down with something. Or had been crying. It left me feeling uncomfortable, like I'd seen her naked.

"Viv hasn't heard from him in a couple of days. He...he passed the test, right?"

"I don't know. He was supposed to arrive Saturday night and he never showed. He fled from the enforcers I sent to remind him of his...appointment. I take that as an admission of guilt."

"Lucia! He might...it could be anything..."

"I've issued a warrant for his arrest. We'll test him and then we'll know for sure. Until then," Lucia said, her voice even raspier, "I consider Washburn one of the enemy."

12

"He's *not* a traitor," Viv insisted for at least the hundredth time. She sat perched on the stool behind the cash register and twisted her skirt in her hands. "He can't possibly be."

"What worries me are the ones who turn up dead," Judy said. Viv turned a stricken look on her. "Sorry. That was insensitive. I just mean, if he's not a traitor, his life could be in danger."

It was twelve-thirty, and the Nicollien morning rush was over, but none of us felt much like lunch. "We should find him," Viv said. "He needs to prove he's innocent. Couldn't you get the Kellers to find him? Or Harriet, I guess."

"Harriet's still in custody. And even if she found him, he'd have moved on before we could get there," Judy said. "Jeremiah's a wood magus and a front-line fighter. They're all good at staying concealed, even here in the city. And there are places as overgrown as the countryside here, too."

"What about his phone?" I said. "He'd have that on him, right?"

"Unless he ditched it to keep from being tracked."

"Oh. Good point." I paced from the counter to the front door and back. "Viv's right. We have to do something."

"I'm not saying I disagree," Judy said, "but what can we do?"

"What about his familiar?" I said.

"What about it?"

"We could track its harness, right? I mean, Jeremiah said it had to be attached to him, and that sounds to me like it has to be unique to him. If we had some way to follow that attunement..."

Judy was silent. "It would work," she said, "but I've never heard of anyone doing it before. And I bet Lucia would tell us to mind our own business if we asked for her help."

"Do we need her help?" Viv asked. "We could just ask whoever's in charge of...of familiar binding, or whatever it's called."

"I don't know," Judy said. "We should probably leave this to the professionals. If Jeremiah's a traitor—"

"Which he *isn't*."

"*If* he's a traitor, and we find him, he might try to kill us. He could turn his familiar on us if he wanted. None of us are fighters, in case you've forgotten."

"I can't imagine Jeremiah turning on us, even if he is a traitor," I said.

"Helena, you've only known a fraction of the people who turned out to be part of the shadow cabal," Judy said, her voice bleak. "I had close friends who failed the tests. The woman who tried to kill my father the other day was a trusted ally. These people have spent years hiding in plain sight and they're really good liars because of it. Their lives are at stake if they're found out. If Jeremiah's a traitor, he will probably think his life is more important than ours."

"I'd know if Jeremiah believed the invaders are right," Viv declared. "I think he didn't disappear on his own. I think he's being held captive somewhere and he needs our help. Come *on*. We have to do this."

I looked at Judy. "His life could be in danger."

"*Our* lives will be in danger," Judy said. She sighed. "All right. Let me make some phone calls. At the very least, Father needs to know this is a possible way to track down our missing magi."

Viv squealed and hugged Judy, who flushed red. "Can we go tonight? We shouldn't waste more time."

"I'll see what I can find out. It's not a waste of time if we're careful." Judy strode off in the direction of the office.

Viv returned to her seat behind the register. "I'm so worried about him. You don't think he—"

A snap like the world's biggest bug zapper cracked the still air outside. I whipped around to see a woman dressed in faded jeans and a thick sweater, her hand still on the doorknob, sagging to her knees outside the door. "What—" I began.

Realization struck like the bug zapper. "Stay away from the door!" I shouted at Viv, who'd taken a few steps toward the injured woman. I yanked out my phone and called Malcolm. "The door trap caught an invader," I said when he answered. "It's paralyzed for now, but we need someone here *immediately*."

"On my way," Malcolm said, and the line went dead. I stuffed my phone into my pocket and moved to where I could see the fallen woman. She still had hold of the doorknob and was on her knees with her head pressed against the wooden frame. A young man had stopped and was trying to remove her death grip on the knob, to help her lie down. I wanted to shriek at him to stay away, but that would just make me look crazy. Instead, I gripped Viv's hand and watched for signs of returning life.

"It looks just like a person," Viv whispered. "How can you know it's an invader?"

"The security system only works on invaders. Could you imagine if it zapped all our customers?"

"Like you don't have some customers you wish you could zap."

I giggled nervously. Had the woman twitched? The man looked up at us and shouted, "Call 911! She's not breathing!"

I waved my phone at him, realized if I'd called 911 I'd still be on the phone, and pretended to punch numbers. I held the phone to my ear and said, "I hope Malcolm gets here soon. The installers didn't say how long it would keep the thing inert. If it wakes up first..."

Minutes passed. I heard Judy's footsteps tapping along the linoleum toward us. "I set it up," she said. "What are you looking at?"

"The security system caught an invader," I said without turning around. I was afraid, irrationally, that if I took my eyes off it, it would leap to its feet and run away, and I wanted it caught.

"Where are they?" the young man shouted at me. I shrugged and hoped I looked sufficiently terrified. If the invader woke, it might kill the young man. It suddenly occurred to me that I'd never asked if the door trap reset itself after discharging. If it was dormant, the thing could enter the store, leave its human suit, and trigger Abernathy's wards, destroying the store and taking all of us with it. I scanned the street, looking for Malcolm's car—but his car was wrecked in the accident, and I had no idea if it had been salvaged or what he might be driving now.

The young man crouched beside the fallen "woman." "She's still not breathing. I think she's dead," he called out. More people had gathered, increasing my tension and fear. Someone else tried removing the thing's hand from the doorknob, with no success. *Malcolm, hurry.*

The crowd exclaimed and took a step back. I looked down at the invader and saw it twitch, its shoulders jerking back like an insect's legs. Judy grabbed my hand and crushed it. The thing stood slowly, all its joints moving independently of each other like a creaking ladder. It seemed to be having trouble freeing itself from the doorknob, as if the knob were coated in something sticky, but finally it broke free and stood there, shaking its hand like it hurt. It glared at me through the door. "*Well played, custodian,*" it hissed. "*Don't think you've won. We'll think of something else.*"

It took a few wobbly steps away from the door. The crowd, possibly sensing something strange had happened, backed away to give it room. The thing glanced over its shoulder at me. Its human mouth smiled widely, revealing teeth stained black. Its arm whipped out, and it grabbed an onlooker by the collar, dragged the helpless man close, and pressed its lips to the man's mouth in a horrible kiss.

The crowd murmured, shifting in a confused way. The invader released the man and shoved him aside, staggering a bit as if drunk. I flung the door open and rushed out, not thinking of the danger. "Stop it—her!" I shouted.

The thing turned around. Its solid black eyes gleamed. "*Foolish girl*," it said, teetering on unsteady feet. "*You should have stayed inside.*"

I backed up and tripped over the fallen man the invader had kissed. He was elderly, and he looked confused. I staggered and managed to keep my feet under me, putting the old man between me and the invader. The thing took a few more staggering steps, its foot coming down on the man's hand and making him cry out in pain. Everyone else just stood there like statues, leaving me defenseless before it.

Someone took me by the shoulders and thrust me behind him. "Get back inside," Malcolm said. He was dressed in suit and tie, but he took up a fighting stance, both his hands empty. I thought briefly about disobeying him, helping him somehow, then remembered I wasn't a fighter and I'd probably just get us both killed, me for being incompetent and him for worrying about me. I ran back inside and slammed the door.

"What's he going to do?" Viv said.

"Fight the creature, of course."

"But how? He can't make an illusion to protect himself from all those people watching, and if he kills it, won't it look like he killed a woman?"

I swore. Viv was totally right. Malcolm was in an untenable position. He didn't even have a weapon—or, more likely, he had a weapon he couldn't use in public. I pressed my forehead against the newly-replaced glass and prayed for a miracle.

It was a still tableau: Malcolm facing off against the "woman", whose face and hands were stained dark now with a viscous liquid oozing from her eyes, ears, nose and nailbeds; the old man lying helpless on the ground between them, struggling to get up; the crowd of onlookers, completely useless. Malcolm balanced lightly on the balls of his feet, his arms held at the ready, his fists loosely closed. The invader swayed drunkenly, but its black eyes were still fixed on Malcolm, weeping oily tears.

It happened so suddenly I jerked back from the window in shock. Malcolm leapt at the invader, driving one fist into its stomach and wrapping his arm around the creature's neck in the next motion. The thing howled and tried to break free, but Malcolm bore it to the ground and pinned it. One or two people screamed, and someone went forward to try to drag Malcolm away from the "woman." Malcolm elbowed him sharply in the chest.

"This woman is ill," he said, his voice muffled by the glass. "She is extremely contagious. I suggest—"

I screamed, "Malcolm, *look out!*"

Dark tendrils that glistened in the afternoon sunlight emerged from the thing's widening mouth. For a moment, Malcolm's grip on the thing tightened. The tendrils flailed about, feeling for a victim, and one brushed Malcolm's face. He cried out and released the invader, taking a few stumbling steps away from it. With one hand he gingerly touched his cheek. Then he snarled, drawing a long knife from his sleeve and provoking cries of alarm from the useless onlookers. If only they'd have the sense to run away!

Distantly, I heard sirens approaching. Wonderful. Someone had actually called 911. Now there would be deaths. Malcolm stood, his knife held ready. The invader's human body twitched, its mouth growing even wider, and the thing continued crawling out of it. It was a dull rust-orange color with a rough, pimply exoskeleton and tendrils where its legs should be. The human body tore as it forced its way through. I realized I was holding Viv and Judy's hands and released them, rubbing feeling back into my hands.

The ambulance pulled up even with the front door. A couple of paramedics jumped out of the rear door, armed—*armed?*—with long, skinny rifles they brought to bear on the invader. Two shots echoed in the street, and darts erupted from the thing's arm and throat. Immediately the paramedics began reloading, and Malcolm leaped forward to grab the invader before it could fall. I might have been the only one in a position to see Malcolm's knife pressed against its side, poised to kill if that became necessary.

But the invader sagged in Malcolm's arms, its black eyes still wide open, half its disgusting body falling out of its host's mouth. Malcolm lifted it, keeping well away from the limp tendrils, and carried it to the back of the ambulance. The paramedics joined him there, and I saw them having a conversation I was too far away to hear.

I saw one of the onlookers, a scruffy-looking young man with a long striped scarf wrapped several times around his neck, kneel beside the old man, who had gone unconscious. Long streaks of watery black extended from the corners of his eyes, like he'd wept tears of black oil. I gasped and pounded on the window. "Don't touch him! He might be contagious!"

The scruffy young man looked up at me in confusion. "Contagious! Like the woman!" I shouted, pointing at the ambulance. The young man jerked away and wiped his hands on his pants, though I was pretty sure he hadn't touched the fallen man.

Malcolm finished his conversation with the "paramedics" and returned to the unconscious old man, bending to lift him into his arms. "Nobody leave," he commanded, and carried the old man to the ambulance. Sure enough, people began drifting away. "Hey!" Judy shouted, "he said to stay here!"

"Do we really want them to stay?" Viv said.

"Probably not. But Campbell might have something in mind."

We watched Malcolm shut the doors of the ambulance and wave to the driver, who let out a few squawks with the horn and drove away. A few people remained, among them the scruffy young man. "Did any of you touch one of them?" he said. They all shook their heads, the scruffy man most vehemently. "You're all very lucky," Malcolm continued. "The disease is contagious, and you all saw how it affected that woman. I'll need your contact information, and someone will be in touch with you. Don't breathe a word of this to anyone, do you understand?"

"If there's an outbreak, people deserve to know," the scruffy man said.

"One ill person does not an outbreak make," Malcolm said. "But I assure you the public will be informed. Watch the news at six. If there's danger, it will be announced then. If not...then we've contained the problem. Now, your contact information."

Malcolm scribbled in a small notebook he pulled from inside his suit coat. Then he said, "Thank you for your cooperation," and came inside, shutting the door behind him. I took a step toward him, and he held up his hand, stopping me before I could throw my arms around his neck. I flushed with embarrassment. One invader attack and suddenly I'd forgotten all the caution we took in our secret relationship.

"Your suit is ruined," Judy pointed out.

Malcolm looked down at the streaks of watery black liquid smearing his coat and white shirt. "It will have to be burned," he said, and removed the coat and loosened his tie before taking it off entirely and putting it in his pants pocket. "I apologize for undressing in public, but I'm unwilling to have this residue so close to my skin."

"We don't mind," I said, then blushed again at the look Judy gave me.

Malcolm balled up the coat inside-out and wrapped the ruined shirt around it, then held it in front of him like a basketball. "I was useless," he said. "Had my security team not arrived when it did, I would now either be in custody for murder, or I'd be dead."

"You kept the invader from attacking anyone else," I said.

"I couldn't keep it from attacking *me*." He was looking into the distance at something no one else could see. "I've never felt the touch of an invader before. I had no idea how agonizing it is. I didn't dare subdue it fully, and risk having it drain me."

I risked putting my hand on his arm, which was tense and rigid. "Malcolm, you told me there would be great adjustments. This is just one of them. Maybe you need to rely more heavily on firearms?"

He looked down at me, half-smiling. "A polite way of pointing out my weakness?"

Stung, I snatched my hand away. "I'm just being sensible while I wait for you to pull your head out of your ass. You're still a fighter. Stop dwelling on what you can't do and figure out what you can."

Malcolm's eyes widened. Out of the corner of my eye I saw Judy's mouth drop open. I didn't care if it was rude. I wasn't going to put up with the man I loved being such a complete whiner baby.

Then he laughed. It pissed me off further. "You'd better not be laughing at me," I said.

"Of course not," Malcolm said. "I'm laughing at myself. I swore I wouldn't fall into self-pity, yet here I am...ah, Helena, what would I do without you?"

"Live a life of bleak despair and hopelessness, probably," I snapped. I was still irritated, though I was having trouble holding onto that emotion.

"I fear you're correct. Ladies," Malcolm said, inclining his head to Viv and Judy, "the custodian and I need to speak privately. Helena, your office?"

I followed him, somewhat grumpily, into the office, where I shut the door behind us and, after a moment's thought, locked it. Malcolm tossed his ball of clothes into the metal trash can and leaned against the desk, staring at the can for a long moment. "I didn't think you'd need privacy to stare at the trash," I said.

Without looking at me, Malcolm said quietly, "I forgot again. I tried to set the ruined clothes on fire, and..." He sighed and pinched the bridge of his nose. "Helena, I hope it's not too weak of me, but I don't know if I'll ever adjust to this new life."

The sadness in his voice dispelled my irritation and left me feeling nothing but compassion for him. I put my arms around him and rested my head on his chest. "You're not weak," I said, "and you'll get past this. I wish I could tell you how long it will take, but I don't know. And neither do you. You just have to keep going, one day at a time."

"I've never been afraid before, facing an invader. I feel like a stranger to myself." He put his arms around my waist and drew me closer.

"I bet you've never faced one of the intelligent invaders before, either."

"No. True. Though I'm not sure it should make a difference."

"I was actually thinking that you went after it without hesitating, and how most people probably wouldn't. That makes you brave, in my opinion."

"I like your opinion. I think I'll use it."

I lifted my face toward his. "I'm sorry I yelled at you."

"I'm not. You were right, I was feeling sorry for myself. And that will get me nowhere." He leaned down and brushed my lips with a kiss, feather-light and tingling. "Particularly since I crave your approval and good opinion."

"You have it." I twined my fingers in the hair at the base of his neck—he needed a haircut—and pulled his head down so I could kiss him deeply. His mouth tasted sweet, like honey, and I stepped closer as he ran his hands down my back and over my hips. "Mmm," I murmured. "Tell me you're coming back tonight."

"I can't. I promised my mother I'd stay home." He moved from kissing my lips to nipping at my earlobe, making me sigh with pleasure. "I am seriously considering manufacturing a hunting emergency."

"No, don't do that. She might get suspicious. We'll just have to exercise restraint."

He hooked his thumbs through my belt loops and tugged me so close I could feel every inch of his body pressed against mine. "I spent two weeks of enforced separation from you. I am not interested...in exercising...restraint."

The low growl of his voice made me giggle, and I dropped a kiss on his jaw, hard and angular. "We can wait another night. Waiting makes it better."

"I'm not sure that's true." He caught my ponytail between his fingers and twirled my hair around his thumb. "But I'm willing to make the experiment."

I kissed him one last time and stepped away from the comforting circle of his arms. "You should probably go. Much as I'd rather you stay. Judy can handle anyone who comes in...actually, we probably have time for—"

Malcolm laughed and silenced me with a finger across my lips. "Exercising restraint, remember?"

I made a face. "That was my idea, wasn't it? Sometimes I have stupid ideas."

We walked back to the front of the store, close enough to hold hands but separated by those few inches, and Malcolm coolly said his goodbyes just as if he and I hadn't been kissing feverishly just moments before. I watched him stride away up the street, looking rather odd in expensive suit pants and a white undershirt, and said, "He is so hot."

"Can we talk about Jeremiah now? You know, the one who might be in mortal danger?" Viv said.

"Oh. Right. Judy, what did you say about setting something up?"

"Viv and I were talking about it while you were having your... private discussion...with Campbell," Judy said. "I spoke to Seth Richards, explained what we had in mind, and he said he could help us."

"It can't have been that easy."

"I may have misrepresented our interest in tracking Jeremiah's familiar. Seth *might* think we're doing this with Lucia's authority, testing the theory before she implements it broadly."

"You *lied* to him?"

"Misrepresented, Helena. If anyone finds out we're doing this, they'll put a stop to it, and that'll be it for helping Jeremiah. Or am I wrong, and you told Campbell the plan?"

"I—no." I'd forgotten about it, honestly, but even if I'd remembered...no, I wouldn't have told him. He would have felt it his duty to come along, and I had a feeling that even if Jeremiah wasn't a traitor, a confrontation between Nicollien and Ambrosite could not end well for anyone. I crushed feelings of guilt and added, "Look, we find out where Jeremiah is and if he's being held captive, nothing more, all right? We aren't equipped to bring him in if he's—"

"He's *not* a traitor," Viv said.

"This worked out *so* well for us before, with the serial killer, remember?" Judy said. "The plan was just to locate *him*, too. And Jeremiah's also a wood magus and accustomed to working alone. If he catches us—"

"Which he *won't*."

"We need to be prepared to run. All that matters is we get news of his location to Lucia. Let's just hope it doesn't cost us our lives."

"You're such a pessimist," Viv said, sticking her tongue out at Judy.

"I'm a realist. Aren't I, Helena?"

"A realist, yes," I replied absently, remembering being caught in skinny, wire-hard vines, remembering too the feel of Mitch Hallstrom's soft hand lying flat against the skin of my belly. I hoped with all my heart Jeremiah wasn't a traitor.

13

Judy had called it "the kennels," but it looked like a cement block bunker, long and pale gray in the moonlight. Its low windows made it seem sunken into the earth, a cut-rate hobbit hole for low-income hobbits. Lights flanked the wire mesh of the gate we'd come in by, illuminating the fence for a few yards before it disappeared around a corner. More lights shone over the metal door at the far end of the building, yellow and flickering like candles. It was the most depressing thing I'd seen in weeks.

I sat with both hands on the steering wheel of my elderly Honda Civic and shivered. I'd been stupid not to anticipate what had happened. Walking into that long, long chamber lined with steel mesh cages, that moment of perfect silence as if the world was holding its breath, and then the screaming, the howling, and worst of all the clawing as dozens of invaders all tried to break free to reach me. I'd shrieked and retreated as fast as I could into the waiting room, where a couple of Nicolliens regarded me curiously. Then, with a quick word to Judy, I'd retreated all the way to the car. I shivered again. It was the cold, just the cold. I should turn on the car and keep it warm. Just the cold.

The door opened, and Viv and Judy emerged. "We've got it," Viv said, dropping into the seat next to me. She held out her cupped hands and displayed a plastic hamster ball, slightly cloudy with long use. Inside was a glowing yellow sphere, fuzzy around the edges, that quivered in the center of the ball.

"How does it work?" I asked.

"When I trigger it, it points the direction toward the harness." Viv held it up to eye level. "We could be driving for a while. I hope you have a full tank of gas."

"It's better than nothing," Judy said irritably.

"Of course it is. That wasn't a criticism. It's still going to be hard to find him."

"Then let's get moving," I said.

Viv held the ball to her lips and whispered a word I couldn't make out. The sphere stretched, spun into a coil, then flattened out into a rough arrow shape that turned a sickly pale green like a phosphorescent grub. "It's pointing...which way are we facing?...southwest. Toward downtown."

I groaned and put the car in gear. "If he's somewhere downtown, it really will take forever."

"Less bitching. More driving," Judy said.

The arrow kept pointing steadily southwest as I passed the entrance to the 5. "I thought you wanted to hurry," Judy said.

"If we're on the freeway, we could speed right past him and then take forever working our way back." I made a left turn and the arrow spun to compensate. "This makes more sense."

"Logical," Judy admitted. "Wait, it's moving."

"It's pointed due west now," Viv said. "Definitely downtown."

I grumbled, but obediently crossed the river and made my way into the warren of one-way streets that was Portland's city center. Viv gave me directions. "Stay on 6th—no, sorry, take the next left—"

"I can't take the next left!"

"Then the *next* next left."

"This place wasn't made for cars," Judy said. "Not that walking is a hardship, if you live nearby."

"I don't believe you ever walked anywhere in your life," Viv said.

"I walked to school when I was in fourth grade."

"That doesn't count."

"Would you both stay focused!" I demanded. "Burnside's coming up and I need to know right or left."

"Right," they chorused. I put on my turn signal and made the turn.

"Okay, I think we need to get on Broadway," Viv said.

"Why Broadway?"

"I've got a hunch." She wouldn't be any more specific than that. I turned onto Broadway and headed roughly southwest again.

"The arrow's steadied," Judy said. "I think we're getting close."

"I know we're getting close," Viv said.

"Why?"

"Because this is the way to Jeremiah's apartment." She pointed ahead to where a confusing intersection led in five directions. "Stay on Broadway."

Almost immediately the city vanished. Broadway, which hadn't exactly been broad in the first place, narrowed down to one lane in both directions, and trees and bushes rose up thickly on either side of the road. It was like a quiet country lane in the middle of the city, dark and overgrown and sinister, with the leaves silvered by the moonlight. Branches lashed in the wind, promising a storm to come. I slowed instinctively, feeling like an intruder in this space.

Houses and condos flashed past on both sides, with cars occasionally parked at the side of the road in complete disregard for possible collisions. I could see the shoulders were wide enough, but that didn't keep me from cringing every time I came close. I slowed again. The arrow still pointed straight ahead, if you could call the winding road "straight."

"Get ready to turn right," Viv said.

"Viv, what if you're wrong?"

"Then we get back on the road and follow the arrow." Viv was leaning forward, peering into the dimness. "It's the next right. It's hard to see—turn now!"

I cranked the wheel and turned up a driveway that was so overgrown it was barely recognizable as such. It sloped upward alarmingly; getting up it after a winter storm, with ice covering the ground, would be almost impossible. I gunned the engine and slowly made it up the incline and out of the green tunnel surrounding it.

At the top of the slope was a wide gravel yard with a couple of cars parked in it. Beyond the yard, a row of two-story apartment units backed into a hedge of rhododendrons, beyond which were enough trees to be called a forest. The apartments were gray in the moonlight, warmed in places by lit windows, and looked as out of place in that wilderness as the cars did. I pulled into a spot near the driveway and turned off the engine. "What now?"

"Look," Viv said. The arrow pointed toward the apartments. "I was right."

"I can't believe Jeremiah's still here," Judy said. "He has to know they're looking for him."

"Let's check it out." Viv dug in her pocket. "I've got a key."

We crunched across the gravel toward the apartments. I didn't bother trying to be stealthy, because I was terrible at it, but I did my best not to be too noticeable. Viv strode ahead of us, stuffing the hamster ball into one of her capacious pockets. Aside from our footsteps, the air was still, singing with the high-pitched whine you can only hear when everything's really quiet. My breath puffed out of me in pale clouds. I glanced at Judy, who had her gloved hands stuffed in her coat pockets. She looked annoyed, probably because she hadn't worn a heavier coat.

Viv stopped at the second door from the end on the ground floor and knocked. The windows of this apartment were dark, with no light coming from deeper within, no movement. She knocked again, then inserted the key into the lock. Quietly, she turned the knob and pushed the door open. "It smells empty," she said.

"What does 'empty' smell like?" Judy said.

"Unused. No cooking smells, no body odors—I mean like soap or cologne or stuff like that, though Jeremiah doesn't wear cologne."

Viv held the door open and gestured to us to enter. The room was completely black except for the lighter rectangle where the moon shone through the drapes. Viv shut the door and turned the light on.

"Viv!"

"There isn't anyone here. And I bet Lucia's people have already searched this place and moved on." She sounded disappointed. I looked around. It wasn't a large apartment. The front room was divided in half by a leather sectional, and a table and chairs stood on the other side. The small kitchen, visible from the living room, had dark wooden cabinets and a white refrigerator that looked too big for the room. A couple of fridge magnets held coupons to its unmarked surface. A short hallway with four doors led deeper into the apartment. "Jeremiah's bedroom, and his familiar's room. The hall closet. And the bathroom."

I gingerly peeked into the first room. It was bare of furniture and the carpet and pad had been rolled up and stowed in the closet, leaving the floor bare concrete. A wire cage stood in the far corner. Its door was open. The room stank of paint thinner, the smell of a familiar. I pinched my nose shut and closed the door.

Viv was standing in the doorway to Jeremiah's bedroom. It was a wreck—the bed unmade, clothes heaped on the floor, drawers pulled out and dumped on the bed. The closet was empty except for a few hangers. "Is this...this isn't how it always looks, is it?"

Viv shook her head. "They must have tossed the place. But where is he?"

"Come and look at this," Judy said.

We joined her in the small bathroom, which also smelled of paint thinner. "He was too smart for us," Judy said, twitching aside the Wonder Woman shower curtain. A puddle of green goo, a couple of scales, and a limp harness lay in a pile at the bottom of the tub. "He destroyed his familiar."

"But...why?" I asked. "You said no one's ever thought to do what we did."

"That doesn't mean he couldn't think of it too. And if he's on the run, a familiar is a liability." Judy dropped the curtain and rubbed her palms on her thighs. "So much for our cunning plan."

Outside, branches scratched at the small bathroom window, which creaked in the rising wind. "I'm not giving up," Viv said. "We're going to find him and...and convince him..."

"Of what? I hate to say it, Viv, but this looks increasingly like he's guilty."

"He can't be!" Viv shouted. "He loves me. How could someone that evil love anyone?"

The window creaked again. Then it shattered, showering us with glass shards. We all shrieked and covered our faces. I looked up in time to see thin branches thrusting their way through the window opening, slithering along like bark-covered snakes bristling with leaves. The branches grabbed us, bound our hands and pressed us against the walls. I ended up with one foot in the tub and the other awkwardly outside it, straddling the edge and hoping I didn't have my foot in what was left of Jeremiah's familiar.

Jeremiah appeared in the doorway. I'd never seen him wear hunter's fatigues before and was surprised at how well they suited him. His familiar smile was gone, replaced by a hard, cold expression. "You shouldn't have come," he said, his voice matching his expression. "Don't you know how dangerous I am?"

"You're not dangerous," Viv said. "Jeremiah, let me go."

"I don't think so." He moved on past the bathroom door and I heard him go into his bedroom. There was a sound like wood moving across wood, and the tinkle of glass. Then a thump, like a trap door closing, and Jeremiah reappeared, tucking something small into his thigh pocket. "Did they send you to appeal to my better nature?"

"Nobody sent us," I said. "We were worried about you. That you might have been captured."

"I know you're not a traitor," Viv said.

"Oh, I'm a traitor, all right." Jeremiah smiled, a lopsided, cynical thing that bore no resemblance to his usual brilliant smile. "Or was. Not that it will make a difference."

"What are you talking about?" Judy said. She'd been struggling against her living bonds, but had given up and was now regarding Jeremiah coldly.

"The trees will release you once I'm gone," Jeremiah said. "Tell Lucia not to bother looking for me. I'm fleeing two sets of people who want me dead, and I don't intend to let them catch me."

"Who else wants you dead?" I said. "Jeremiah, did you break with the traitors?"

Jeremiah ignored me. His attention was all for Viv, who was crying. "You were the one good thing in my life," he said, "the one innocent thing. I do love you, Viv, and to prove it, I'm leaving here before they figure out how they can use you against me."

"Don't you *dare,*" Viv snarled through her tears. "You owe me an explanation, if you're not just going to duck out of here like a coward."

A smile touched his eyes. "I might have known that's what you'd say," he said. "I should—" He turned away, shaking his head. The thin branches binding my hands withdrew, and I found myself free and able to step away from the remains of the familiar. "Don't make the call," he warned Judy, who had her phone out. "I'll tell you my sad story, but in exchange for that I'll have to insist you let me leave. I have no interest in being executed by Lucia's henchmen."

"You think you can make demands?"

"I think I could have had those branches strangle you. Put the phone away. Now."

Judy scowled, but put her phone back in her pocket. "Why don't you three sit on the couch," Jeremiah said. "You might as well be comfortable."

"Why are you still here?" I said. "You should already be running. You killed too many steel magi for them to let you live."

"I wasn't part of that magic. Wasn't approached to be part of it, fortunately, because I would have refused and they would have killed me."

"So you say. Why didn't you leave when Lucia's summons came?"

"They came for me unexpectedly, while I was destroying my familiar," Jeremiah said, "and I left behind a couple of essentials I wanted to take with me into exile. If you'd come last night, you'd have run into Lucia's watchdogs. Good timing all around, eh?"

"I don't care about that. I want to know why you're a traitor." Viv wiped her eyes with the back of her hand.

"Because it made sense, once upon a time," Jeremiah said. He paced a tight circle in front of us. "The Wardens are fighting a losing battle. We barely hold our own against the invaders, the small, stupid ones, and we have no chance against the intelligent ones. I met one of the latter one night while I was hunting, and we had a long conversation about what they want from our world. What we can do for each other. And I was convinced."

"But they want to treat us like cattle! Kill some of us like...like sacrifices," I exclaimed.

"That's what they say, yes. And I'm ashamed to say I fell for it. Small sacrifices for the lives of all of humanity. It seemed a fair price to pay for everyone else's freedom." Jeremiah shook his head. "But it's not what they want. Once they get us in a subservient position, once we stop fighting, they will slaughter us all and move on to the next world. It's what they've done for millennia. They have no compassion, no kindness, no sense of justice. There is only kill or be killed."

It felt as if he'd sucked all the air out of the room. "How do you know this?" I asked.

"Years of investigation. I know I look like a happy-go-lucky guy, but I don't trust easily and I certainly don't trust anyone who claims such naked altruism on the part of someone else's race. I joined the invaders' human allies expecting to learn things they weren't telling us. When I discovered just how much they weren't telling us, it was too late. They'd already marked me as one of their own."

I shot out of my seat. "But, Jeremiah, don't you see how valuable that makes you? Lucia needs the information you have. You should tell her the truth!"

"And say what, exactly? I have no way of proving I've left the Mercy—such a pleasant name for the enemies of mankind, don't you think? All I have is a marker in my head that says I'm one of the traitors. Lucia already knows I'm the enemy. My former masters will figure it out soon enough. I'm a dead man unless I flee."

"Lucia can protect you. And she doesn't want to kill anyone if she can help it."

Jeremiah's smile became even more bitter. "She killed her own lover when it turned out he was a traitor. She'll have no problem killing me."

"You should have told her as soon as you decided to break with the...Mercy?" Judy said. "She might have believed you then."

"I was afraid she'd just think I was crazy. Besides, it was when the familiars were breaking their bindings, and things were a little busy. I did what I could. I steered the Nicolliens in the right direction to figure out what was wrong with the bindings."

"How did you know that?"

"I sacrificed my familiar to study the binding. I would have had to anyway, since my masters could use the familiar to monitor me."

"And yet you took another familiar." Judy's voice was flat, emotionless.

"I had to. They were becoming suspicious." Jeremiah let out a long, deep breath. "That's about it. I realized I couldn't belong to an organization that ultimately would allow the destruction of mankind, and I started looking for a way to free myself that didn't include my death. Then Lucia started rounding up traitors, and my time was up. Now, do I need to tie you up again to keep you from following me, or can you give me your word you'll let me go?"

Viv stood. "No."

"Viv, I don't—"

"No. You're not leaving. You're going to tell Lucia what you told us and work to reverse the damage you caused."

"I can't do that."

"Yes, you can." She turned to look at Judy and me. "We'll talk to Lucia first. Explain what we learned. We'll get her to promise she won't just kill you out of hand, and then you can arrange a meeting in a safe neutral place, if that's what you're worried about. That would make sense, anyway."

Jeremiah shook his head. "Nowhere is safe."

"Stop talking like you've already given up!" Viv shouted. "I love you. I'm not going to watch you throw your life away and go on the run forever when you could actually do something to help the Wardens!"

"Lucia will *never* listen to you."

"She will. She's not irrational. I think she would rather have the advantage of your knowledge than see you dead."

"I think Viv's right," I said. "And Lucia can protect you. Please, Jeremiah."

Jeremiah looked at Judy. "You've been awfully quiet."

"If I were you, I'd run," Judy said.

"*Judy!*"

Judy held up a hand to forestall Viv's next outburst. "But that's because that's how I work," Judy said. "I'm no fighter. I have to strike from the shadows to protect myself. You're a front-line fighter and you're no coward. Go on the run now, and you might live a long life. It's up to you whether it's happy or not. But stay and fight, and you might make a difference. Plus, it will make Viv happy, and I think that's something you want."

"Viv's in danger the moment the Mercy finds out I've betrayed them."

"Then I'll have to find a way to protect myself," Viv said. "I'm not going to be a hostage before anyone's even tried to hurt me."

Jeremiah's face was a mask of indecision. "I shouldn't," he said, and reached out to Viv, who put her arms around him.

"I have faith in you," she whispered. "Everything else, we can figure out."

Jeremiah sighed and closed his eyes, putting his hand on Viv's bright magenta hair. "This may be the stupidest thing I've ever done."

"Well, it doesn't come close to the stupidest thing *I've* ever done," I said, "so you're all right."

"Do you have your phone?" Viv asked. Jeremiah shook his head. Viv dug in her pocket for her phone and pressed it on Jeremiah. "We'll call you when we've spoken to Lucia, and you can set up the meeting time and place. In the meantime, do you have someplace safe to go?"

"Safe enough that I won't tell you where it is." Jeremiah kissed her, and Judy and I turned away to give them a little privacy. I could hear them speaking in voices too low to make out, then Viv said, "We'll go to Lucia right away. Be safe."

Jeremiah turned off the light before we left his apartment, and when I looked back, the place looked as empty as it had when we'd arrived. "I hope this is the right thing to do," Judy said as I drove down the steep driveway.

"Of course it's right. Think how much Jeremiah can help Lucia in this fight." Viv hammered her fists on her thighs, a nervous, erratic movement. "I was so scared!"

"That's definitely not what I expected," Judy said. "I guess we were both right."

"Now we just have to convince Lucia," I said. "That ought to be..."

"Difficult?" said Viv.

"Terrifying?" said Judy.

"A challenge," I said.

14

With Judy's help, I navigated to the entrance to the Gunther Node. Viv and I stood in the middle of the thorny white circle painted on the floor while Judy spoke into the old-fashioned telephone on the white metal wall. "I'm so excited," Viv whispered. "I've never been here before! Are you sure you won't be in trouble for bringing me?"

I eyed Judy, whose conversation with whoever was on the other end of the line was increasingly emphatic. "Either they let you in, or they don't, and if they let you in, we aren't in trouble." *Probably*. "Viv, how can you be excited when Jeremiah's life is at stake?"

The smile fell away from her face. "If I start thinking about him, I start to panic," she said. "I'm trying to distract myself. And now it's not working anymore."

"Sorry."

Judy hung up the phone and strode to the circle. "I think Lucia's in a good mood," she said, "at least, a—"

The world twitched, and we were elsewhere. Even at this hour—it was probably after nine in the evening—the node was busy. Men and women crossed between doorways, talking rapidly or carrying bundles of notebooks or strangely-shaped parcels wrapped in brown paper. A few people were pushing carts that seemed to weigh hundreds of pounds.

"—better one," Judy finished. "We're to wait here for a guide."

We took a few steps to one side—I didn't know if people could teleport in while the spot was still occupied, and I didn't want to find out—and waited. Viv stared at everything in wonder. "You think of magic as being, sort of, allakazam!" She waved her fingers in what was meant to be a mysterious way. "But this is all like some kind of manufacturing business. A drab one. Couldn't they paint murals on the walls or something?"

"It *is* a manufacturing business, in a way," Judy said. "They collect the *sanguinis sapiens* from the node and process it for use in semi-magical technology, or for healing, or...there's lots of uses."

"It just seems so far removed from what Jeremiah does." Viv walked over to a stack of plastic crates and peeked inside the top one.

"Viv!"

"I'm not *touching*. And it's nothing interesting. Just a bunch of empty glass vials."

"For use in collecting *sanguinis sapiens*," a new voice said.

Viv jumped and took a few hasty steps away, putting her hands behind her back. Dave Henry smiled at her. "Don't worry, you're not in trouble," he said. "Not for that, anyway."

"Dave..." I couldn't think how to end that sentence. The smile fell away from Dave's face.

"Come with me," he said, and we followed him in silence.

Now that we were here, I was having trouble remembering all the reasons for coming that had made so much sense an hour ago. I had no idea what Judy had told whoever she'd spoken to, whether it had even been Lucia—probably not—but Lucia had to know, now, that we'd found Jeremiah, and that he wasn't with us and hadn't killed us. What she might make of that, I didn't know, but it made me nervous, going in to see Lucia without all the facts at my disposal.

The hallway to Lucia's office—the usual one, not the insanely long one that was the test for the neurological marker—snaked a little and had no doors or windows. That last made sense, because I was pretty sure the Gunther Node was deep underground. Where else could something this size be without drawing all sorts of attention? I walked beside Judy and behind Viv, who was still looking about her with curiosity, as if this weren't a boring, cold passageway that smelled faintly of gardenias. Except for the gardenias, it could have been some Cold War bunker, designed to withstand a nuclear blast.

Eventually, we came to the short hallway lined with metal doors I was becoming familiar with, and Dave opened the third door on the right. "Inside," Lucia said, and we all dutifully filed in.

To my surprise, Lucia's office was tidy for once, with the stacks of paper on the metal bookshelf replaced with two-inch-thick binders and the plastic milk crates filled with hanging file folders. Lucia sat behind her desk, her fingers steepled in front of her. "Well, if it isn't Nancy, Bess, and George," she said with a wry smirk.

"Who?" I asked.

Lucia rolled her eyes. "Nobody reads the classics anymore," she said. "Tell me why I shouldn't tear each of you a new one for going after a dangerous criminal on your own."

"He's not a criminal!" Viv exclaimed. "He's not a traitor, either."

"He fled apprehension. That doesn't make him innocent."

"It's more complicated than that," I said. We'd agreed on the way over that I would do the talking, but now I wasn't sure Viv could keep quiet. I glared at her, and she glared back at me.

"Is it," Lucia said. "I'm listening. I might not be listening for long, so make it quick."

I nodded, and skipped over the part where we figured out how to track Jeremiah and started in where he'd surprised us in his apartment. Lucia's eyes narrowed as I revealed that Jeremiah was a traitor, narrowed further when I said he was a reformed one, and by the time I reached the end of the story, her lips were thin and pressed tightly together. "He's playing you," she said finally.

"No!"

I elbowed Viv in the side. "I don't think so. He wanted to leave, go into hiding. He didn't see any benefit to coming to you."

"Neither do I. You expect me to believe his story?"

"Yes, I do."

Lucia raised her eyebrows. "Just like that?"

I braced myself against her desk. "Jeremiah had a lot of opportunities to hurt the Wardens. Instead, he steered the Nicolliens toward the solution to the failing bindings. You know the invaders were taking advantage of that catastrophe. If he were still loyal to them, why would he have helped the Wardens instead?"

"We have only his word for that," Lucia said with a frown.

"You can corroborate it," Judy said. "Seth Richards spearheaded that research. He'd know if Jeremiah were involved, and how."

"True." Lucia nodded at Dave, who left the room. "Do you have *any* idea how much damage Washburn could do if I took him at his word? He's a self-admitted traitor and we have no way to prove he's reformed. The Board would take me apart if I were to appear lax toward traitors."

"After...what happened the night of the purge," I said, unwilling to say Martin's name, "I doubt anyone will believe that of you."

Lucia stiffened and wouldn't meet my eyes. "All the more reason for me to be strict in my enforcement of the new policy."

"Then meet with him. Make up your own mind. We told him we could set up a meeting in a neutral place, somewhere you both can feel safe. Please, Lucia. Think of how much he knows that might give us an edge."

Dave came back into the room. "Richards confirms that Washburn gave him the critical information he needed to solve the failing bindings."

"Well, that's something." She pulled out her phone. "What number?"

Viv recited it for her. Lucia crooked her finger at me. "No more detective work, all right? You realize you risked the future of the oracle tonight. You and Rasmussen both going off to potential death...did you have a third candidate for custodian waiting around somewhere?"

I gulped. "Um..."

"That's what I thought. Nevertheless...good work. Now, get out."

Dave shepherded us into the hallway and pointed at the door. "She's pleased," he said. "She wants to believe Washburn is on our side. It would make for a huge morale boost, after...Martin."

"I'm really sorry about that," I said.

"It was a huge blow. She won't even talk about it with me. Maybe someday..." He shook his head and went back into Lucia's office.

"So, does that mean we won?" Viv asked.

"I hope so. Let's go home."

"I'm not tired. I feel like I could take on the world." Viv punched the air a couple of times like a victorious prizefighter.

"Movie night?" said Judy.

"Movie night," I said. "But it's my turn to choose."

They groaned. "Please, *please* let it not be Hitchcock," Viv said.

"*To Kill a Mockingbird,*" I said. "Brilliant screenwriting, wonderful acting, and bonus points for how sexy Gregory Peck is."

"Well, if you put it that way," Viv said.

WEDNESDAY WAS EVEN BUSIER than Tuesday had been, though thankfully no more invaders in human suits tried to enter the store. Everyone wanted auguries related to identifying traitors. Some of them even tried asking "who?" and I had to gently remind them not to waste the oracle's time. They eyed each other furtively, rarely engaging in conversation, and it left Abernathy's feeling cold and quiet and tense.

A couple of Wardens wore small pins on their lapels or shirts, ribbons like the ones people wear for breast cancer awareness, but white instead of pink. After the third Nicollien with one handed over his augury slip, I asked, "What's the ribbon for?"

"It's to show I'm free of the marker," he said, tapping it with his fingernail. "So people know I can be trusted."

"But there's nothing keeping a traitor from wearing it."

He blinked at me. "Um...I guess not."

"I don't know. It doesn't seem like a good way to reduce tension, reminding everyone of the ongoing tests."

"Every little bit helps."

I wasn't sure that was true in this case, but I smiled and retreated into the oracle, where I found his augury immediately. Maybe that meant the oracle thought it was dumb, too.

We had Nicolliens in the store right up until quarter to two, filling me with anxiety at the possibility of the two factions encountering one another. I ushered the last one out the door and smiled at the waiting Ambrosite, though I had no intention of letting her in early. I hadn't had my lunch yet.

"It's like a fishbowl," Judy said, handing me half a tuna fish sandwich and biting into hers. "Only I'm not sure whether we're the fish, or they are."

"The way they press their noses against the glass, they're definitely looking in at us fish." My sandwich was moist and filled with crunchy bits of celery, which was the only way I'd eat celery. "I don't think it's been this busy since last summer, when all the Nicolliens were looking for Malcolm. And the Ambrosites weren't as active then as they are now."

"It's frightening, not knowing who might be a traitor. I can see why they'd want the comfort of an augury."

"You know what's weird?" I took another bite. "That there haven't been reports of shadow cabal members attacking Wardens. Just that one massive attack, and then of course they fight back when they're arrested."

"Do you have any idea how much magic it must have taken to pull that off? Striking all the steel magi at once? I think their reserves were exhausted."

"But not everyone was involved, according to Jeremiah. And now they can't conceal their existence anymore, so why haven't we seen more killers like Mitch Hallstrom?"

"I don't know and I don't care, so long as they keep quiet or flee. I wonder if Lucia's met with Jeremiah yet."

I stuffed the last bite of sandwich into my mouth and checked the time. "Do you think she'll call us?"

"I doubt it. She seemed pretty serious about keeping us out of any more detective work." Judy snorted. "I looked up Nancy, Bess, and George. Apparently it's Nancy Drew and her two best friends. I have trouble picturing Lucia as a young reader of detective stories."

"Well, we wouldn't have to be detectives if she'd do the work herself."

"That's not fair. You know how much she's had to deal with."

I gaped at her. "You just said something in defense of Lucia. I didn't know that was possible."

Judy shrugged. "Maybe I appreciate her job a little better now. I believe in being fair."

"Well, I'm sorry I was critical. You're right, she's had a lot on her plate recently." I wiped my mouth and went to open the door to the mob outside. "This is going to be a long afternoon."

But the mob hung back, making room for the tall, olive-skinned figure at the head of the line. "Ms. Davies," Acosta said, "how are you?"

"Fine." He stood hovering in the doorway, his hands jammed into his coat pockets. "Are you coming in? Because you're in the way of all these nice people."

"How do you know they're nice?" He sauntered in, followed more slowly by the Wardens, who had umbrellas and hoods up against the drizzling rain. "It's impossible to tell a person's character from his face. Or hers. They might be felons. They might be murderers. That book thief, Hallstrom, wasn't it? He looked perfectly innocent."

"That's true. But I think the percentage of murderers and felons in the general population is small enough that I'm safe assuming these people aren't going to try to kill me or steal my stuff." I saw a couple of Wardens wearing the white ribbon and wondered if that was true. Acosta was right about one thing; you couldn't tell a traitor just by looking.

"Probably." Acosta shrugged.

"Well, how can I help you, detective?" Maybe I could get him out of here quickly.

"You can give me an augury," Acosta said.

The room went very still. It had already been quiet, with the Wardens unwilling to speak to anyone who might be a traitor, but this was a frozen, rigid silence, painful and hard. "Excuse me?"

"I want an augury."

Answer his questions honestly, Lucia had said, but could she possibly have anticipated *that* request? Knowing Lucia, yes, she might well have. "You have to write it down in the form of a question," I said, though my mouth was dry and my throat felt numb.

"I don't care who knows it," Acosta said. "My question is—'What is Abernathy's?'"

He'd spoken loudly, and the question hung in the air like a gauzy curtain, drifting away on invisible currents. "Just one minute," I said, and walked into the oracle.

I'd hoped, in the instant between stepping from one world to the next, that the oracle would refuse to answer, throwing up a red light like the glow from a dying star. But the air was blue-tinted and cool, not cold, and in the distance I saw a brighter gleam, blue light haloing a bookcase some ways away. I walked down Abernathy's narrow aisles, some so narrow only one person could pass at a time, until I reached the spot that was the center of the oracle. Four bookcases at least ten feet tall stood facing each other in a square, surrounding a small open space big enough for me to stand comfortably within.

High on one of the bookcases, a large book shone with blue light that traced its edges. I climbed on the lower shelves, gingerly, feeling the bookcase shift under my weight, and carefully removed the book from the shelf. *The Revelation Unveiled*, the title page said, and written in silver ink below that were the words *Gregory Acosta, $1000*.

"You actually want this guy to know things about you?" I said, closing the cover. "He's our enemy! He wants you destroyed!"

Silence. I hadn't expected anything else. The oracle never spoke except under extreme duress, which this wasn't. "Fine," I said. "It's your choice. I wish I knew how he knew to ask for an augury. Makes me wonder who else he's been harassing."

I returned to the front of the store. Acosta was browsing the shelves facing the window, the ones that weren't part of the oracle, as far as I knew. The Wardens all had their eyes on him, which I would have found unnerving, but Acosta either didn't notice or didn't care. He turned to me and said, "Is that it?"

"$1000. And I'm going to have to ask for cash."

"My check's not good here?"

"No. And I'm sure you remember we take payment in trade, but you don't look like you have a box of books under your arm."

"That's all right. I came prepared." Acosta pulled out his wallet and counted out one thousand dollars in hundreds. I handed it off to Judy, who'd been watching this in silence, and handed the book to Acosta. Judy wrote him a receipt.

"Detective," I said as he turned to go, "what do you expect to find there?"

"Answers," he said, and let the door swing shut behind him.

The Wardens erupted in noisy argument. Fears were forgotten in their common shock and horror that an outsider had known to use Abernathy's. I didn't tell them my sister, also an outsider, asked for auguries frequently—that was different in every way. "All right, calm down," I said, though I felt anything but. "Assuming he knows how to interpret that augury, it's not like it would be admissible in court or anything. He's not going to bring the mundane authorities down on us."

"He's police," said Evelia Duclos, who'd stood by the window watching the detective walk away. "You've just given him proof that Abernathy's isn't what it seems to be. Of course he's going to bring the authorities down on us!"

"Lucia told me to answer his questions if he came back, and I did. She wouldn't steer me wrong." But a niggling doubt crept into the back of my mind. It hadn't exactly been a question; what if I was wrong? "Besides, if he knew enough to ask for an augury, that means someone else was loose-lipped, and we've got more to worry about than one detective."

That silenced them, or at any rate reduced their outrage to low murmurs. "I'm going to make a quick phone call, and then I'll take your auguries, so if you'd like to form an orderly line..."

I ducked into the office and called Lucia. "Detective Acosta came in and asked for an augury. I gave him one. Please tell me I didn't screw everything up." Then I went back and accepted the first augury slip without making any exasperated noises. It wasn't the Ambrosites' fault I might have given control of the store to my enemy. And there wasn't anything else I could do about it.

But as the afternoon wore on, I became increasingly tense about my encounter with Acosta. I'd been so stupid. Of course Lucia hadn't meant me to reveal everything to him! What was I thinking? He now not only knew that Abernathy's was special, he had an augury that would answer his questions about what Abernathy's actually was. It was too much to hope for that Acosta wouldn't know how to interpret the augury. He wasn't stupid, just single-minded and wrong-headed. I stopped before leaving the oracle with the latest augury and banged my head gently against the nearest shelf. What if the Board heard about this? I was going to be in so much trouble they'd have to invent new words to describe it.

My phone rang just as I took the final augury slip in hand. Lucia. "Wait just a minute," I said to the customer. "Hello?"

"So our friend has made some discoveries," Lucia said.

"I'm sorry, I shouldn't have—"

"You did just fine. We want Acosta to learn the truth, one baby step at a time."

"But why? He's our enemy!"

"When he thought you were a front for the Mob, sure. Once he knows the truth...I've been thinking about cultivating a contact inside the police force for some time now."

"With all the Wardens we have, how do you *not* have a contact inside the police?"

"Police work is the same kind of full-time job the Wardens have with the Long War. The two are mostly incompatible. Any Warden with an instinct for police work funnels it into front-line fighting."

"I guess that makes sense. But why now? Is Acosta really the best you could do?"

"With the shadow cabal no longer lurking in the shadows, we can expect them to start striking at us once they've recovered from their attack on the steel magi. Another set of eyes, particularly one privy to things I can't see, can only help us. And Acosta's intelligent and driven—a perfect tool."

"Lucia, I don't think Detective Acosta is the kind of person you can manipulate."

"Don't underestimate me, Davies. And I don't intend to manipulate him. Much. If his partner Green comes in, steer him toward asking Acosta any questions he might have. Don't tell him the truth about Abernathy's. He won't believe it unless it comes from his partner. And don't worry. I have everything under control."

"You sound unusually optimistic."

"I am. We just cleared Ryan Parish of being a traitor. I don't mind telling you I'm relieved. Having to replace the Ambrosite leader in addition to all of this would be a pain in my ass I do not need."

"I'm glad to hear it. What about Jeremiah?"

There was a pause. "We're meeting in an hour in a mutually determined spot. I have to say I'm impressed he's willing to take this risk."

"Impressed enough to believe his story?"

"Don't push, Davies. I agreed to listen. That's all."

"That's enough for me."

"It warms my heart to meet with your approval. Now, get back to work." She hung up.

I smiled politely at Doug Schrote, patiently waiting for his augury. "How does it feel, being right about the attack on the steel magi?" I asked.

"Weird," he said. "Like I caused it somehow. I mean, I see connections everywhere, you know? But I'm not used to them being right."

I read his augury slip: *Where is Nathan Morris's fortune buried?* "Maybe you're more insightful than you think," I said.

15

Once Doug was gone, I busied myself for the last half hour cleaning, mostly dusting shelves that constantly seemed to need it. Judy hurried past, wrapped in her coat. "Father's hosting a party tonight," she said. "Call if you hear anything about Jeremiah."

"I will." I picked up the broom and swept the front area clean. I couldn't call Viv, since Jeremiah presumably still had her phone, and Lucia would just yell at me for pestering her, so all I could do was wait and hope. I checked my watch, then locked the front door and turned the sign to CLOSED. One more day done. Would anything ever return to normal? Or at least a new kind of normal, given that the revelation of the shadow cabal—the Mercy—had shaken the magical world to its foundations.

My phone rang while I was in the basement, putting the broom away. "Come let me in," Malcolm said. "I brought dinner."

I squealed and darted up the steps, flinging open the back door with such haste I had to catch it before it bounced. Malcolm stood there with a pizza box in one hand and a six-pack of beer in the other. "Lowbrow cuisine, I know," he said, "but I'm too tired for anything else."

I followed him up the stairs to my apartment. "I don't mind. I was going to have boxed macaroni and cheese."

He shuddered. "I don't know how you can stand to eat that when your palate has supposedly been honed by years of exquisite meals."

"You underestimate my commitment to not liking to cook." I found plates and helped myself to two slices and a can. "Bill's Pizzeria is as close to heaven as takeout pizza comes."

"Even if your idea of heaven is a little strange. You must have an iron-clad digestion to eat that many jalapeños on your pepperoni."

"Someday, it will catch up to me, but until then, I'll eat my spicy pizza with gusto. Did you want to watch a movie, or something?"

"A movie would be nice."

We settled on *Stagecoach* and cuddled up together on my couch, eating and drinking and occasionally (me) burping jalapeño-scented burps. Malcolm didn't seem to mind. I knew we were comfortable with each other when I felt I could eat spicy food with impunity.

I set my plate down on the floor and snuggled closer. "Any other year, and this would have won the Academy Award for best picture. 1939 was an amazing year for film, don't you think?"

Malcolm was silent. "Malcolm?"

He startled. "What?"

"I said...are you watching the movie?"

"Of course. I was just...thinking of something else."

"We don't have to watch it if you're distracted."

"I'm enjoying it."

I sat up, making him turn to look at me. "Something's bothering you."

"I'm fine."

I paused the movie, leaving John Wayne standing up straight with his mouth open. "I can tell you're not."

"I'd rather not talk about it, if you don't mind."

The rebuff hurt. "All right." I unpaused the movie and settled back in next to him, stiffly, my hands folded in my lap.

"And now you're angry."

"I'm not angry."

"You're sitting like you have a board strapped to your spine and your jaw is set. You're not happy."

"I'm as much not angry as you're fine."

He took the remote from me and paused the movie. "I don't know how to untangle that sentence."

"You're supposed to be able to share your unhappiness with me, Malcolm."

"I don't want to burden you."

"You're never a burden. Talk to me. Maybe it will help."

Malcolm sighed. He set the remote on the arm of the couch and took my hand in his. "The team and I were in training all day," he said. "We have to rework all our tactics to...accommodate me."

He sounded so bitter I squeezed his hand and said, "Don't feel sorry for yourself."

"I don't. But I don't think it's unreasonable for me to be angry that it's necessary. At night I lie awake wishing I had those magi in my power, the ones who did this to me. They're not pretty fantasies."

"I'm not sure—" I stopped before I could complete that sentence.

"Not sure of what?"

"I don't want to tell you how to feel. I'm just not sure it's healthy to dwell on wanting revenge. Though the truth is I feel a little bloodthirsty about them myself, so I shouldn't criticize."

"I try to direct that anger into fighting invaders. Mostly I'm successful. Anyway. Training is never fun. It's exhausting. But today was just...discouraging. So much of what we used to do is useless now. I can't just point myself at the enemy and let fly anymore. I actually—Helena, you won't understand how significant this is, but I had to disarm myself of my knives so I wouldn't go for them instinctively."

I squeezed his hand. "I can imagine. Malcolm, I'm so sorry."

"We were fumbling all over the place. If we tried to go on the hunt, one or more of us would be seriously injured. It was discouraging, and infuriating. Based on my performance today, I have no business leading a team in the field."

"But—that's just temporary! You'll figure it out, and soon you'll be as efficient as ever. Maybe even more so, if this forces you to develop new techniques."

"The Wardens don't have time for that. So many teams have been devastated by the loss of their steel magi, there's been a push to put more candidates through the Damerel rites, create new magi to take their places. If I really cared about the Long War more than my own selfish desires, I'd retire and let someone else head my team."

An astonished breath hissed out of me before I could contain myself. "Malcolm, you can't do that!"

"I can, and I probably should. But...Helena, love, I don't want to! This is who I am, magic or no, and it's where I should serve."

"So what are you going to do?"

Malcolm looked away from me. "I'm going to undertake the Damerel rites again."

It was so unexpected it took me a moment to understand his words. "Malcolm, you *can't*," I finally said. "No one's ever survived it a second time."

"This afternoon, after training, I went to talk to Darius Wallach," Malcolm said. "He's the bone magus who supervises the Damerel rites. I told him what I've told you and I told him what I wanted. And he told me—he said he's been waiting for someone like me to come along."

"Someone with a death wish?"

"I have never had more to live for, Helena," Malcolm said, finally looking at me again. "Wallach has invented a new kind of steel aegis, an alloy he says makes a steel magus ten times as capable of wielding magic as the current one. But it's expensive, and the two times he's tried it before, the magi died and the aegises were lost."

"Were you trying to fill me with confidence? Because it's not working."

"The Damerel rites are dangerous even for a first-time magus. Wallach believes the reason no one has ever survived them twice is that the previous aegis sets up a resonance within the magus that a second aegis has to match. He can create an aegis using the new material that resonates with my lost aegis and won't kill me outright.

There's even a possibility that the second implantation will go more smoothly than the first."

"But he's never done this before."

Malcolm hesitated. "No."

"And all this is theoretical. He doesn't even know if the new steel aegis can implant properly."

"Yes."

I felt as if he'd slapped me. "Malcolm, are you out of your mind? This will almost certainly kill you!"

Malcolm clasped my hands in both of his. "Helena, what is certain is that without this, I will no longer be a fighter in the Long War. I will be reduced to working from the sidelines, and the thought fills me with abhorrence. Can't you see that this is my only hope?"

Tears filled my eyes. "Can't *you* see that you'd be throwing away your life for nothing? What's so wrong with working from the sidelines?"

"It would be a waste of my training. And Wallach is convinced—"

"He's not the one who'd be mourning you in secret for the rest of her life!"

Malcolm put his arms around me and drew me close. "I know," he said. "This affects you as much as it does me. I wasn't going to tell you tonight—I wanted to think it through a little more, work out what I intended to do—but you were right, I should be able to share my problems with you."

"Damn straight," I said, my voice muffled a little.

"I wish I could introduce you to Wallach. He can explain it better than I can. It might reassure you to know I'm not leaping into this blindly. Wallach has convinced me that with his new procedure and the alloy aegis, my chances of survival are as good as a first-time Damerel candidate. It's still dangerous, but not foolhardy."

"But..." I couldn't think of a way to end that sentence that wasn't whiny. I didn't want Malcolm to risk his life at *all*, let alone on an untested procedure with an unproven aegis. But before this crisis, he'd gone into the field almost every night, putting his life on the line for the sake of everyone, including me. "If I asked you," I said instead, "would you give this plan up?"

I felt him stiffen. "I would," he said after a moment's pause.

"Why?"

"Because you would never ask it of me."

I nodded. "You're right. And the truth is, this is exactly the kind of risk you were made to take. I couldn't ask you to abandon it without making you someone other than you are."

He relaxed, and I felt him kiss the top of my head. "I never want to hurt you."

"I know. This isn't about me."

"It is, a little. You're right. If this kills me, you'll be unable to grieve openly."

I sat up to look him in the eye. "That's why I'm going with you."

His eyes widened. "You can't go with me."

"I can. I know they let loved ones accompany the candidate as a sort of anchor, a reminder of what they're fighting for."

"Yes, but *you* can't go without revealing our relationship!"

"Then maybe it's time to reveal it. Or did you think we could just go on in secret for years?"

Malcolm gripped my wrist. "Helena, I can't let you do this."

"It's my decision."

"I won't be the reason you lose your life."

"They won't kill me. I've done too much for Abernathy's for them to feel justified in executing me." I was mostly confident of that.

"But you'd certainly be stripped of your custodianship."

"Maybe. If I could convince them otherwise—"

"With what? The evidence from the Accords you've so far failed to find?" Malcolm stood and paced to the window, where he gripped the sill and stood staring down at the street. "No, Helena. Please."

The quiet desperation in his voice stopped my quick response. I stood and went to join him at the window, putting my hand on his shoulder. "I want to be with you."

"And I don't want you to lose something so essential to who you are because of me." Malcolm looked over his shoulder at me. "How will my regaining my aegis matter if it means you losing your custodianship?"

I closed my fingers tightly on his shoulder. "Malcolm—"

"You were meant to be the hands of the oracle. For whatever reason, Nathaniel Briggs chose you—a non-Warden outsider to the Long War, the least likely candidate anyone could imagine. But what happens if you reveal everything, and I die anyway? You'll still lose Abernathy's, and for nothing. *Please,* Helena. I won't tell you I don't wish you could be with me. But I can't indulge that wish. Not at that cost."

The anguish in his eyes startled me. I knew how much Abernathy's meant to me, but I'd never realized how much my custodianship mattered to him as well. "All right," I said. "But you'd damn well better come back."

He smiled and caressed my cheek. "I will always come back to you," he said, turning to take me in his arms.

"When will you do it?"

"I'll give him my answer tomorrow. Then...it will happen Saturday afternoon. It takes them a day to make the new aegis, and then time for him to build up a resonance in it...Saturday is the soonest it will be ready, and I don't want to wait around for no reason."

I put my arms around his neck and ran my fingers through his hair. "I'm not in the mood for a movie anymore."

"Neither am I." He kissed me, his lips lingering on mine, making me shiver with delight. "But I will show you what I am in the mood for, if you'd care to adjourn to the bedroom?"

I kissed him back. "Lead the way."

Doug Schrote came bounding into the store at 2:15 the next afternoon, shouting, "Did you all hear? Malcolm Campbell's going through the Damerel rites again!"

I clutched the augury slip in my hand harder as the murmurs

went up all around. "How do you know that?" I asked, calmly. I hoped.

"Everyone's talking about it. Darius Wallach finally found a test subject for his wacky theory."

I forbore to comment on how wacky something must be for Doug to find it crazy. "I'm sure you're wrong. That seems like something very private."

"No, the Damerel folks are making the aegis right now. It's a special kind of steel that's never been used successfully before. I think Campbell's nuts for trying it. No one's ever survived Damerel twice."

At least Malcolm hasn't been spreading the news. I silently cursed Wallach and his team. Malcolm was a private man, and I was sure he didn't want his business the subject of gossip throughout all of magery. "I'm sure if Malcolm's doing it, he has a good reason."

"Desperation, most likely." Doug turned and went to the end of the line, where he started sharing his news with his neighbors. I smiled at my current customer and hoped I didn't look insane.

As I searched the stacks for the woman's augury, I found myself going over what Malcolm had told me. I wished I was in a position to grill Wallach on the details—what other metals went into the alloy? How was the resonance established? What did "resonance" even mean? What were the chances of death? My knowing those things wouldn't make Malcolm more likely to survive, but I needed something, anything to hold onto when the rest of my thoughts whirled around and around the terrifying central fact that no one, in all the centuries of magery, had ever survived what Malcolm proposed to do.

Judy was at the counter when I returned with the augury. "Is Doug telling the truth?" she asked in a low voice. I nodded. Judy's lips set in a taut, angry line, but she stayed silent. For now. I was sure she'd have plenty to say once the store wasn't so full.

At five, when the store was finally empty of Ambrosites, Judy said, "Why didn't you talk him out of it?"

"I tried. He gave me all the facts and his reasoning, and I couldn't convince him otherwise."

"Of course you could! Threaten never to sleep with him again! It's practically your duty to keep him from doing something stupid like that."

"I couldn't do that without making him someone other than he is. I love him too much for that."

Judy threw up her hands and turned away. "He's out of his mind."

I followed her. "I'm not sure. He's done a lot of research—"

"All prompted by Darius Wallach, no doubt. The mad scientist of Gunther Node."

"Is that really what they call him?" I asked, surprised.

"It's what he calls himself. He's always experimenting—not just with the Damerel rites and aegises, but all sorts of electromagical doodads. Sometimes he comes up with something great, but mostly he just has explosive failures."

"But...the great things are great?"

Judy scowled. "Not the point. The point is—"

"I don't know, I think it might be the point. If his successes are so wonderful, doesn't that point to them being worth the explosive failures?"

"We're talking about your boyfriend here. Do you want to use his name anywhere in conjunction with the words 'explosive failure'?"

"No, but I choose to have hope. Malcolm's made his decision and I support him."

"You have weird ideas about what it means to be a girlfriend." Judy hopped up on the stool and put her elbows on the glass countertop. "I hope he survives. From what I hear, the magi could use that kind of morale boost. Things aren't going well, what with losing almost eighty steel magi."

"Malcolm thinks the new technique could benefit first-time Damerel candidates as well."

"That would be wonderful. They're already pushing the steel magi candidates through too quickly—there haven't been any fatalities yet, but it's only a matter of time."

The door opened, jingling the bells. I was caught with my mouth open, surprised not only at the intrusion but at the man who came through the door. "Detective Green," I said, "how are you?"

"Better than you," he said in his gruff voice. He went to the nearest bookcase and began feeling around underneath its shelves.

I glanced at Judy. "Um...can we help you with something?"

Green grunted and straightened. He extended his hand toward us, displaying something small and matte-black. I heard Judy gasp.

"What is that?" I said.

"A bug," Judy said. "His damned partner bugged us, probably illegally."

"Legally, illegally...it's a gray area," Green said. "He didn't intend to use the information he gathered to send anyone here to jail, at least according to him. Could one of you please tell me what the hell is going on?"

Judy and I looked at each other again. "You'll have to be more specific, detective," I said, but my words felt like they were coming from far away. How long had that thing been there? No wonder Acosta had known about auguries—oh, *no*, we'd talked about Malcolm freely in front of it! Probably Acosta had no idea of the magnitude of the potential for blackmail he had, but if it was recorded somewhere—

"I haven't seen him for more than a couple of hours at a time, this past week," Green said. He tucked the little device into his pocket and patted it absently. "He's put a lot of time into this Abernathy's case, only I find out yesterday he was ordered *off* the Abernathy's case. Worse, there no longer is such a case. And when I finally cornered him, he was cagey as hell and only admitted to having bugged you because I saw the equipment. Who *are* you, Ms. Davies? And what exactly do you do here?"

Judy and I exchanged glances. Green looked thoroughly perplexed, his brow shining with sweat though the store was as comfortable as ever. *Don't tell Green the truth,* Lucia had said. *Steer him toward asking Acosta.* "I sell books," I said. "I sold one to Detective Acosta yesterday. Why don't you ask him about it? In fact, tell him I told you to ask why he bought it."

"That's not good enough."

"It will have to be, because that's all I can tell you." I crossed my arms over my chest and stared him down, hoping I didn't look as frazzled and nervous as I felt.

Green scowled. "If I don't start getting some answers, I'm arresting both of you."

"On what grounds?"

"I'll figure something out." He pulled the door open and stomped away.

As soon as the door shut, I slumped against the counter. "He can't arrest us, can he?"

"I guess he could manufacture evidence," Judy said. "I have no idea whether it would stick. I'm sure my father would intervene."

"For you, maybe. Probably not for me."

"You're a Warden. He'll support you over a non-Warden, even a police officer, however he feels about you personally."

"That's comforting."

A few more Ambrosites came in during the last hour, but they seemed more interested in talking about how insane Malcolm was than in getting auguries. I smiled politely until my face hurt, told them all my support for Malcolm's decision, and managed not to burst into tears. When I finally put up the CLOSED sign and locked the door, it was with a profound sense of relief. Only two more days —not even two full days—and it would all be over. One way or the other.

"You're tougher than you look," Judy said.

"How so?"

"I'd have punched Lucy Yearsley in the throat for twittering on about all the horrible deaths people have suffered during the Damerel rites. Death's really very rare these days."

"Except for a second-time candidate." I leaned against the counter and scrubbed my eyes with the heels of my palms.

"Hey, no falling into despair. You said Crazy Wallach—I mean Darius Wallach had good support for his theory, right? And Campbell's not stupid. He wouldn't do this if he wasn't confident."

"It's the waiting—the not knowing. Worse, not having a right to know. I should be with him for this, Judy."

"That really would be crazy." Judy gathered up her purse and headed for the back door. "I'll see you tomorrow. Just two more days, right?"

"One and a half, really. I can endure for thirty-six hours." *And then I will run mad in the streets.* I locked the back door behind Judy and trudged upstairs, where I planned to eat ice cream for dinner and watch re-runs of *The Donna Reed Show.* Mindless entertainment, a window on a world that had never existed.

My phone rang ten minutes into the first episode. "Hey, Viv. Have—"

"Yes, I've heard from Jeremiah," Viv said, her voice practically squeaking with excitement. "It's going to be all right, Hel!"

"That's great? Um—what does 'all right' look like?"

"Well, I guess it's not totally all right. He's been locked up in the Gunther Node—for his protection, he says, and he didn't sound sarcastic so I think it really is for his protection. And I'm here too, for now, until they figure out how much of a threat the Mercy is to me. But he and Lucia met, and he said he was completely open with her, and she asked all sorts of questions, but not as many as she probably had, and in the end Lucia said she would give him a chance to prove his loyalties. Personally, I think he's already done that, but you've always said what a hard-ass Lucia is—"

"I've never said that!"

"Not in those *words*, but I know what you meant. Anyway, we're in a very nice little apartment that doesn't look at all like a cell, except for being—yes, all right, there are no windows and I think the lock is on the outside, thank you, Jeremiah—he's so pessimistic sometimes."

"Can I talk to him?"

"Sure, he's right here."

A fumbling sound, then Jeremiah said, "Helena?"

"Are you all right? I mean, she didn't rough you up or anything?"

"If by 'she' you mean Lucia, no. I think she came completely alone to our meeting, though probably armed. Just between us, I can admit she terrifies me, and I've faced invaders the size of half a city block.

But she was remarkably civil. Probably because she was prepared to kill me if I moved wrong."

"She's not that bloodthirsty."

"For all she knew, I was a dangerous rogue magus, and killing me would save lives."

"You're far too reasonable for a man in your position."

"Well…the truth is, I had instructions from my former 'masters' to assassinate her."

"*Jeremiah!*" For a moment, my heart raced, terrified that I'd betrayed Lucia to her death.

"Instructions I never had any intention of carrying out, Helena. I think my being open with her about it made her inclined to trust me. She actually laughed about it. It was chilling."

"She would. Are you…glad, now, that you didn't run?"

"I am. I just regret involving Viv."

"*I don't!*" Viv called out.

"She shouldn't have to be trapped here with me, but I'm afraid as soon as my status is revealed to my former allies, she'll be in danger. Some of them would have no trouble hurting her just as revenge, not even to force me to act."

"Viv is fiercely loyal. I guarantee you she doesn't see this as a hardship."

"I don't know if Lucia realizes how much of my motivation to help the Wardens stems from a desire to keep Viv protected. And I don't know if our relationship will survive enforced confinement together."

I laughed at the rueful tone of his voice. "Viv's creative. She'll keep you both occupied."

"That sentence fills me with dread. Here, talk to her again. And… thank you."

"Hey, I heard a rumor, something the Wardens who brought us here were talking about," Viv said. "Something about some kind of rites, and Campbell undergoing them. Were they talking about Malcolm?"

"Viv, remember Jeremiah doesn't know the truth about us."

"I know, I'm not pushing for details, I just wanted to know if you'd heard anything."

"Malcolm's going to undergo the rites to replace his aegis so he can be a magus again." Such a simple sentence, but it left me feeling dizzy, as if there weren't enough oxygen in the air.

Viv gasped. "I thought no one—"

"There's a new procedure. It's still very dangerous."

"Helena—" There was a long pause, and I could picture her peeking over her shoulder to see if Jeremiah was listening. "When?"

"Saturday afternoon."

"That's a long time to wait."

"It's actually the shortest time they could manage it."

"I see. I hope everything goes well."

"Me too."

"Well." Viv sounded suddenly more chipper. "I have to go, but I'll call you again tomorrow. I'll go crazy if I have to stay indoors for too long, even if it is for my safety."

"Just don't be *that girl* in the movies who eludes her Secret Service protection so she can go dancing, and then the serial killer gets her."

Viv snorted derisively. "As if."

16

Saturday morning I dressed in a pleated skirt of warm red and brown plaid, a white shirt with a Peter Pan collar, and a fitted vest that matched the skirt. I buttoned the vest feeling like I was armoring up for battle, though I wasn't the one facing death today. Malcolm and I had spent the previous evening together, not making love, just holding each other and talking quietly about everything but the Damerel rites, and I'd managed to forget about them for a few hours. Now I faced my reflection and practiced a smile. When had I started needing to practice those?

In the kitchen, my phone buzzed with an incoming text. I set down my hairbrush and trudged down the hall to pick it up. A squishy infant face beamed out at me when I turned on the display. ISABELLA SAYS MAKE A SMILEY FACE AUNT HELENA, my sister Cynthia's text read, and I smiled at my niece, a real smile that felt natural and good. I texted back I REALLY NEEDED THAT TODAY THANKS and put my phone in my pocket. I couldn't help Malcolm by being miserable. Couldn't help him at all, really, but I could keep him in my heart today and offer up what prayers I knew how to utter. I straightened my lapels, let out a deep breath, and went downstairs to open the store.

The first two Nicolliens through the door were having a conversation that immediately expanded to include me. "You're his friend," the woman said, "why couldn't you talk him out of it?"

"Excuse me?"

"I hate Campbell, but now there's this shadow cabal running around, we can't afford to lose any more Wardens," the man said. "He's out of his mind to even think of it."

"He knows it's dangerous, but the reward is worth the risk," I said, feeling vaguely proud of myself for coming up with such a neat catchphrase on the fly. Probably I'd read it somewhere I'd forgotten now. "I'm sure Mr. Wallach knows what he's doing."

The two Nicolliens looked at each other. "It's possible you're not familiar with some of Crazy Wallach's earlier plans," the man said. "He tried to breed houseflies with cameras so he could get mobile observational units, I think was what he called them. Damnedest thing I ever saw. They were the size of ponies and kept running into walls."

"And sticking their proboscises into other people's drinks," the woman said.

"But at least he succeeded," I said.

They both shrugged, and the woman handed over her augury slip.

I tried not to think of houseflies the size of ponies as I wandered the oracle looking for her book. Okay, so maybe that wasn't something Wallach had intended, but breeding insects with inanimate objects ought to be impossible, and Wallach had accomplished that. Malcolm had sounded confident about the new alloy aegis—though I wasn't sure how much of that had been trying to reassure me. But reassurance or no, I trusted Malcolm not to lie to me about anything, particularly anything this important.

The blue glow appeared in the distance, and I strode faster. I could focus on trying to beat my record for number of auguries in an hour—that would give me something else to think about. I removed the book from the shelf and flipped to the title page. *A Charmed Life*, by Liza Campbell. Only $750, of which I would earn enough to buy lunch. That was another fun, distracting thing I could do—count up how much my one percent of the augury price came to over the course of a day.

The woman's companion had a request as well. I glanced over the crowd, which was medium-sized and less frightened-sounding than it had been the past five days. Of course, most of them were carrying on conversations about Malcolm, but I shut my ears to that and hurried back into the oracle. This time it was *Braving It*, by James Campbell, $475. It looked interesting—something about a father and his daughter having an Alaskan adventure. I made a mental note to look it up at the library.

I sidestepped having a conversation with the next customer and hurried back into the oracle. If I was going to beat my record, I didn't have time to chat. $500, *The Power of Myth*, Joseph...Campbell. I stared at the title page for a few seconds. That was weird. I closed the book and examined the spine and cover. The author's name—I vaguely remembered the book from somewhere—was embossed on both. Puzzling.

I handed the book over to its recipient and said to Judy, "Would you do me a favor? Get a piece of paper and write the authors of the books we sell this morning. I know we don't usually keep that information."

Judy raised an eyebrow, but tore a page from the back of the ledger—it was looking pretty ratty from the number of times we'd done that—and wrote *Joseph Campbell* at the top of it. I took the next slip and hurried away, thinking I was being stupid. This was just coincidence.

The next book, glowing blue, was *Joker One.* Author, Donovan Campbell.

Judy wrote the author on her page, then gave me a puzzled look. "What's going on?"

"I don't know. The two before those were also Campbells."

"It has to be coincidence." Judy pointed at the stacks with her pen. "Try again."

A Nun on the Bus. Simone Campbell

Pathways to Bliss. Joseph Campbell again—or was it a different one?

The Iron Lady. John Campbell.

Weird Things Customers Say in Bookstores. Jen Campbell.

"It's no coincidence," I said, ignoring the waiting Warden who was waving his augury slip in my directions. "Every augury this morning!"

"So what does it mean?" Judy ran the pen across the page, making dark lines under each Campbell. "The oracle's trying to talk to you."

"I just don't understand what it's saying." With all the Wardens in the store, I couldn't talk openly about Malcolm, but I was increasingly unnerved by the repetition of his name.

"Do it again. Maybe it will get clearer. Or maybe we should be examining the titles, as well."

I snatched up the augury slip, making a face at the impatient man. "You do that. I'll hurry back."

The new augury was just around the corner, ready to hand. *Winners and How They Succeed,* by—I dropped the book in my astonishment. Alastair Campbell. Malcolm's father's name. I was pretty sure Mr. Campbell had never written a book, but even so—I swept the book up and ran out of the oracle, thrusting it at Judy. "Look at that one," I demanded. "Look at it!"

"I'm looking," Judy said, scribbling out a hasty receipt and shoving it and the book at the Nicollien. "Helena, this is creepy."

"But I don't know what it *means,*" I wailed, drawing the attention of the nearest Wardens. "What does it want me to do?"

"You have to keep going. I still don't see a pattern in the titles."

I grabbed an augury slip at random, ignoring the startled protest of the person next in line, and hurried into the oracle. The blue-limned book was on the shelf immediately opposite me, as if the oracle, tired of my fumbling, had put it where even I couldn't miss it. Gingerly, I slid it off the shelf, feeling the electric tingle of a live augury. The cover was stark black, like a book missing its dust jacket, and I opened the cover and turned a few pages.

Hear Me, the title read. By Malcolm Campbell.

I screamed, turned, and ran out of the stacks, feeling as if something were chasing me. "I have to go," I told Judy.

"Go? Go where?"

"To the Gunther Node. Everyone, I'm sorry, but Abernathy's is closing early today."

A displeased murmur went up. "I know, but this is a...a custodian emergency. Please hang on to your augury slips, and come back on Monday, where you'll receive a discount as an apology for making you come twice." *Do you hear that? Don't make me eat my words.*

Judy was scribbling the final man's receipt. "Stop grousing and go already," she called out, handing the receipt and the book to the man and shutting the ledger. "Let's get locked up so we can go."

"We? I don't think it meant you to come." I shut the door behind the last protesting customer and vehemently turned the dead bolt. "I think I should write a note so people will know why we're closed."

"Make it quick. And I'm coming with you," Judy said, "because it's almost 11:30, and you will never make it in time with the way you drive."

I stopped writing on another sheet of paper from the ledger and hugged Judy hard. "Thank you for not arguing with me."

"What's to argue about? I have no idea what you intend to do."

"Neither do I," I said, "but I've got about forty-five minutes to figure it out."

WE FLEW along the freeway in my car with me resolutely keeping my eyes forward. Knowing just how fast Judy was going wouldn't make me happier. "I think Malcolm needs me somehow," I said. "I think that's what the oracle was trying to tell me. I *hope* that's what the oracle was trying to tell me."

"But how can you possibly help him without standing up and shouting your secret to the world?" Judy said.

"I don't know." I was beginning to have a feeling, though, and it filled me with anxious dread. Everything we'd discussed Wednesday night still made sense. Revealing our secret wouldn't make Malcolm more likely to survive, and if he, God forbid, died during the Damerel rites, I'd have given it away for nothing. I couldn't help him by telling the truth.

Unless I could.

Breaking the Accords hadn't bothered me at all at first, back when I'd been so blithely assured I could find a loophole. But the longer we'd gone in our secret relationship, the worse I'd felt. Not because I felt bad about breaking the rules, because I thought they were stupid rules that deserved to be broken, but because the rules shouldn't exist at all. They were unjust and unfair and I had no idea how many other people, innocent people, had suffered because of them. So maybe...I leaned my head against the cold glass of the window. I didn't want to reveal the truth. The consequences were too harsh. But what if it was what the oracle wanted?

Judy took the freeway exit at speed and came to a screeching halt at the stoplight at the end of the ramp. "Come on, come on," she chanted, "change, change."

"How much of a hurry are we in?"

"Don't know. He said 'afternoon,' right? Well, it's officially been afternoon for thirteen minutes, and at this point we have to—" She floored the gas pedal, and my poor car jerked forward—"assume we might already be too late."

I gripped the door handle tighter. "If the oracle had been clearer—"

"Or if we'd been smarter."

"I like my version better. It removes culpability from us."

"Let's hope we're on time. Who knows what the oracle might think if it went to all the trouble to warn you, and you were too late?" Judy rounded the turn onto the long, nearly-abandoned road that led to the entrance to the Gunther Node.

"Oh, great, Judy, thanks tons for giving me something else to worry about."

Judy grinned, a manic expression completely at odds with her demure pantsuit. "Is it working?"

"...Actually, yes."

"Then you're welcome." She skidded to a halt, spraying gravel everywhere, and we leaped from the car and scrambled across the concrete to the teleportation circle. I stood inside, jigging in my impatience, while Judy spoke to someone on the phone. It was taking far too long. Why did we have to go through this every time? Couldn't they just issue us a pass or something?

Finally, Judy hung up the handset with some force and ran toward me. "I lied," she said. "I told them Lucia summoned us."

The world blinked, and we were in the vast concrete chamber. "I guess you were believable," I said. "Now what?"

Judy took a few steps and collared a black-jumpsuited figure. "The Damerel rites," she said. "Where do we go?"

"Are you supposed to be present?" the tech said. He had a flat face with a very snub nose and a suspicious air.

Judy rolled her eyes. "Would I be asking directions if I wasn't?"

The tech looked briefly confused. "Lucia summoned us," I said.

"I don't—"

"The custodian doesn't like to be kept waiting," Judy said.

The man's indecision briefly deepened, then he said, "Through the blue door and down the hall to elevator D, press the button for the lowest floor. Hey, if you were summoned, shouldn't you already know this?"

"Thanks," I said, and Judy and I took off running. "That was close."

"Notice I didn't say which custodian," Judy said.

We darted around a couple of people pushing what looked like a mining cart full of purple glowing ore, and it had just registered with me that that was probably *sanguinis sapiens* in unprocessed form when we reached the blue door. It was actually a big opening, with a frame painted royal blue, and two stripes, one blue, one purple, snaking down the center of its floor. It was busier than the main chamber had been, and we had to dart and twist past people who weren't at all inclined to give way. It slowed us to a walk, making me want to scream with frustration. None of them sensed the urgency of our mission at all. I got stuck walking behind a couple of really big men who were strolling along like they'd been issued extra buckets of time at the company store and were using it all at once, until finally Judy grabbed my hand and shoved past them.

"Thanks," I said.

"You're too nice," she said. "I say that as a friend."

"No, it's true. It's a flaw."

We reached the elevator bank and located elevator D. There were a handful of people already standing in front of it, awaiting its arrival. "It's not too late," I said.

"Not too late."

"And it will be obvious what the oracle meant once we get there."

"Obvious."

The elevator door slid open, and I grabbed Judy's hand so we wouldn't be separated in the flood of people who emerged. It reminded me of the New York City subway, not that I'd ever been to New York City, but this was like what you saw in movies—fifty people trying to get off, another fifty trying to force their way on while the first fifty were exiting. This was no time for politeness.

"Out of my way!" I shouted, and shoved forward, weaving and dodging my way through the crowd. Judy's hand slipped, and then it was gone, but I didn't have time to worry about her, I had to get on that elevator. Someone stepped on my foot, and I cried out and kicked the offender, who swore at me. As if I cared at all about that.

I wedged myself into the crowd and made it in with just seconds to spare before the doors slid shut again. Shoving some more, I managed to push the button for the bottom floor, which appeared to be number 1. Then I tried to take a deep, relaxing breath, but the elevator was too crowded. It smelled, not just of a few dozen bodies crammed together in a small space, but of musty, unused air that had been locked up for far too long. The lights were dim, possibly because they were blocked by so many of those bodies, but it felt to me like it was light that had been seen by too many eyes over the years and was now worn-out, yellowish-orange and faded.

Floor 3, said a pleasant female voice I recognized as that of the Athenaeum, repository of all the knowledge of mankind. Apparently the woman took on side jobs. Maybe she made recordings for all the Neutralities. I wondered how much that paid.

The door slid open, and there was another mass exodus. I clung tenaciously to my post near the control panel and therefore near the door. What I did not want was to be stuck at the back of the elevator when we reached my floor. More people pushed past to get on, not as many as before—well, with luck, the deeper we got, the fewer people would want to continue down.

Another ding, and *Floor 2*. More shoving. Someone else stepped on my foot, and I yelled, "Watch it!"

"Sorry," a sheepish female voice said, and the doors slid shut. My heart was beating so fast I was sure everyone around me could hear it, the smell was starting to make me feel sick, and my foot throbbed. I still had no idea what I was supposed to do. Judy was gone, I was alone...I closed my eyes and cursed my weakness. Now was not the time to go all weepy. If Malcolm needed me, I couldn't be weak.

Floor 1.

I shoved my way out through the men and women trying to enter the elevator, or tried to—the pressure of so many bodies kept me locked in place. In desperation, I shouted, "Come *on*, people, were you all born in a barn or something? Stand back and let us out first and *then* you can stampede wherever you want!"

It stilled the crowd long enough for me to slip past and stand, gasping for breath, just outside the elevator door. I was in another corridor illuminated by fluorescent bulbs, cold and clammy and smelling of damp concrete. People flowed past me in both directions, and it wasn't until the elevator door closed and most of the people who'd gotten off with me had walked away that I realized I didn't know where to go next. "Wait, please!" I shouted, running after them. Two women stopped and turned around. "The Damerel rites," I said. "Where do I go?"

"I don't know," one woman said.

"I think you follow the red line," the other said, pointing at the floor. Sure enough, there were three painted lines, one red, one yellow, and one green like a time-elapsed stoplight. "That should at least get you to someone who can give you better directions."

"Thanks," I said, and bolted off along my painted guide.

17

After only a few strides I was sure she'd directed me wrong. The red line led me a merry chase through halls and rooms where I startled the occupants, sometimes leaving its green and yellow companions, sometimes paralleling other colors like lilac and cyan. But I had no other guide to follow, and by that time I was feeling manic and confused, unable to remember why I'd come—but it was the oracle that had sent me, wasn't it? That was why I'd come. That, and to help Malcolm.

I turned a corner and found myself in a long hall identical to the one outside the elevator. I stopped and bent over to catch my breath, cursing the unknown woman who'd "helped" me. I was going to need a guide dog and a Sherpa to find my way out of this place.

I lifted my head. At the far end of the hall, a small group of people was standing outside a door, apparently chatting. I recognized Lucia immediately, and then my heart leaped at the sight of Malcolm, standing next to her. "Wait!" I shouted, and ran toward them, pushing myself harder than before because my fuddled brain was certain if I didn't catch them *immediately*, they would vanish, and I'd be lost in this maze of twisty passages forever.

The people all turned to look at me with varying expressions of interest. Lucia wore a look of disgust, as if I'd done something vulgar like burping in public. Malcolm's expression looked completely indifferent except for his eyes, which were blazing a warning. Two strangers, an old man and a young woman, regarded me with the kind of attention you'd give a strange dog—wary, but prepared to be charmed. And—*gulp*—Timothy Ragsdale, member of the Board of Neutralities, looked puzzled at my appearance. Well, I probably looked like a madwoman; my hair had to be falling down after all that time in the elevator, and I had a feeling my skirt had rotated back to front from the running I'd done.

"What do you want, Davies?" Lucia said. "You have *no* business here." Her expression said clear as day that I needed to get out, right now, and not be a total idiot.

"The oracle sent me," I said, which startled all of them, even Malcolm, whose mouth fell open a little in surprise.

"The oracle?" Ragsdale said. In his black suit, he looked like a prosperous banker, and the look on his face was pure incredulity. "You're not permitted an augury on your own behalf, Ms. Davies."

"It wasn't an augury. It has other ways of communication. It clearly wanted me to be here."

"Helena," Malcolm said. His voice was a warning.

"I'm not lying, Malcolm. Every augury today had your name on it. It wanted me to be here."

"I see," said Ragsdale. "And why is that?" He looked curious now, like he'd asked me a riddle he hoped I could answer.

I looked at Malcolm. I could practically hear him begging me to walk away. To say nothing, and let him go through that door. And knowing that told me, finally, why I was there.

I turned to face Ragsdale. "Because I love Malcolm," I said, "and if he dies today, I'm not going to grieve in silence."

Ragsdale's puzzlement deepened for just a moment. Then my words registered. A look of intense fury crossed his face so swiftly I almost thought I imagined it. Beside me, Malcolm closed his eyes and let out a long, thin stream of breath. Lucia swore viciously. "Did you know about this?" Ragsdale demanded of her.

Lucia eyed me. "This is the first I've heard of it," she said, and I relaxed a little, because I really didn't want Lucia getting in trouble for turning a blind eye to my relationship.

"How long has this been going on?" Ragsdale said.

"Eight months," I replied, though my mouth was dry and my heart continued to beat like a timpani.

"Eight *months?*" Ragsdale sputtered. "You've been in violation of—you were—during the Conference?"

"Yes, sir. Malcolm and I have been together for eight months, and I was in love with him before that." Saying it was getting easier, since I hadn't been struck dead immediately. It was probably a mistake to think that was a good thing.

Ragsdale's lips thinned with anger. "Arrest her," he told Lucia. "Immediately."

"Excuse me," the strange man said, "but this young lady is your girlfriend?" His voice was stronger than I'd expected from his appearance. If I'd had my eyes closed, I wouldn't have guessed his age from hearing him speak.

Malcolm put his arm around my shoulder and drew me close. "She is." He sounded impassive, which frightened me. If he was angry with me, what was I going to do?

"Well, I don't know what kind of forbidden love thing you've got going on, but arresting her is going to have to wait," the man said. "Unless you want the rites to fail entirely."

"I don't know what you're talking about, Wallach," Ragsdale said.

"We like to have loved ones participate, if they can stomach it. Gives the candidate something to hang onto in the dark times. Taking her away just before...might as well stab the boy in the heart and get it over with."

Ragsdale still looked like he wanted to string me up right then and there, but he said, "You're the expert. Let's get this over with. And *you*," he said, pointing at me with a trembling finger, "don't think you're getting out of this. If he—"

"Please don't jinx this, Mr. Ragsdale," I said. "Malcolm's going to live."

To my surprise, Wallach extended his hand to me. "Darius Wallach," he said. "And you are...?"

"Helena Davies."

He didn't recognize my name. "Come with me, and I'll explain the procedure." He swiped his identification badge, which hung on a lanyard around his neck, across a sensor, and the door swooped open like something in a science fiction movie.

The room beyond was brightly lit, not with fluorescent bulbs but with LEDs that made the room gleam with whiteness. It wasn't very big and was mostly empty, with only a few cabinets along the far wall and a long padded table in the center of the room, all of them white. A closer look showed me the "table" was actually more an operating table, with a disturbing number of leather straps with buckles dangling from it.

"He has to be strapped down for his own protection, and to keep the rites from failing, of course," Wallach said. I took a moment to observe him instead of the room. He was old, not as old as my friend Iakkhos Kalivas who ran the Neutrality called the Labyrinth, but at least seventy, and his snowy white hair was a stark contrast to his lined dark skin. He wore his hair pulled tightly back from his face so it made a fluffy pouf at the back of his head. Like the woman, he was dressed in surgical scrubs, but where hers were a plain maroon, his were black with hundreds of multicolored palm trees printed on them. I nodded as if any of that made sense. Protection from what?

"The Damerel rites—the new and improved rites, I should say—alter the human body to accept an aegis, which allows a magus to tap into his personal reserves of magic and direct them outward," Wallach said. "A team of magi, steel magi in Mr. Campbell's case, since he proposes to become a steel magus, build up a resonance within the aegis that matches his own body. Then another team of bone magi enhance the resonance of his body so both are strong and perceptible."

"I'm not sure I understand what the resonance is. Is it like a vibration?"

"A metaphysical one. You're not a magus?"

"No." So he really didn't know who I was. It was comforting that there was at least one person in the room who didn't think I'd just thrown my life away.

"Then you won't be able to perceive it. That's all right, it's not necessary. Then the last set of bone magi open a path to his heart and the aegis is inserted—and from there it's up to him."

"Is that metaphysical, again?"

"No, it's a literal opening. Non-surgical, pure magic. A scalpel would interfere with the resonance. Let me show you the aegis. I'm very proud of it," Wallach said, guiding me toward one of the cabinets. The upper doors were frosted glass, and Wallach opened one and removed a Plexiglas ball, holding it out to me. "Don't touch it, just look. Isn't it beautiful?"

Floating in the center of the ball was a slim needle that was pointed on both ends. It was about an inch long and shone like silver in the many, many lights. It looked like something an assassin would coat with poison and put in a blowpipe. "It's a tungsten-molybdenum steel alloy that until now has had mostly manufacturing uses," Wallach said. "But we're still just calling him a steel magus. Tungsten magus doesn't have the right impact."

"Malcolm said something about...resonance being a new concept?"

"Ah." Wallach winked at me. "It will change the nature of the Damerel rites entirely. A magus's resonance...frequency, to use your vibration metaphor...changes when the aegis is implanted. Identifying the new resonance is crucial to the success of a second Damerel. Now the procedure won't kill him outright."

"But it's still dangerous."

"We're sticking a damned great needle into his heart. Of course it's dangerous. But much of that danger can be mitigated, and some of it the candidate can overcome. That's your part, if you aren't the squeamish type."

"Um..."

"'Squeamish' is the wrong word," the woman said. She looked like she could be the old man's granddaughter, down to the pouf of hair at the back of her head. "He means, can you bear seeing your loved one in pain without freaking out?"

"I think so."

"You have to know so, or we can't let you stay."

I looked at Malcolm, who was standing beside the operating table fingering the straps. "I know it," I said.

"Fine. Mr. Campbell, if you're ready?"

"No," Malcolm said, and with a few quick strides he was at my side and holding me close. I wrapped my arms around him and buried my face in his chest. "I'm glad you're here," he whispered. "Everything else, we can figure out."

My heart felt as if it might burst out of my chest with happiness. He wasn't angry, he was going to live through this, and then...we'd figure it out. Together. "I love you," I whispered, and let him go.

Malcolm took off his black T-shirt and handed it to me. I wadded it into a ball and clasped it between my hands, resisting the urge to hold it to my face so I could breathe him in. He walked back to the table and lay down on it. The woman began strapping him to the table, starting at the ankles and working her way upward. She pulled a couple of padded boards to swivel out from beneath the table, then handed Malcolm a mouth guard, which he fitted between his lips before stretching his arms out to either side. The woman strapped his arms to the padded boards, put a final strap across his forehead, then went around again, quietly talking to Malcolm. I saw him put pressure on the restraints, which gave a tiny bit in places; the woman tightened the bindings, then stepped back, satisfied.

Wallach, in the meantime, was leaning against one of the walls, evidently praying. At least, his lips were moving soundlessly, and he had his hands pressed together in front of him. "What's he doing?" I quietly asked Lucia, who with Ragsdale had come to stand near me.

"I have no idea," Lucia said. "What are *you* doing? Have you completely lost your mind?"

"The oracle sent me," I said. Nothing that had happened had changed my conviction that I'd done what I was meant to do.

"Then the oracle has lost its mind," Lucia said, and wouldn't say anything more.

The room was silent and still, with Wallach's soundless speech the only movement. A whiff of ozone reached my nose, sharp and fresh. I wished I could go to Malcolm's side and remind him I was here—but he already knew that, and I didn't want to disrupt the rites. I caught myself tapping my toe and stilled it.

I glanced at Ragsdale, who wasn't looking at me in a way that said he was entirely too aware of my presence. My courage failed me briefly. I'd always thought Ragsdale liked me, or at least respected me. *Maybe that makes your betrayal worse*, I thought, and was surprised by it. I hadn't betrayed anything...had I? It was possible Ragsdale had respected me so long as he thought we shared the same values, and now he knew how long I'd been flouting the rules...no wonder he was pissed off.

Finally, Wallach pushed off from the wall and pressed a button on the side of the cabinet. "This shouldn't take long, but I have to remind you all not to interfere from this point on, no matter what you see or hear."

The door opened, and a handful of magi filed in, all of them dressed in scrubs of one color or another—no, there were only three colors, the maroon the first woman wore, a traditional teal color, and pure white. There were only two of the latter, and they held back from the others, who all grouped around the table, obscuring Malcolm from view. Some shifting, and then they all went still. The two in white hovered by the door, like guards, though I couldn't imagine what they were guarding against. I hoped all these magi had been cleared by Lucia. The thought of a shadow cabal magus interfering in Malcolm's Damerel rites made me feel dizzy. I swallowed hard and focused on his hand, which was all I could see of him. It was loosely closed and even looked relaxed.

I still felt dizzy, and closed my eyes for a moment to clear them. When I opened them, the fuzzy, dizzy feeling had grown, but now I recognized it was coming from outside me, that the air itself had gone fuzzy. I blinked and kept looking at his hand. The smell of ozone was growing, just strong enough to be perceptible, and a slight vinegary tang joined it. Malcolm's hand closed more tightly.

"Very good," Wallach said, his voice muffled as if he were speaking through gauze. "Now let's increase his body's resonance. We want to get him up to speed."

Malcolm's hand clenched, and the tendons stood out on his arm. I covered my mouth to hold back a cry that would surely disturb the magi at their work. The dizzy feeling subsided, but the ozone and vinegar smell increased until the air was sharp and hot and electric. The lights began to take on a purple tinge, like a black-light bulb. "Excellent," Wallach said, and this time I could barely make out his words, he sounded so distant. "Now, the aegis. Mr. Campbell, feel free to scream. Don't fight this."

The two magi dressed in white came forward to stand at Malcolm's head. For a long, long moment, nothing changed. Then Malcolm's arm, his whole body, strained against the straps, and he screamed, an agonized, garbled sound. I gasped and clenched my own hands tight, my nails cutting into my palms. The magi stepped away from the table like they were giving him air, but to me it looked as if he were dying, trapped on that table with a piece of metal embedded in his heart, and only Wallach's warning kept me from rushing to his side to free him.

Malcolm thrashed once more and went horribly limp, his hand relaxing all at once. The magi quickly began freeing him from the straps while Wallach bent over him, thumbing up his eyelids and checking his pulse. I made an involuntary squeak, and Wallach looked up at me. "Come," he said, and I flung myself at Malcolm, taking his hand and clutching it.

Malcolm didn't move. He wasn't breathing. He was so still I began to cry. "Malcolm, wake up," I begged him. "Remember what you said? You promised you'd always come back. Malcolm, wake up!" I looked up at Wallach. "He's dead!"

"Don't give up," Wallach said.

"This was *your* fault! You gave him hope in something that could never happen!"

"His body has to decide whether to accept its new destiny. Talk to him. Remind him why he's coming back."

I stared at Wallach, whose lined face was creased in a compassionate smile. "Malcolm," I said, swallowed, and began again. "Malcolm, you have to come back. Remember? You did all this so you can be a magus again. Don't let it be a waste. Come back. You promised—promised you'd come back. It's not working!"

His chest was so still. There was the original mark of his first aegis, a round white scar the diameter of a walnut, and the long red line of the heart surgery that had removed it. And now, another flat white knot of scarring, smaller than the first and just centimeters above it. I touched it; it felt ridged and rough. I leaned down and rested my cheek on those scars. "You're the strongest man I've ever known," I said in a quiet, conversational tone, "and you've never backed down from a challenge. Maybe that's why you had to do this. I couldn't have talked you out of it without making you other than what you are. But damn you, Malcolm Campbell, don't you dare back down from this one!"

I slammed my fist onto his chest and burst into noisy sobs, clutching his shoulders to keep my balance. It couldn't be true. He couldn't be dead. Not after all this. Why had the oracle sent me if it hadn't meant me to save his life? I cried so hard I had to stop for breath. I'd misunderstood, the oracle *hadn't* wanted me to come, I'd sacrificed my life for nothing, and Malcolm was dead.

Hands touched my shoulders, tried to pull me away, and I clung to my dead love and sobbed. Why couldn't Ragsdale give me a few minutes to mourn? I couldn't believe I'd ever liked him.

"Davies, you're choking him," Lucia said in my ear, and I jerked upright, swiping an arm across my eyes. Another hand rested on my forearm, the fingers closed gently on my sleeve. Malcolm's hand. He drew in a ragged, shallow breath, then another. I let out a cry and gripped his hand, hard, and began to cry again when he smiled, the slightest twitch of his lips.

"...don't cry..." he whispered, so quietly I had to lean over to hear him. "...enough to make a man think he was dead..."

I laughed through my tears. "Which of course you're not."

His eyes fluttered open, and he smiled at me, a real smile. "I don't remember weakness before," he said.

"It's a side effect of the resonance technique, which by the way was a complete success and I plan to gloat about it to everyone for at least a week," Wallach said. "The weakness will pass in a few minutes, and in an hour you'll be back to normal."

"And...my magic?"

"You've got that now."

Malcolm closed his eyes again. The next moment I found myself hovering six inches off the ground and had to fling my arms wide to keep from overbalancing. "*Malcolm!*"

It was Malcolm's turn to laugh. "Ah, love, I feel whole again," he said, "and ready to take on the world."

"Enough," said Ragsdale. "Pontarelli, do your duty."

I felt a hand close around my wrist, bringing me back to earth. "Helena Davies," Lucia said, her voice husky, "you're under arrest for violating the Accords."

18

The cell was a concrete cube about twelve feet on a side that smelled clean and cool, lit by a couple of bulbs set into a recess in the ceiling. The recess was covered by wire mesh so I couldn't touch the bulbs, not that I wanted to; they glowed hot and would probably burn my fingers. I guessed the cell's designers hadn't wanted prisoners to be able to break the glass and, what? Fight their way out with thin shards of lightbulb? Or was it potential suicide they were worried about? Either way, the bulbs were in no danger from me.

There was a bench on one side long enough for me to lie down on, if I felt tired, with no pillow or blanket, and a sink with only one handle on the tap. No bathroom, so I guessed this was just a temporary holding cell rather than an actual prison. This was good news. It meant I hadn't been condemned out of hand, which I knew from my exhaustive study of the Accords was illegal. But Ragsdale had been angry enough that I hadn't been totally sure he'd abide by the Accords in this case.

I fixed my skirt and finger-combed the tangles out of my hair, then put it back up in a messy ponytail and sat on the bench, staring at the door. It was metal painted institutional beige and had a line of rivets all around its edges. For lack of anything better to do, I counted them: thirty-one. *Why an odd number? Why not thirty or thirty-two?* There was a tiny window in the top, about three by five inches, with a metal slider closing me off from the outside. I got up and pried at it, but couldn't get it to move. I'd just have to sit here and wait. They'd—

—wait a minute, Lucia hadn't taken my phone! I pulled it out and checked the signal. No bars. My excitement faded. Well, at least I could play solitaire. That would keep me from going crazy from waiting.

I'd played about fifty games of solitaire and lost all of them by the time the window slid open. I quickly tucked my phone away, though it was probably too late to keep it hidden. "I'm coming in," Lucia said. "As ludicrous as this sounds, I have to warn you that attacking me will make your situation worse."

"I'm not going to attack you."

"What's ludicrous is the idea of you trying." The key clanked in the lock, and the door swung noiselessly open. Lucia's face was tense and drawn. "You just had to be a hero," she said bitterly. "Couldn't you have come up with a better story than that one? Like that the oracle sent you to witness history being made?"

"It felt like the right thing to do."

Lucia rolled her eyes. "God save me from noble idiots. Your 'right thing' is going to get you dismissed."

"Not...executed?"

"Not likely. With all these traitor deaths, the Board is reluctant to murder one of its own. What did you do to piss off Ragsdale? He's foaming at the mouth, wanting you dismissed immediately without trial."

"I think he feels he's gone to bat for me so many times, I should have respected that by not violating the Accords. I'm sorry about it."

"Nothing you can do about it now. But he's not a good enemy to have."

"I know. Lucia, what happens next?"

"The Board will convene for your trial. The *full* Board. I insisted on it."

"You did? Why? Couldn't they participate from a distance?"

"Because having them face you directly will give you an advantage. Easier to dismiss someone who's just a voice and an image on a computer screen."

"Oh. Thank you."

Lucia waved that away. "It will take a few days for them all to gather. Your trial will be next Tuesday morning. You'll be free on your own recognizance until then, and you'll open Abernathy's as usual on Monday."

"You're not going to keep me locked up?"

"Judy Rasmussen argued persuasively that you are still Abernathy's custodian, and Abernathy's should stay open for as long as that's true. Stirlaugson admitted you were unlikely to make a run for it, what with your whole life being here."

"It's true. And I wouldn't run anyway. I want to argue my case before the Board."

"There's not much to argue. You stupidly admitted to your guilt in front of a Board member and a fellow custodian."

"Not that. I'm going to ask them to change the Accords."

Lucia raised both eyebrows. Then she laughed. "You're guilty as hell, but you're going to argue they shouldn't punish you *and* should make your offense legal? I never knew you had that kind of nerve."

"I don't know about punishing me. I do know the Accords are wrong, and I'm going to convince the Board of that."

Lucia shook her head, her laughter trailing off. "You want to roll the dice again, it's your funeral. As it is, you're free to go. The Board will send word as to when and where you're to meet with them." She swept me a humorless bow and I scuttled out the door, vaguely afraid of having it close on me and trap me in that boring cell again.

Lucia and I walked down the short corridor lined with cells—actually, there were quite a few, which made me wonder how many were occupied and how often they were used—and through another beige metal door whose rivets I didn't have time to count. Beyond, a curving hall with a black stripe painted down its center stretched out before us. "Follow the black line to where it joins the magenta line, then follow the magenta line to the transit hub. Someone will be waiting for you there."

"Who?"

"I don't know. Campbell, probably. He wasn't too happy to see you led off in metaphorical chains while he was still helpless. And I think Judy Rasmussen is around here somewhere." She made a little shooing motion and turned around. "I've got a crapload of paperwork to do that *someone's* little speech generated."

"I'm sorry—"

"Don't worry about it. Just...don't be afraid of the Board." Lucia let out a long sigh. "You know you've got no chance, right?"

"And *you* know I have to try, right?"

"I do. I'll try to be there on Tuesday, but if not...good luck, Helena."

"Thanks, Lucia."

I strode down the black line, then the magenta line, barely noticing my surroundings except that the gardenia smell was stronger now. I had two days and a few hours to figure out what I could say to the Board. Avoiding punishment was probably pointless, and I had to admit I was guilty even if the rules I'd broken were stupid, unjust ones. That meant I could focus on what I increasingly felt was the purpose the oracle had sent me for: getting the Board to change the Accords.

I emerged into the central chamber and looked around for a familiar face. The display on my phone told me it was almost six o'clock, and apparently that was the node's busy time, because the chamber was thronged with black-clad men and women, some wearing fatigues and bearing guns or knives, others in jumpsuits pushing carts. No one I knew appeared, so I began walking the perimeter of the chamber.

There were seven great openings, each painted a different color, and the lines on the floor made an enormous tangled spider's web near the center of the room. I'd never noticed the tangle in all the times I'd been here before. I was so fascinated by it I didn't at first hear my name being called, and looked up just moments before

Malcolm swept me into his arms and kissed me in full view of everyone. Someone passing nearby let out a long whistle, which made me smile. Malcolm released me, though only to arm's length, keeping hold of my hand. "You're all right?" he said.

"I'm fine, except for the Tasers and the beatings. No, I forgot, you people use jolters."

"How can you joke at a time like this?" Judy said. "The Board is still out for your blood."

"Yes, and I've got a few days before I have to face them." Judy's choice of words dampened my courage. What if all of them felt, as Ragsdale did, that I'd betrayed their trust in me? Which in a sense I had.

"That will be plenty of time for you to plan your defense," Malcolm said. "I think we should leave this place and start on that immediately."

"I'm not sure I have a defense, given that I'm guilty."

"Of violating an unjust law."

"That's what I plan to say. I'm going to ask the Board to repeal that provision of the Accords."

Malcolm's hand closed tightly on mine. "You're not serious."

"I am serious."

"She is," Judy said. "When she gets those two little lines between her eyes, you can tell she's going to be stubborn."

"I will remember that," Malcolm said. "I have a feeling it's information I'm likely to need in the future."

SUNDAY MORNING I re-read the Accords and made notes, though I'd memorized all the key points of it, chapter and verse, back when Malcolm was on the run. Then I went to the Athenaeum and did a little more research, this time on the circumstances surrounding the drafting of the Accords. It probably wouldn't matter, but despite my brave words I was starting to feel desperate. By three o'clock Sunday I'd fallen into despair. I'd only been a Warden for sixteen months; the

Board members had been Wardens their whole lives. Who was I to demand they change the document that for more than seventy years had kept the peace in the magical community, just for selfish reasons?

I lay on my couch and stared at the high, white ceiling. There were patterns there, too distant to make out. Why did people texturize their ceilings, anyway? Maybe for insulation? Or so the sunlight wouldn't reflect off them so easily? Or...it was pointless guessing when I had no understanding. Much like trying to guess which way the Board would jump.

Harrison, I knew was my enemy, and had been from the start. Ragsdale, I'd made my enemy. Would Chukwu, the Board member from Nigeria and someone friendly to me, come down on Ragsdale's side? After what had happened at the Conference of Neutralities, I trusted the Board to do what they thought best for all of magery, but I didn't kid myself that that meant they'd do what was best for me. Helena Davies was just another cog in the machine, important only to herself.

The door opened. "Helena?"

"I'm in here."

Malcolm came down the hall and bent down to kiss me. "I never realized how much it chafed that you had to let me in."

"Are you really a stronger magus, thanks to the new alloy?"

"I'm not sure. I'm still experimenting, and the team hasn't done any training yet. Nor will we, until this is over."

I moved my legs so he could sit next to me. "You shouldn't stop on my account."

"I'm stopping on mine. I am far too distracted to safely train, and I believe Canales, Quincy, and Tinsley would say the same. Tuesday night, it will all be over."

"One way or the other. Malcolm, what will we do if they take Abernathy's away from me?"

"You mean, will I suddenly stop loving you and find myself a beautiful magus to keep my bed warm?"

I slugged him. "Be serious."

"I see nothing else changing except that you and I, love, will no longer have to sneak around. You will still be a Warden, with full knowledge of the magical world, though without responsibilities. You might even take Judy's place, if you could bear it."

"I don't know which would be worse, being separated from the oracle entirely or being relegated to opening the mail. I just don't want to think about it."

"Then don't. Let's go to your parents' house for dinner like an ordinary couple, then return here to spend the night."

I gasped. "Will you stay the night?"

"There's no longer any reason not to. I would like nothing more than to hold you while you sleep, knowing I don't need to sneak away before morning."

I sat up and hugged him. "I can't imagine anything more wonderful."

And it was.

19

I woke slowly, lazily the next morning, gradually becoming aware of the other person sharing my bed. Malcolm lay sprawled on his back, his mouth slightly open, his hair messy across his forehead. I scooted over and snuggled up next to him. He stirred, rolled a little, and brought his arm around to draw me closer. "Is it morning yet?" he murmured.

"I have no idea."

"Let's pretend it's not, and stay like this for a few more hours."

"Or all day. They can hardly try me twice for breaking the Accords, if I just don't open the store."

I heard a distant pounding on the apartment door and groaned. "It's probably Judy."

"She'll go away if you ignore her."

"No, she really won't." I freed myself from the circle of Malcolm's arms and found my bathrobe hanging on the back of my door, then stumbled down the hall and opened the door. "Finally," Judy said, and pushed past me with her box of donuts. "You and Campbell get dressed, and I'll make coffee."

"Not to be ungrateful, but what if we wanted a private morning together?"

Judy rolled her eyes. "You can have that tomorrow. Today, we have to plan."

"Plan what?"

"Your campaign of public support." She disappeared into the kitchen. I stared after her in disbelief. Then I returned to the bedroom, where Malcolm was already half-dressed.

"Did you hear that?" I asked.

"No. But I surmise that Miss Rasmussen has something on her mind."

"She called it my 'campaign of public support.'"

Malcolm raised an eyebrow. "I see. She may be onto something."

I hung up my bathrobe and put on my clothes. "I don't understand either of you."

Seated at the table with my coffee and a maple-glazed donut, I still wasn't more enlightened. "The Board doesn't act according to public opinion. What good will it do for me to have an upwelling of public sympathy?"

"The Board doesn't change if it might seem to be bending to the masses' whims," Judy said. "They can't afford to look like they just do whatever's popular. But that doesn't mean they don't pay attention to what the Wardens are saying. If we can get enough testimony as to your stellar qualities as custodian, we might be able to get the Board to keep you on."

"It's a long shot," Malcolm said. "You shouldn't get your hopes up. But Miss Rasmussen—"

"Judy."

Malcolm glanced at her and nodded. "Judy is right. Enough people attesting to your impartiality as custodian should sway them, hopefully enough."

"We've got one day. That sounds impossible."

Judy shook her head. "I was working on it all day yesterday. The Nicolliens are going to be a hard sell, given your relationship with an Ambrosite, but by the same token they'll be the most convincing. If *they* think you've been impartial, it means more."

"Okay, but—"

"Look, just let us worry about it, all right?" Judy nodded at Malcolm. "You run the store and be your usual friendly self. Act like nothing's wrong, and maybe it will come true."

I took a ferocious bite of my donut, spraying crumbs. "Let's hope so."

Judy made a face. "Can't you get her to stop eating that way?"

"She puts jalapeños on pepperoni pizza. There's no stopping someone like that," Malcolm said.

I finished eating, then readied myself for the day, putting on makeup and styling my hair a little more elaborately than my usual ponytail. It felt once again like going into battle, only this time I was fighting for my life. I gripped the sides of the sink and leaned forward until I was close enough for my breath to mist white on the mirror. "You can do this," I told myself. "You have right on your side." My reflection mimicked me perfectly. I didn't know what I would have done if it had talked back.

Malcolm had brought a suit with him and now stood at the back door to say goodbye. "What happened to not sneaking around anymore?" I said.

He smiled and touched my cheek. "No sense inflaming Nicollien feelings by having an Ambrosite walk through the store during their time, or in presenting them with a living reminder of why you are on trial. We want them to remember everything you've done for them."

"You make sense," I grouched, "but I don't have to like it." I put my arms around his neck and drew him down for a deep, satisfying kiss. "I'll see you tonight?"

"I would like to spend the night again, if you don't mind."

I laughed, my irritation dispelled. "If I don't mind. I think that was the most restful sleep I've had in weeks."

"Agreed." He kissed me once more, then let himself out. I locked the door and leaned against it for a moment, then straightened and drew a deep breath. Half an hour, and I'd face...not my accusers, really, but certainly the Wardens most likely to be angry about my violation of the Accords. This might be a difficult four hours.

The mail was early, so I busied myself with mail-in auguries, feeling increasingly nervous until by 9:57 my hands were shaking too badly to hold a pen. I set the little bundle of envelopes down and practiced calming breaths. Outside, a line of Nicolliens waited. I caught the eye of the woman at the head of the line and smiled. She gazed at me, expressionless, and my smile faltered and fell away. Well, there was no point in waiting any longer. I turned the sign to OPEN, unlocked the door, and opened it. "Good morning, and welcome to Abernathy's," I said cheerfully, though my heart was going like a hamster on a treadmill and my palms were sweaty.

No one answered. They all filed in, taking up places in the usual orderly line, all of them staring at me. I held out my hand toward the first woman. "Do you have a question?"

"I do," she said, but made no move to give me her augury slip. "Are you sleeping with that Ambrosite?"

The hush was so deep it felt like the room was buried in velvet. "If you mean Malcolm Campbell, then yes, he and I are in love," I said, and my inner self gave me three cheers for how steady my voice had been.

"You expect us to believe you're impartial?" the woman said. A murmur went up among the waiting Wardens. I kept my eyes fixed on the woman, who despite her words didn't look angry, but curious.

"I've always been impartial," I said, raising my voice, "and you all know it. Remember last July? How many of you came in here wanting auguries so you could find Malcolm and kill him? And I gave every single one of you the auguries you wanted, even though it broke my heart."

"We don't know you gave us the right ones," said a short, tubby man from somewhere near the center of the line. "You could've lied."

"If you knew anything about Abernathy's, you wouldn't make that accusation," I said, taking a few steps toward him. "I don't lie about auguries. I think the oracle would reject me if I did. And if that were true, Judy Rasmussen would be the custodian now. Do you think she'd pretend *not* to be the custodian if it had passed to her?"

The little man swallowed hard as the people nearest him took a few steps away, as if he had a contagious disease. "All right, maybe you didn't lie," he said weakly. "That doesn't make you impartial."

"I say it does," said a strong voice, and Harry Keller pushed his way through the crowd, followed closely by Harriet. Physically, he'd never fully recovered from the attack by his familiar, and he now walked a little bent over, leaning on a cane. But his voice was as powerful as ever. "Helena's made close friends here, and I'm proud to be one of them. The idea that she'd let her affections, however strong, affect her judgment is just ridiculous, and I'll tell anyone who asks so."

Tears prickled my eyes. "Harry," I said, and flung my arms around him, making him wobble. I hugged Harriet, who was carrying a Tupperware container. "Harriet, you're free!"

"As of three days ago. It was quite the ordeal—but I've decided to put it behind me."

"I'm just so glad. Did you come for an augury?"

"For moral support," Harriet said, "and Chocopocalypse cake for two. Dear, why didn't you tell me you were dating Malcolm? I wouldn't have pushed so hard for you to date Manuel!"

"I couldn't—you know it had to be a secret."

"I know. I just think you could have trusted us." She handed me the cake and patted my cheek. "But that's all behind us, and Friday I want you and Malcolm to come to dinner. Bring your appetite. You look like you could use some feeding up."

I carefully blotted the tears from my eyes. "Thanks, Harriet. Thanks to both of you."

"Don't worry," Harry said. "Everything will work out for the best. I've always believed that. And don't mind that squidgy little Ragsdale fellow. He got his feelings hurt and he's lashing out at you because he feels like a fool. The rest of the Board will be more reasonable."

"I hope so."

"We're praying for you, dear," Harriet said.

When the Kellers were gone, I returned to the woman at the head of the line. "Augury?" I said. "Or more questions?"

She held up her slip. "Augury."

I escaped into the oracle. My hands had stopped shaking, my heart rate had slowed, and I felt cheerful, like Harry was right and the Board would be reasonable. I had friends on my side, and I couldn't fail.

But the rest of the day wasn't nearly so cheerful. I had to repeat my speech about impartiality and the auguries about Malcolm seven more times, whenever enough new Nicolliens who hadn't already heard it came through the door. Responses were mixed. Some people turned and left without an augury when they heard me admit I was in love with an Ambrosite. Others nodded in agreement when I pointed out that I'd filled all those auguries without refusing one. By lunchtime, the flow of Wardens hadn't slowed at all. Maybe someone had posted an announcement on the Warden Facebook page—come see the Accords-breaking custodian, today only! Though I was fairly certain the Wardens didn't have a Facebook page.

At 1:34, when the final Nicollien had her augury and was out the door, I was exhausted and hungry and wondering where the hell Judy was. *She'd better be creating that upwelling of sympathy, because I could really use a sandwich and a Diet Coke.* I ran upstairs to put the cake away and find a container of baked ziti, one of the many meals my mother had pressed on me Sunday evening. I opened it as I went down the stairs; even cold, it smelled heavenly. I put it in the microwave and went back to the front of the store, just in case someone had come in, but it was still empty.

The microwave *ding*ed. I zipped back to retrieve my food, juggling it because the container was hot, and hurried back to the front counter. I felt, superstitiously, that if I weren't there to greet every customer, the Board would see it as one more black mark against me, and I didn't need any of those.

On my way through the stacks, the bells above the door rang, and I hurried faster. "Sorry," I called out, "be right there," and emerged into the front of the store to find Acosta and Green standing there. "Oh," I said. "Um. Good afternoon."

"Did we interrupt your lunch?" Acosta said, pointing at the ziti.

"Um, yes. Sort of." I took a small bite, chewing carefully around how hot it still was, to give myself time to think. Acosta *and* Green? What had Acosta learned? What had he told his partner? Why were they even here? "It's been a busy morning," I said around my mouthful of food. I really had the worst table manners. Not that I cared what they thought of me, but I sort of did.

"I read the book you sold me," Acosta said. "Well. Not so much read as studied. It was...enlightening."

"I'm glad. Um, how so?"

"This store isn't a store, is it?"

Lucia said answer his questions. "No."

"It's a prophet. It sells books of prophecies."

"That's more or less true. We call it an oracle, and it gives auguries."

"And there's no criminal connection at all."

"No."

"Except Nathaniel Briggs was a criminal. We weren't wrong about that," Green said.

"Right. He was blackmailing people. But it had nothing to do with the store."

"And magic is real," Acosta said. "You and everyone associated with this store are called Wardens, and you fight a magical battle against evil."

"That's...more or less true."

Green and Acosta looked at each other. "What are you going to do," Acosta said, "if we tell people what goes on here?"

"Me? Nothing. It's Lucia Pontarelli you'd have to worry about. And I have no idea what lengths she'd go to to protect the oracle."

"Are you threatening me, Ms. Davies?"

"Of course not. I'm just stating facts. You remember the kind of trouble you ran into when you tried to get a search warrant for Abernathy's? And that was just a minor annoyance."

Once again the detectives exchanged glances. "Will you go on selling us auguries?" Acosta said. "In the future, that is."

"I guess so. I don't have any instructions to the contrary."

"No matter what the subject, or what we do with them?"

"The oracle's meant to be impartial, detective. It won't help you commit a crime, and there are certain questions it won't answer. But beyond that, it leaves the interpretation and implementation of the augury to you."

Acosta nodded slowly, his eyes alight with possibilities. "Tell me about your Ms. Pontarelli," he said. "Who is she?"

"She's in charge of the largest magical node in the western United States. She controls law enforcement in the magical community here in the Pacific Northwest. Supervising the magi—that's what people who can work magic are called."

"She's got no authority to do that. She's a vigilante."

"Wardens have to police themselves. Can you imagine an ordinary cop trying to apprehend a rogue magus?"

"Still, she ought to have official police sanction," Acosta said with a scowl.

"And how do you suggest she get that?"

Acosta's lips thinned with disapproval. Green said, "I think we've heard enough."

Fear touched my heart—fear for them, not of them. "Don't tell anyone what you've learned. Your lives could be at stake."

"You let us worry about our lives, Ms. Davies," Green said.

"Besides, who would we tell?" Acosta said. "If Ms. Pontarelli didn't come after us, we'd no doubt be stuck in a psych ward for evaluation. Don't worry. Your secret is safe with us."

"Then help us," I said impulsively. "You both know the secret now, so why not work with Lucia? It could benefit both of you."

"We'll consider it. Good day, Ms. Davies." The bells jingled as they let themselves out. I took another bite of ziti, lukewarm thanks to that conversation, and turned my back on the window where Ambrosites had already begun to gather. What on earth would Acosta and Green do next? I hoped they took my warning seriously, because much as I disliked and, yes, feared them, I didn't want them to die. But I couldn't begin to imagine what Lucia might have in mind for them.

I wandered back to the break room, eating as I walked, and helped myself to one of Judy's Diet Dr. Peppers from the fridge. Call it payback for her disappearing when I needed food badly. I washed down the last of the ziti with a healthy swig and wiped my mouth. Four more hours to go. At least the Ambrosites were less likely to want to lynch me. I tried not to think about how the Board might use their approval against me.

20

The woman in the mirror looked like me, though she was confident and professional and I was a writhing ball of nerves. I'd invested in a nice suit and pinned my hair up in a tight roll at the back of my head, cleaned my one good pair of pumps, and now I turned one way and the other, trying to see all of myself at once.

"Hold still," Malcolm said, and I felt a tug on the back of my jacket. He was still dressed only in boxers—well, I'd woken unnaturally early, couldn't fall back asleep, and had decided to cut my losses and get dressed. Now I had about three hours of waiting before the time appointed by the Board for me to stand before them. I needed to pee. Again. Nervous peeing, that was what this day needed.

"You look beautiful," Malcolm said. "Beautiful and competent and deserving of respect."

"Thank you. I wish I didn't feel so nervous. I don't look nervous, do I?"

"Not at all." He kissed my cheek lightly. "I'll make breakfast. You have eggs, right?"

"I'm not a total savage."

We sat and ate eggs companionably, just like any couple. "I'm coming with you," Malcolm said.

"You weren't invited."

"No, but there's nothing in the Accords that says you can't have someone waiting for you, and I plan to be there when you return. I don't think I could bear to sit around somewhere else, not knowing what happened immediately."

I sighed and took his hand. "I'll feel better knowing you're there. You're sure your family doesn't need you?"

"Ewan was cleared last night, and Mother is throwing a celebration today. But I picked him up from the node yesterday, and we had a long conversation."

"About what? If it's not prying to ask."

"About the business, and his role in it. Being confined gave him plenty of time to think about who he is and what he wants to do with his life. He's decided to leave Campbell Security and take a position with a hunting team in Seattle."

"That's a big change."

"I told him I approved. I haven't ever felt as close to my brother as I did yesterday. But he's telling Mother his decision today, and I've decided I don't want to be there for that little explosion. It will make my break-up with Andria seem like nothing by comparison."

"I can imagine."

"Which is nothing compared to what you're about to endure."

I sighed again. "I just wish the whole thing were over."

"It will be, soon enough." He kissed the back of my hand. "Let me get dressed, and I'll drive you there."

Malcolm's new car was a late-model Mustang, cherry-red, that practically screamed "pull me over, copper!" "I'm sad about the Jaguar," I said. "You didn't want another one?"

"I drove that one in memory of my father, and replacing it with another E-type felt like adultery," Malcolm said. "I'm still not used to this one. I think red was a mistake, but..."

"...it's just so compelling, isn't it?" I ran my fingers over the black leather seat. "It must be hard driving it in Portland."

"I'd like to take it on a cruise up the coast someday, really open her up." Malcolm revved the engine with a wicked smile. "But today, alas, we're just going downtown."

The tribunal building was an undistinguished red-brick office building on the waterfront near the Morrison Bridge. Its many large windows caught the light and reflected it back at the sky, which today was covered with great gray clouds like corrugated steel. Geese thronged the waterfront park, crowding the bike lane with complete disregard for the bikers. Malcolm slowed to avoid one or two that strayed into his path. "I'd honk, but I'm afraid they'd turn on us."

"Geese are vicious. I saw one attack a man once. It was scary."

The parking garage adjacent to the office building was mostly full, but Malcolm narrowed his eyes and a space appeared as if by magic, right near the exit. "Did you do that?" I asked.

"Yes. No, I'm joking. I could have, at the expense of rearranging everyone else's parking, and that seemed a trifle selfish for an unimportant thing. We're both young and strong and walking a little ways won't hurt us."

"But you won't give up that space."

"Of course not. I'm pragmatic as well as principled."

We held hands as we walked across the tiny plaza between the parking structure and the building. The atrium was as tall as the building itself and unlit by anything but the gray skies outside, which made it feel gloomy and tired. The gray-flecked white granite tiles, two feet wide and outlined in dull, unpolished brass, looked humped in the middle, though I was pretty sure it was an optical illusion. My pumps made sharp tapping noises against them. Malcolm's feet in their hand-stitched Italian leather shoes made no noise at all, which was either magic or Navy SEAL training, or, more probably, both.

We approached the white reception desk, which curved in an elongated S midway between the doors and the bank of elevators facing one another. I vaguely remembered the woman who stood there, her dark hair coiffed much the way mine was, her suit a lovely rose color. She smiled as we approached and said, "Your appointment?"

"Helena Davies to see the Board of Neutralities."

Her mouth fell open. She looked from me to Malcolm and back to me again. "Ms. Davies," she stammered, "I...here." She thrust a laminated badge toward me that I clipped to my lapel. "Take the first elevator on the right all the way to the top. And...good luck."

"I'll wait here," Malcolm said, and kissed me, his lips warm and soft on mine. "Good luck."

"I love you," I said, and walked at a measured pace toward the indicated elevator without looking back.

It was only my imagination, again, that everyone I passed stopped to watch me go. I didn't look any different from the other women in the atrium, at least I didn't think I did, and the badge with my name on it wasn't large enough to be clearly seen from more than a few feet away. Yet I felt more eyes on me than just Malcolm's as I crossed the atrium to the elevators.

The first one on the right looked like all the others, except it only had one button, pointing up. Nobody else stood waiting with me for the elevator, which made me feel even more as if I were in a *Twilight Zone* episode, one with an elevator that opened on Hell or something. People moved past me, and *now* I knew they were staring, because I could see them out of the corner of my eye. I turned my head and smiled pleasantly at an older couple standing next to me. They swiftly turned their attention to their elevator. So I was interesting, but also poison. Given my current standing with the Board, that made sense.

The door slid open with a quiet *whoosh*. I stepped inside. Here, there were only two buttons, both embossed with arrows. I pushed the Up button. The doors slid shut, and the elevator made a rapid ascent. I looked at my feet, examining the faded pattern of the carpet. I couldn't make out whether it was paisley or floral, but in either case it was a tacky turquoise and pink and it made me feel better, like the Board couldn't possibly have that much power over me if it had such terrible taste. The silence in the air stifled me, and I yawned, hoping to make my ears pop, though that probably wasn't it. The worst elevator music in the world would have been preferable to the still, unnerving silence.

The doors slid open on a short hallway with floor to ceiling windows along one of its sides. I looked out over the Willamette, down on the park several stories below. The geese were a moving smudge along the parkway. I spared a thought for the bikers who had to pass them and walked to the end of the hallway, pushed open the door, and cautiously entered.

The enormous room beyond probably took up half the top floor, but was mostly empty. Pillars stood at regular intervals throughout the room, propping up the relatively low ceiling and making me feel claustrophobic despite the many windows. On the far side of the room, near one bank of those windows, stood an executive table surrounded by low-backed leather chairs. All but one of the chairs were occupied. The nine members of the Board of Neutralities regarded me dispassionately.

I straightened my spine and walked forward until I stood at the foot of the table. Laverne Stirlaugson, seated at the head, gave me a long, considering look. "Ms. Davies," she said, "be seated."

I took my seat and crossed my hands in my lap. I wasn't about to be the first to speak. And I really wanted to know how this was going to play out.

"Ms. Davies," Stirlaugson said again, "the Board has chosen to hold this hearing here rather than in the Blaze as a consideration to you. We remind you that you are still bound to speak the truth, even if we cannot compel it out of you."

"I understand. Thank you." The Blaze, a magical device for assessing the truthfulness of a speaker, was a white-purple flame that blinded me because I could see through the illusion put on it. The fact that they'd decided not to use it heartened me. They couldn't be *that* angry if they were considerate of my needs, right?

Stirlaugson's next words dispelled that feeling. "You stand accused of violating the Accords and demonstrating partiality toward the Ambrosite faction in your romantic relationship with Malcolm Campbell. How do you answer this charge?"

"I admit to violating the Accords. I deny that this makes me partial."

A faint susurrus of movement swept across the table. "Ridiculous," Ragsdale said. "If you violated the Accords, you're partial. End of story."

"With respect, Mr. Ragsdale, I disagree. I've demonstrated through my actions in the last sixteen months that I am committed to being nonpartisan. For half that time, I've been romantically involved with Malcolm Campbell. I contend personal attachments are not de facto evidence of partiality, and I'm here to ask the Board to amend the Accords to reflect that."

Everyone began speaking at once before I'd finished, forcing me to raise my voice. Stirlaugson shouted, "Be still, all of you!" Gradually the room quieted, though Ragsdale looked like he was forcibly restraining himself from speaking. "Ms. Davies, you are *on trial*," Stirlaugson said. "You are not in a position to make requests."

"My defense hinges on my proving I'm still impartial. If it's true my love life hasn't prevented that, then it's true others can do the same, and the Accords ought to reflect that."

"Impossible," Ragsdale said. "You're not seriously considering this."

"I am," said Chukwu. "Ms. Davies has earned a great deal of goodwill from us. I say we listen to her defense and make a *reasoned* decision, not one based on anger and spitefulness."

"Ayodele—"

"I said *be still*," Stirlaugson said. "Ms. Davies. Convince us."

I took a moment to look each Board member in the eye, gauging where my support lay. Harrison was an old enemy and he looked pleased to see me in this position. Ragsdale, of course, was livid. Chukwu was apparently on my side, though for how long, I couldn't tell. Chao Min, the elderly Chinese woman, was an enigma, but I knew she would respond to any argument that increased the Board's power.

The others, I didn't know their names, but the redheaded American woman looked intrigued and the white-bearded Frenchman looked cross. I didn't even know the nationalities of the final two women, just that they were both middle-aged, one was white, one darkly tan, and they looked at me as if waiting for me to get on with it. Right. I'd stared long enough.

"The Accords were written to keep the peace between the Ambrosite and Nicollien factions," I began.

"We're not interested in a history lesson," Ragsdale said.

"I'm just setting the stage, Mr. Ragsdale. My point is that everything in the Accords is intended to serve that purpose. The Wardens who wrote them put a lot of thought into the rules, which is why we have things like Article IV, Section G, subsection 2, paragraph ii—mandatory *sanguinis sapiens* harvesting must occur on the sixth day of the fourth week of every month. To an outsider, that may look silly, but it was life or death to those Wardens."

"Are you mocking us by quoting the Accords?" the redheaded woman said. She was smiling like it was all a great joke, so I didn't let her throw me.

"No, ma'am. I've just studied the Accords thoroughly for the last eight months, looking for a loophole, and now I know them very well for someone who wasn't a Warden until just over a year ago." I swallowed and wished they'd provided water. "The reason I bring up that provision governing *sanguinis sapiens* harvesting is I looked up why it was there at all. Why such a specific date? And I learned that it was because of their accounting procedures and the fact that February is short. So there's always a reason for even the pickiest of details."

"That does not excuse you. In fact, it rather condemns you," the Frenchman said.

"I don't think so. Would you like to know why there's a provision in the Accords stating that romantic relationships between a custodian and a faction member are illegal?"

"It's irrelevant," Ragsdale said.

"Shut up, Timothy, we all know how you feel," the redhead said. "I'm interested, Ms. Davies. Tell us more."

"It's a longer story than the other, so bear with me. It has to do with a man named Tracy and his wife Glenda. Mr. Tracy was one of your forebears—"

"We know who Steven Tracy was," Chukwu said.

"Oh. I guess that makes sense. Then maybe you know the story. It's in the Athenaeum and I found it easily. Mr. Tracy was one of the Wardens who wrote the Accords, and Mrs. Tracy was custodian of the Gingher Node. They were both busy people and I guess they didn't see much of each other. Anyway, there was a Nicollien named Fred Sparks who was a frequent visitor to the Gingher Node, and...well, things went the way they often do, and Fred and Glenda became lovers. They ran off together, abandoning the node and throwing it into turmoil. Mr. Tracy was angry and humiliated. And when it came time to delineate the relationships between the Neutralities and the factions, he insisted it be written in that no custodian could have a romantic relationship with a faction member."

I leaned forward a little in my seat, keeping their attention fixed on me. "See, the thing I never understood was why it doesn't say we custodians can't have close friendships with faction members. I'm close to lots of people on both sides, like the Kellers, and yet the Accords aren't concerned I might display partiality toward them. But if you look at poor Mr. Tracy's story, it starts to make sense. One man is hurt—badly hurt, and I feel so sorry for him—and he turns around and enshrines that hurt in law. And the rest of us have to suffer for it."

The Board was silent. I swallowed again, trying to moisten my mouth. "Another thing," I said. "My predecessor, Nathaniel Briggs, was killed because he wouldn't falsify an augury for a close friend. If he'd done it, the Accords would punish him for giving a false augury —that's Article I, Section C, subsection 4, paragraph i—and it would punish him for being partial. It would *not*, however, punish him just for having that friendship. And I think that's right. I think the Accords should give custodians more credit. We take our duties very seriously, ladies and gentlemen, and expecting us not to make friendships, or even romances, across faction lines is expecting us not to be human. Don't condemn us for the possibility that we *might* be partial. Only condemn us when we actually *are*."

More silence. I sat back in my chair and gripped the armrests loosely. My palms were dry, for a miracle, and my heart beat a nice steady pace. Chukwu sat forward. "You have been involved with this

Malcolm Campbell for eight months," he said. "How will you prove that you have not been partial?"

"Malcolm was accused of murdering a high-ranking Nicollien, and the Nicolliens all wanted auguries so they could find him and kill him. I could have refused to give those auguries. I could have lied about them—maybe. I've never seriously thought about lying about any augury, and I don't know what the oracle would do if I did. But I did neither. I performed every augury brought to me during those days, even though it hurt more than I can say. I wanted so badly, every time I walked into the oracle, to see it tell me there was no augury. I did a lot of crying and a lot of shouting. But I also did my duty. Ask the Nicolliens. They'll tell you."

"They already have. At length," the Frenchman said grouchily. "We have heard much in support of you." *Thank you, Judy.* "All irrelevant, of course."

"Evidence," the redheaded woman said. "None of it truly irrelevant."

"You think you should be allowed to get away with this, just because of some old story and a handful of auguries?" one of the unknown women said. She had an Australian accent and frizzy, windblown hair that made her look like a goddess of the harvest—a hardscrabble harvest.

"I don't know what kind of punishment I deserve, and I'm not going to choose one for myself. I probably should have come before the Board petitioning for the change before I started dating Malcolm. I made mistakes. I was in love and I didn't want to wait to have the man I wanted. I'm sorry for that. But I don't regret the decisions I made."

"Impenitent," Ragsdale said, "impertinent, bold, disrespectful—I'm shocked that you feel entitled to ask the Board anything, let alone to overlook your transgression."

"I haven't asked you to overlook it. And if I don't ask, who will?"

"Nobody else seems interested in dating a faction member," said the other unknown woman, whose accent was lightly Hispanic. "This all sounds very self-serving to me."

I didn't have an answer to that. It had always been the problem, that no one had ever challenged this part of the Accords before, and for all I knew I was the only one who ever would. "It's not," I said, and hated how weak I sounded.

"We're not going to change a seventy-year-old document just so you can have the social life you want," the Frenchman said. "Are we ready to deliberate?"

"Does anyone have any more questions?" Stirlaugson said. No one spoke. "Then I do," she added, and leaned forward in her chair.

"Ms. Davies," she said, "how will you respond to the verdict of the Board?"

I swallowed yet again. Really, the lack of water made me feel more like a criminal than any amount of grilling. "I will abide by your decision," I said, "because it's what I swore to do."

"Good," Stirlaugson said. "Wait outside that door until we call." She pointed at a door on the other side of the room from where I'd entered. I walked slowly across the textured Berber carpet, feeling a flaw in my left heel catch on the nap every other step, and went out the door. Once I shut it behind me, I leaned against it and drew in a deep breath, then let it out again, closing my eyes against the remembered nightmare.

Eventually, when I'd become lightheaded from all the breathing, I opened my eyes and stood upright. I was in a little reception area with two chairs and a curved desk about armpit-high to me. There was also, thank God, a water dispenser and a stack of those cups that are pointed at the bottom. I snatched one up and filled and drained it three times without stopping. Then I filled it a fourth time and stood sipping and looking out the tiny window that showed only the roof of the building next door, and let my mind go pleasantly blank. It was over. Sure, the Board had yet to decide my fate, but there was nothing more I could do to change their minds.

A couple of water birds coasted in from the left, where the river was, and landed neatly on a pipe protruding from the roof. Where were they going? What could they hope to find on that barren roof? Were they mated, or just chance-met friends? One of the birds pecked at the back of the other, who didn't freak out, so probably it was a desired pecking. I wished I could see beyond the roof. Even the geese would be more interesting.

I sat and stretched out my legs, eased off one of my pumps and scratched the sole of my foot with my toe. I felt so tired. All I wanted now was to go home, take off my suit, and curl up in Malcolm's arms and fall asleep. Even sex felt like too much work.

The door scraped open. I hopped to my feet, then staggered a bit trying to get my shoe back on. The redheaded woman peered in at me. "You can come back now," she said with a smile. I gulped down the rest of my water, dropped the empty cup on my chair, and followed her, my heart once again pounding. It seemed I wasn't as calm about this as I'd thought.

The Board watched me closely as I returned behind my guide. I tried to judge the decision by their expressions and gave up; they all looked stern and unfriendly, even Chukwu. *Sit, stand, sit, what do I do?* Finally, I reached my chair and dropped into it. If this were a real courtroom, they'd ask me to stand, but my legs were shaking badly enough that I wasn't sure I could stay upright.

"Ms. Davies," Stirlaugson said, "the Board has considered your case, and your petition, and has made the following decision. Your reasoning with regard to the Accords is sound, and we acknowledge that there is more to considerations of partiality than simple rules. Given that friendship is not forbidden by the Accords, we choose to amend the law to permit romantic relationships—"

I let out a squeak. Half the Board members laughed behind their hands.

"As I said, the Accords will now permit romantic relationships, though we will also be revising the punishments for partiality to reflect this. The Board thanks you for your diligence in bringing this to our attention."

"Don't get so excited," Ragsdale said. The evil little smile on his face sobered me instantly.

"This decision is not retroactive. You are still guilty of violating the Accords and must be punished accordingly." Stirlaugson stood and put her hands palm-down on the table, leaning far forward like a puma poised to launch herself at her prey. "Helena Davies, you are fined one hundred thousand dollars and will be under close scrutiny by the Board for the next twelve months. You will have your actions audited once a month by a Board member—" Her eyes briefly flicked toward Ragsdale, who looked positively blissful. "And *any* violation of any provision of the Accords will be viewed with extreme displeasure and the fullest prosecution of the law."

"And you have to pay that fine yourself. No having your rich boyfriend throw money at it," the Australian woman said.

Stirlaugson shook her head slowly as if in warning. "Do not misunderstand me, Ms. Davies. This was not a unanimous decision. Some of us wanted a much harsher punishment. Fail us, and you may yet lose your custodianship." She leaned back. "You're dismissed."

I gaped at her. "I'm still Abernathy's custodian."

"For now," Ragsdale said.

"I expect you to be there this afternoon. I have an important augury to receive," Stirlaugson said.

I pushed myself up and had to hold onto the back of the chair. "Thank you," I said, and strode away as fast as my wobbling legs could carry me.

Safely outside the elevator, I leaned against the button and closed my eyes again. One hundred thousand dollars. I had a little more than half that saved up, thanks to frugal living and the one percent bonuses from the auguries, which really added up over time. I'd just have to scrimp harder for the next...oh, five or ten years? But it was just money. I was still the custodian. And I was free.

My excitement grew as the elevator descended, until I was practically bursting with it. I needed to call Judy. And Viv. And Lucia, and the Kellers, and *everyone*. I'd done the impossible, and I'd survived to tell the tale.

At first I couldn't find Malcolm, but the receptionist helpfully pointed me toward a sitting area, where Malcolm waited. He was leaning forward with his elbows on his knees and his head bowed, looking down at the floor. I trotted over to him and waited for him to look up. The grim despair on his face gradually gave way to hope—well, I was grinning like a maniac and bouncing on the balls of my feet. "Well?" he said.

I smiled even more broadly and put my arms around his neck. "I won," I said, and kissed him where everyone could see.

21

"The place is as clean as it's going to get," Judy said. "Stop the nervous sweeping."

"I'm almost positive Ms. Stirlaugson voted in my favor. I feel like I owe her gratitude."

"But you don't owe *anyone* servility." Judy took the broom away from me. "You're wearing a groove in the floor."

"All right. I'll stop."

"Only because I took the broom away. And no dusting either. You're getting that suit all dirty. Why didn't you change?"

"Because she said she was coming and…I'm being servile again, huh?"

"Little bit." Judy disappeared with the broom. I settled on the stool and fingered the cash register keys. It all felt so unreal to be back in Abernathy's as if I hadn't nearly lost it forever. Only a few magi had come in, mostly ones who lived in caves and hadn't heard about my tribunal, and I'd laughed and joked with them until they started to look a little nervous. Now I made myself sit quietly. I was composed and calm and everything. I just couldn't stop smiling.

"What are you and Campbell doing to celebrate?" Judy said when she returned.

"I don't know. Malcolm said it was a surprise, and just to be ready to be picked up at 6:15. He wouldn't even tell me what to wear—said it didn't matter. I'm a little nervous, honestly. I'd be satisfied with staying in and watching a movie."

"You're sort of boring, you know that, right?"

"I like boring. Boring is nice. Nobody ever gets eaten by invaders when it's boring."

"Invaders don't generally happen to people even when they're not boring."

My phone rang, startling me. "Congratulations," Lucia said. "You live a charmed life."

"Thanks. I feel fortunate right now. I almost can't believe I won."

"Neither can I. The Board changes for no one, especially not a disobedient custodian. You must have some powerful allies."

"If I do, I don't know who they are. I mean, I think Ms. Stirlaugson was in favor of me remaining custodian, but as far as changing the Accords goes, I don't know how that voting went down."

"I'd bet a month's salary at least a few of them were already inclined toward your point of view."

"I can't afford to take that bet, but you're probably right."

"Yes, I heard about your fine. I don't suppose even your famous chutzpah extended to asking for a raise?"

"How do you know about that?"

"I have my sources." It sounded sinister enough I decided not to press. "I called to see if you're open today, given the extreme stress you were probably under."

"I am." I decided not to bitch about Ragsdale to Lucia. She couldn't do anything about it, and if it got back to him, he might decide to double down on the hell he intended to rain down on me. Not that I thought Lucia was loose-lipped at all. I was just paranoid. "Do you need an augury?"

"Do I need an augury. Davies, I need all manner of things, starting with more enforcers and including an augury telling me how best to use them. I'm satisfied we've either uncovered all the traitors in my jurisdiction or forced them to flee. But that doesn't tell me what they plan to do next, and Washburn only knows so much."

"What about the factions? What are they doing?"

"Parish is still having to defend himself against rumors that he's secretly a traitor. It's stirred up the Ambrosites to the point that some of them have petitioned the Archmagus to replace him. If the Mercy wanted disruption, they got it."

"They also got seventy-six deaths. What I don't understand is why they didn't follow up that attack with something else."

"According to the ones we've interrogated, the magical cost was higher than anticipated. It threw their organization, such as it is, into chaos. And for all we know, some of the ones who fled are like Washburn—changed their mind about their loyalties. But it left us weakened enough that we can't press the attack either."

"So what are you doing? If it's not too nosy of me to ask."

"Your nosiness pleases me. We're retro-engineering the magic that affected the steel magi and investing every magus with protection against similar attacks. I've got my people investigating the names the traitors gave us—under duress, so who knows how valuable that intelligence is, but we can't afford to ignore any information."

"I thought I read somewhere that torture was useless."

"You ought to remember we don't use torture. Magic to encourage someone to speak, sure, but even that can only go so far. And those traitors were resistant to influence. Some of them suicided rather than talk, and I think it might have been an induced response. Like Matt McKanley last year. We thought it meant he had an accomplice working with him on the illusion attacks on the oracle, but now I wonder if it wasn't something his masters embedded in him."

"I remember." I'd never forgotten the mottled face of the man who'd kidnapped me and tried to kill me.

"At any rate, once we've finished protecting our people, it's time to take the fight to the Mercy. Stupid name. They're no longer in a position to operate secretly among us, so they'll have gathered somewhere—several places around the globe, no doubt. And large gatherings of magi are easier to spot than a few individuals."

"But won't that mean dividing your forces? The teams will still have to hunt invaders."

Lucia sighed. "Try not to mention that logical conclusion to anyone, will you? We're trying to boost morale."

"Sorry."

"I'm not eager for this fight. There's too much about Wardens fighting Wardens, even traitorous ones, that makes me sick. But they won't go easy on us, and God only knows what kind of advantages the invaders give their human puppets. It's not a fight we can refuse."

"What can *I* do?"

"What can you do?" Lucia laughed. "Davies, one of the things I like about you is your absurd willingness to throw yourself into battle, armed with nothing but your sense of justice. Keep doing what you're doing. You're a walking miracle as far as the Warden community is concerned. Don't let them down."

"I..." I swallowed to moisten my suddenly dry throat. "Thanks."

"Don't thank me, thank whatever divine force protects you," Lucia said, and hung up.

"What was that about?" Judy said. She didn't bother pretending she hadn't been listening to my half of the conversation.

"Does Lucia's approval fill you with more dread than her antagonism, or is that just me?"

"I think having her attention at all makes most people walk softly."

"And to think she actually has superiors. If I didn't know better, I'd think she ruled the magical world."

The door swung open, the bells jangled triumphantly. "Good afternoon," Stirlaugson said. She was accompanied by the redheaded woman and Chukwu. "I take it things have been quiet."

"Yesterday I told everyone the store would be closed today on account of not knowing how long the, um, tribunal would take." I hopped off the stool and came around the counter to shake hands. "So there were only a few people."

"Well, this shouldn't take long. I thought, as long as I'm in town, I would come in personally and save a stamp." Stirlaugson removed a folded piece of paper from her purse and handed it to me. I kept myself from bowing and retreated into the oracle.

I stopped a few paces inside and unfolded the paper. *How can we best take the fight to the Mercy?* Excellent question, and one I'd have been happy to deliver an answer for even if I hadn't felt unnatural, yes, even servile gratitude toward the asker. I wandered through the aisles, not exactly taking my time, but not hurrying either. It just felt so *satisfying* to be where I was meant to be, to know the Accords were changing and I didn't have to give Malcolm or the oracle up.

There, in the distance, a blue light burned. I picked up the pace just a little. *Textiles of South America*, the spine read, and I pulled it off the shelf, reveling in the tingling feeling of an augury. I flipped it open to the title page. *Laverne Stirlaugson*, it said, and below that—

I sucked in an astonished breath. *Impossible. She's never going to believe it.* I read the number again, counted the zeroes, then closed the book and headed for the exit.

Ms. Stirlaugson and the Board members hadn't moved, just chatted quietly. Judy sat on the stool with the ledger and receipt book ready to hand. "Ms. Stirlaugson," I said, "I have your augury. But I don't think you're going to like it."

Stirlaugson's eyes narrowed. "Why is that, Ms. Davies?"

"Oh, it's not the augury, it's the price. The oracle—" I swallowed. "The oracle says it will cost you five million dollars."

The redheaded woman gasped. Chukwu's eyes went wide. "Five *million?*" he said.

"I swear I'm not making it up. You don't have to pay for it if you don't want. It's more than it's ever charged for an augury before, even the Ambrosite Archmagus's augury."

Stirlaugson's expression was perfectly calm. "Five million," she said. "Ms. Davies, how much do you make from each augury?"

"Um...one percent?"

"And one percent of five million is fifty thousand dollars, am I correct?"

"Yes, but—oh, you don't think I'd lie to you just to make money?"

Stirlaugson shook her head. Then she laughed. It was the most spontaneous sound I'd ever heard out of her. "Ms. Davies, tell me something," she said when she regained control of herself. Her companions stared at her like she'd lost her mind. "How much money did you need to pay the rest of your fine?"

I joined Chukwu and the redhead in staring at the madwoman. "Fifty thou—" Then it hit me. "But I *really* didn't make it up!"

"I don't believe you did. I *do* think the oracle has some strong opinions about you. Don't disappoint it, young lady." Stirlaugson patted the augury gently. "I'll need to arrange for a wire transfer. Hold that book for me, and I'll return in the morning."

Chukwu nodded politely to me as he followed Stirlaugson out the door. The redhead lingered behind. "I don't think we've been introduced," she said. "Ariadne Duwelt. I admit to some curiosity about what you'll do next." She smiled and waved goodbye, closing the door quietly behind her.

Judy and I stared at each other. "The oracle just extorted money from the Board to pay your fine," Judy said. "That has to be a first in all of history."

"So maybe it really did intend all of this," I said. "Though I can't imagine why it would care about my personal life."

"If it cares about its custodians...you never have learned what prompted Silas to abdicate. Suppose it wanted him to have a different life and arranged for that to happen?"

"Or maybe it just wanted the Accords changed."

"Then why pay your fine with the Board's own money?"

"I don't know." I sighed. "I'm slightly afraid someone's going to see how happy I am and do something to screw it up."

"Way to look on the bright side," Judy said.

It was quiet enough I felt safe scampering upstairs and changing out of the suit, which was pretty but uncomfortable, and into dress pants and a blouse. Malcolm's breezy statement, when he dropped me off at eleven that morning, that it didn't matter what I wore made me even more anxious about the matter. So I dressed as nicely as I could while still remaining comfortable and hoped it was enough.

I called Viv around 5:30. "How are you doing?"

"We're both fine. Jeremiah's off being interrogated again. He's really the greatest guy—so patient about the whole thing. I love him so much."

"Has he been able to give Lucia much information?"

"The revelation that he was supposed to assassinate her was more than enough. They—the Mercy—operate in what he calls cells, isolated from one another, but he gave her what names he could, and one of them was someone Lucia was able to pick up and interrogate. In less nice a way than she did Jeremiah."

I shuddered. "I don't even want to think about that."

"Me neither. But I'm nervous about tomorrow. Jeremiah offered to let the bone magi analyze his brain to see what the invaders did to him."

"Why would he do that?"

I heard a distant thumping, as if Viv were dragging a chair over a linoleum floor. "He says part of the alteration made him more capable of communicating with the intelligent invaders, to let them speak to him in his dreams. He's hoping the magi can shut down that means of communication, just in case they can do more than communicate. Lucia thinks her people might be able to reverse it, use it to communicate with the invaders."

"That seems pointless."

"Not if you're putting thoughts directly into their brains. They might be able to use it as a weapon. But I'm worried about Jeremiah's safety. It doesn't sound like a non-invasive procedure."

That made me shudder. "Jeremiah's braver than I am. I don't think I could do that. Almost as bad as having a needle inserted into your heart."

"Is Malcolm recovered from that?"

"Fully. As far as I can tell, anyway. It's so weird to think how badly injured he was three weeks ago, and now he's walking around like it never happened. And the sex is wonderful—so much better than when we had to be a secret."

"Jeremiah and I have discovered there's a limit to how much sex is enough. Don't tell him I told you that. He's very private and doesn't understand there are things girls talk about with their girlfriends that have nothing to do with their boyfriends, right?"

"I guess that's true. I'm getting nervous about where Malcolm is taking me tonight. It feels so weird not to have to hide anymore."

"I can imagine. Does it feel like everyone's staring at you?"

"Yes. Exactly."

"Well, they're probably staring at how cute a couple you are, so don't worry about it."

Judy passed me on her way out the door and waved. I waved back. "I'm sure I'll get used to it. And there will probably still be Nicolliens who give me the hairy eyeball because I'm with Malcolm, but I can endure that too."

"Hairy eyeball, what a disgusting image."

I grinned. "I got it from Harry Keller, who is a fount of all sorts of disturbing metaphors."

"Ew. Oh, Jeremiah's coming back and we're going to dinner. Talk about being stared at. It's like being the last fish in the bowl when there's a cat in the room."

"How much longer will you have to stay there? Lucia can't expect the two of you to live in confinement for the rest of your lives."

"I'm not sure yet. At least a week, while they finish this brain analysis. Then...do you think it's crazy that Jeremiah and I are talking about moving in together?"

I gasped. "Viv! Isn't that sort of sudden?"

Viv's voice turned serious. "It's been almost three months. That doesn't seem unusual. It's just...I've never thought about settling down in any way, but Jeremiah is more than capable of defending himself, and he's certain I'm going to need protection at least for the next few months. He says if I'm going to need a bodyguard, he wants it to be him. It's romantic, and scary, and...I think I'm going to do it."

"That's wonderful! I'm so happy for you both."

"I'm excited and nervous all at once. I'm not the easiest person to live with. I scare away all my roommates eventually. I think you and I lasted as roommates for all of three days."

I remembered those long-ago days and suppressed another shudder. "That was when we were much younger and stupider. I'm sure you and Jeremiah will do just fine."

"Just so long as we have our own spaces. He doesn't want to hear my music all the time, and I don't want to know what happened on *Battlestar Galactica*, either the old one or the really old one."

"There has to be at least *something* he's into that you like."

Viv laughed. "Surprisingly, it's this cartoon called *Cowboy Bebop*. It has the greatest jazz soundtrack, so if I get bored I just close my eyes and listen."

I laughed. "That's the kind of compromise I can get behind."

22

It was ten 'til six. The sun was turning the clouds pink and gold, sidewalk traffic had almost dried up entirely, and I thought seriously about closing up early. Then I remembered Ragsdale's face, how pleased he'd been at the thought of auditing me, and decided I was safer playing by the rules. So I sat at the counter until exactly six o'clock, then locked up and went upstairs to wait. The apartment was cool and quiet, for once, and I sat on my couch and thought about how nice it was that it was still mine.

6:15 came around, and no Malcolm. I played some solitaire and tried not to fret. At 6:20 I texted Malcolm: NOT TO BE IMPATIENT, BUT WHERE ARE YOU?

About a minute later, I got the reply CAR STUCK IN TRAFFIC, ALMOST THERE. WAIT OUT FRONT.

I sighed and grabbed my jacket. Malcolm was certainly going out of his way to be mysterious.

It was windy and cold outside, the icy breath of an invisible creature tickling the back of my neck. I huddled into my jacket and tried to control my impatience. Streetlamps were coming on up and down the street, making a tracery of light that would be beautiful and delicate from two hundred feet up. I watched a flock of birds wheel and dip above me and wondered what they made of all this human activity. Where were the river birds I'd seen outside the tribunal building now?

Cars passed slowly in both directions. Rush hour hit us even this far from the freeway. I watched as a gray Lincoln Town Car, far too expensive for this neighborhood, approached and then, to my surprise, came to a stop in the middle of the lane. The driver got out and came around to my side, ignoring the honks of the car behind him. He opened the rear passenger door and bowed. "Ms. Davies?"

"Um...me?" I looked around as if some other Ms. Davies were lurking behind me.

"Mr. Campbell's compliments."

"Um..." The other car honked again, long and loud. I scurried to get into the car. The driver closed the door and got back in behind the wheel. "Excuse me, where are we going?"

The driver handed me an unsealed envelope and put the car in gear. I removed a square of notepaper from the envelope and, squinting in the dim light, held it up to my eyes. *I'll join you later,* it read in Malcolm's elegant handwriting I envied. *You have some shopping to do.*

I dropped the note into my lap. Shopping?

The interior of the Town Car was the most luxurious thing I'd ever seen—smooth black leather seats, plenty of leg room, a host of buttons I was sure were after market. I pushed one at random and a sheet of glass began rising up between me and the driver. I squeaked and stabbed it again so the glass would retract. "Sorry!"

"Not to worry, miss," the driver said. "The car is at your disposal for the evening."

"Where are we going?"

"Mr. Campbell instructed me not to tell you, miss. He wanted it to be a surprise."

"Huh." I started texting Malcolm, then deleted it before sending. If he wanted it to be a surprise, I could humor him. Besides, I was starting to feel excited. It was all so mysterious—the car that might as well be a limousine, the attentive driver, and shopping, whatever that meant.

The driver took us out to the freeway and then downtown, and my respect for his skills grew as he navigated the one-way warren without so much as a hint from his GPS. We passed any number of stores, and I sat forward, wondering which one was our destination. But the place where he finally stopped was off the beaten path, with no windows advertising wares, just a door up a couple of steps and beside it a plaque bearing the single name BENVOLIO.

Once again the driver came to a stop in the middle of the street and had my door open before I could react and open it myself. I accepted his hand, though I didn't need any help getting out of the car, and stood uncertain on the sidewalk. A couple of men, their heads bent against the rising wind, passed us with no more than a single incurious look.

"Ring the bell," the driver said. "I will return for you in one hour." He bowed and got back in the car, and drove away. I felt abandoned.

There was a simple brass button next to the Benvolio door. I pressed it, and waited, once more huddling into my jacket. The wind felt like it came straight from the mouth of the devil, deep within Hell—the one image I remembered from studying Dante's *Inferno*. It was an image I had trouble shaking.

The door opened. "Ms. Davies, welcome to Benvolio," said a tall, angular woman with a pleasant smile. "May I take your coat?"

With the door safely shut on the oncoming storm, I shed my jacket and handed it to her. The store, if that's what it was, was little more than a large room with a sofa and chair upholstered in champagne-colored velveteen. The plush maroon carpet had a pile deep enough for me to make footprints in; the woman carrying my coat away left the tiny prints of her stiletto heels that faded almost immediately. The walls were all curtained in rose damask that coordinated with the furniture and carpet and gave the room a hush I felt inclined to match. The scent of roses, faint but distinct, filled the air, and soft lighting made the whole thing look exactly like a lady's boudoir in an upscale home decorating magazine.

"Please sit," a second woman said, coming from behind one of the curtains and startling me. She was round and plump and had a beautiful smile. "Would you care for a glass of wine?"

"No, thank you," I said. My excitement was tangled with confusion, and I wanted—needed—to keep my head clear. "Um...why am I—"

"I'm Elle, and this is Veronica," the second woman said. "Let us show you some of the possibilities."

"Oh! What...possibilities?"

Elle clapped, a couple of sharp sounds, and one set of curtains drew back, revealing another room, less well-lit than this one. "It's really too bad it's so cold tonight," she said, "because with your figure, a short skirt really is attractive." A young woman came forward to stand, no, *pose* in front of me. She wore a long, full-skirted gown in old gold, with beads all over the skirt, utterly beautiful. She turned, making the skirt flare out. I gaped.

"It's beautiful," I said. Then the penny dropped. "I'm shopping for a *dress?*"

"Mr. Campbell instructed us to help you choose something to wear," Veronica said. "I don't know if that's the right color for you..." She clapped again, and another young woman came forward, wearing a white dress with a black lace overlay that made the whole thing look like patterns of shadow over snow.

"Oh, I like that one," I said. Veronica gestured, and the young woman went to stand to one side of the room. Another young woman, this one in pale pink with a plunging neckline, came to stand in front of me. I shook my head. Too daring for me.

More models—at some point the same models started reappearing—trotted out dress after dress for my approval. I nodded or shook my head, and a few more women joined the black and white girl off to the side. It felt just like that scene in *How to Marry a Millionaire*, where Cameron Mitchell has Lauren Bacall and the other models show off a bunch of clothes for his make-believe aunt—and as I thought that, I laughed and had to wave off Veronica's query about what was so funny. Of course Malcolm would recreate that moment for me. Shopping, indeed.

Then I let out an astonished breath. The new dress had a knee-length skirt and a bodice that crossed in front. It hugged the model's hips and showed off just the right curves of her breasts. It was also red, cranberries-in-winter red, heart-of-a-rose red. "That one," I said. "I don't care if it's cold."

Elle looked at me appraisingly. "I think you're right," she said. "Veronica?"

"This way, Ms. Davies," Veronica said.

I needed a new bra because the one I was wearing peeked out of the cleavage of the perfect dress, and then I needed a slip because my panty line showed, but in only a few minutes I was tucked into the dress, and it fit like it was made for me. I could get used to this kind of shopping. Viv and Judy would be in heaven. I slipped my feet into the simple black heels they provided and turned in front of the trifold mirror, admiring myself. "How much?" I said. It had to be hideously expensive, but I was feeling flush with cash and willing to spend some on the perfect dress.

"Mr. Campbell has instructed us to send the bill to him," Elle said.

My cheeks warmed. This was an expensive gift, and maybe...but how rude of me to reject something he'd gone to so much trouble over, something he'd known would make me happy. "Oh," I said. "That's...very nice of him."

Elle and Veronica exchanged meaningful glances. "Normally Mr. Campbell comes here with his mother," Veronica said. "I think he was glad to make use of our services for someone...else."

"Oh." And that cleared up another question, which was *how does Malcolm even know about this place?* and the fear that I wasn't the only girl he'd treated to the full experience. I turned around again. I felt like the most beautiful woman in the world.

Elle and Veronica found me a wrap so I wouldn't freeze, a black satin drape that only partially concealed the perfect dress, and checked outside to see if my driver had returned. He hadn't, so we stood inside and chatted. I learned that Elle and Veronica were in fact

Mrs. Campbell's preferred couturiers, and that Malcolm came in with his mother sometimes. "She insists on discussing business as if we're not here," Veronica said with a grimace. "I think it makes Mr. Campbell uncomfortable."

"Which is probably why she does it," Elle said. "She's...not the nicest lady."

"But we like Mr. Campbell very much. You're a lucky girl," Veronica said, winking at me.

"I know," I said. "I feel lucky."

"And the car accident...is it true he nearly died?"

"Yes, I—he was hurt badly."

"He seems to have recovered quickly."

"He heals fast," I said. "Is that the car?" It was. I hurried into the back seat, grateful not to have to deflect that line of conversation.

The driver handed me another envelope and showed me how to turn on the rear lights (more after-market stuff, and how handy!) to read it. *The crowning touch*, was all Malcolm had written, and I smiled and shook my head ruefully. He'd pulled all this together in half a day?

The next stop was a salon whose posted hours were nine to six, but lights burned beyond its window, and a young man with long curly hair opened the door for me. "Sam," he said, shaking my hand. "I like what you've done with your hair, but I think, with that dress, curls around your face and over your shoulders will be better."

Twenty minutes later I had to agree with him. He'd put something in my hair that made it shine, then used a flat iron to make long curls he brushed out so they twisted gently around my face. "I wish I knew how to do that," I sighed.

"Come back some time, and I'll teach you." Sam gave me a hand out of the chair and walked around me, examining the effect. "Very nice. You're going to turn heads tonight."

There's only one head I care about turning. "Thanks, Sam."

"My pleasure. I've cut Malcolm's hair for five years and he's my favorite customer. Nice to finally meet the woman he's been talking about the last three months."

The Town Car was waiting by the curb. "Another note?" I said.

The driver handed it over. *Hope you're hungry.* After all that work, I was extremely hungry. I hoped whatever meal Malcolm had in mind would be filling, and not one of those stereotypical fancy meals with two julienne carrots and a couple of peas on a big white plate. Thinking that brought the nervousness back. How fancy would it have to be to justify this dress? Why was Malcolm going to so much trouble?

I hadn't been paying attention to our route, so when the car came to a stop, I wasn't sure where we were. The restaurant, La Grenouille, had a low canopy over the door and white Christmas lights outlining its eaves. The driver pulled up to the door and came around to let me out. This time, I did need help getting out of the car without my skirt hiking up. Suddenly the custom of the man opening the door for the woman made sense.

"Have a good evening, Ms. Davies, it was a pleasure," the driver said, and just as I realized I'd never asked his name, he got in behind the wheel and pulled away. I stood shivering for just a moment, watching him go, then came to my senses and hurried inside, hoping my curls weren't too disordered.

A short foyer like an airlock kept the warm air in and the cold air out, and I quickly passed through the brass-bound doors with their dozen square glass panes into the actual restaurant. Warm air scented with garlic and rich buttery goodness met me the instant I passed the inner door, and I stood and breathed it happily in. Oh, this would be far better than a couple of artistically arranged vegetables.

"Your party, miss?" said the woman at the maître-d's desk.

"Um...Campbell. Malcolm Campbell."

The woman gave me a longer, appraising look. "This way, Ms. Davies," she said, gesturing to me to follow.

The restaurant was filled with the murmur of people eating and talking quietly. To my relief, most of them were dressed as well as I was, not that I would have minded looking like this at McDonald's. Much. The small round tables seemed perfectly suited to two or four diners, with their little candles flickering across their faces. I couldn't tell whether or not I was turning heads. Certainly no one dropped their fork in astonishment at my beauty. That would have been embarrassing. The dark carpet, not as plush as at Benvolio, still felt like I was leaving footprints in wet sand.

Then I saw Malcolm. He was breathtakingly handsome in dinner jacket and satin tie, almost like his regular suits but somehow more... formal, was really the only word. He saw me, and his eyes went wide. Then a slow smile spread across his face, and he rose and came toward me. It was so much the reaction I'd hoped for that I blushed and reached to take his hand.

"Beautiful," he said, lightly kissing my cheek. "Did you like Elle and Veronica?"

"They were so nice. It felt just like *How to Marry a Millionaire.*"

He pulled my chair out for me to sit. "I'm so glad you understood the reference. I was afraid you'd think I was reenacting *Vertigo* instead."

I laughed. "You know, you'd make a terrible Jimmy Stewart."

"And you're far superior to Kim Novak." He leaned back for the waiter to fill our wine glasses with something pale and rosy. "You look extraordinary."

"So do you. I've never been here before."

"It was a recommendation by your mother."

My eyebrows went up. "When did you talk about this with my mother?"

"Sunday after dinner. She says she doesn't cook haute cuisine herself, but this is her favorite place."

"I didn't even know she liked haute cuisine."

Another waiter handed me a menu. "Uh-oh. You know it's expensive when they don't print the prices." I read over the offerings, grateful they'd printed English translations next to the French words. I caught the eye of an older woman sitting at the next table, smiled and nodded at her and was smiled at in return. She made me think of what Michelle Obama would probably look like in twenty years.

"I hope you're not worrying about the cost," Malcolm said.

"Not at all, so long as you're paying."

That made him laugh. "It doesn't matter to you at all that I'm rich, does it?" he said.

"I hardly ever think about it." Though I was now, a little.

"That's so refreshing, after Andria—if I dare bring up another woman's name on a date with you. She was constantly maneuvering me into positions where I'd have to buy something for her."

"That sounds awful. I'd have dumped her, too."

"Well, that, and there was this other woman I wanted to date who happens to look spectacular in red—Helena, I can't stop staring at you. That dress is incredible."

"I know, isn't it perfect? I love it. Thank you."

He smiled with satisfaction. "And there it is again. No fuss, no exclaiming over the price—"

"They wouldn't tell me how expensive it was."

"And even that doesn't matter to you. I've never felt less like a walking wallet than when I'm with you."

I blushed again. "That's a lovely compliment."

"It is. We should probably order. Have you had haute cuisine before? I'd be happy to make suggestions."

I lowered my menu. "Only once or twice, and never anywhere like this. Would you pick something for me? Dad says to listen to the advice of the expert. But can we get snails? I've always wanted to try snails."

He laughed. "My adventurous gastronome. Of course. You'll like them." He addressed the waiter in fluent French, of which I caught only "escargots." The waiter nodded and walked away. I gaped at Malcolm.

"You speak *French?* Like a native?"

"My mother is French-Canadian, and I grew up speaking both French and English. So Québécois French, but still."

"'C.K. Dexter Haven, you have unsuspected depth!'"

"We still have so many things to learn about each other. And a long time in which to learn them."

I raised my glass to him. "I'm looking forward to it."

The snails were delicious, slightly chewy and drenched in butter and garlic. I had no idea what whatever Malcolm ordered for me was called, but it turned out to be lamb brochettes with vegetables served with a citrus sauce I adored. "You have to try this," I said, offering him a bite.

"Mmm. Oh, I chose well for you. But—and this is also something you should know about me—I generally choose steak for myself if it's at all a good cut of meat."

"My father loves steak, too. He learned to cook it last summer."

"Wise man."

I caught the older woman looking at us again and nudging her companion, who looked more like Sidney Poitier than President Obama, to my relief. What was so interesting about us? Aside from how attractive we both were. Well, maybe that was enough.

"Ready for dessert?" Malcolm said, wiping his lips with his napkin.

"Something you should know about *me* is I am *always* ready for dessert."

We settled on profiteroles and waited for them to be brought to our table. Malcolm took my hand, smiling. "I hope it's been a memorable evening."

"Very. I'm never going to forget this night."

"Then I've succeeded." He stroked the back of my hand with his thumb. "I want everything to be perfect."

I smiled back at him. It was perfect—

Oh.

The dress, the hair, the car, the fancy restaurant. All perfect.

He was going to propose.

All the blood drained from my face, and I quickly picked up my glass and sipped the pinot noir that had come with my lamb. He couldn't—but why else would he—this was *far* too elaborate even to celebrate our new freedom, wasn't it? I couldn't. I loved him, but I just wasn't ready. And yet, how could I say no? How could we come back from that? I had to be wrong. Malcolm would never do this to me, laying on the luxury in preparation for the big question. And yet... My innocent happiness dissolved like chalk in rain.

I picked at my profiterole until Malcolm laughed and teased me with "Too much even for the Davies iron-clad digestive system?"

"I'm fuller than I thought."

"Understandable. Are you ready to go?"

"Yes," I said with relief. At least he wasn't going to do it here in the restaurant with Michelle Obama and Sidney Poitier watching.

"Then...there's just one more thing," Malcolm said, and reached inside his dinner jacket. The blood drained from my face again. No. Not now.

He pulled out a jewelry box, not a ring box but something long and white. "Oh, Malcolm," I said, feeling panic rise up in me because now I had no idea what he was thinking. "Really, you don't need to do this. It's all been more than enough without that, too."

A smile touched his lips and lit his eyes with wry amusement. "I believe it's customary to give your girlfriend a gift for her birthday."

I gaped at him. "It's not my birthday. That's on Saturday."

"True, but I thought two elaborate celebrations in one week would be anticlimactic." He pushed the box toward me. "Open it."

Stunned, I took the box and opened it. Inside lay a perfect diamond solitaire pendant hanging from a gold chain. It was less than a carat in size, not too big, and the gold warmed it to something other than a chip of faceted ice. "Oh," I said, and couldn't find any more words.

"Simple. Classic. Perfect for you," Malcolm said quietly.

I lifted it out of the box and held it up to the light. It caught the flickering candlelight and threw off a million shattered rainbows. "Malcolm," I said.

"You don't like it."

"I love it. It's perfect. How did you—"

"I guessed you'd be uncomfortable with anything huge. If you want, this is something you could wear every day."

The stone blurred in my vision briefly. "Help me put it on," I said, and Malcolm came around and settled the chain gently around my neck as I lifted my hair out of the way. He sat down, and a broad smile creased his face.

"It is perfect," he said. "So...you do like it, yes?"

I caught the older woman nudging her dining partner, who now seemed uninterested in us. "I do." I felt so relieved I thought I might fly away. I laughed, hoping I didn't sound manic, and pointed discreetly. "Though that woman's disappointed. I think she thought you were going to propose."

Malcolm's eyebrows raised. "Did she?" He looked at me more closely. "And so did you. Are you disappointed, or relieved?"

I blushed so hard I was sure my face matched my dress. "Malcolm—"

"I thought about it. I almost did." Malcolm leaned forward over the remains of our meal. "But you're not ready."

"No. I'm not. I'm sorry."

"Don't be sorry." He reached out and took my hand. "Helena," he said, "someday, I will ask you to marry me, and when I do, it will be the right time. For both of us. Until then—I love you, and I want to share your life as much as you'll let me. And that's more than enough."

My heart felt full to bursting with joy. "I love you," I said. "Let's go home."

HELENA'S MOVIE LIST

Movies referenced in this book include:

The African Queen
The Thin Man
The Philadelphia Story
My Man Godfrey
Notorious
Hollow Triumph (The Scar)
Vertigo
Black Narcissus
The Matrix
To Kill a Mockingbird

ACKNOWLEDGMENTS

Though I was born in Portland, I haven't lived there for many years, and this book required a flying trip over Labor Day weekend to scout locations. All real places appearing in this book have been fictionalized, but I appreciate the kindness of those individuals who allowed me to "borrow" homes and businesses. Abernathy's location, as always, remains undefined to protect the mystery.

Thanks go to Megan Breedlove, who helped me with Chapter Two. Any mistakes in EMT procedure are mine alone.

I'd also like to thank the usual suspects, Jacob Proffitt, Jana Brown, and Hallie O'Donovan, for being willing to read this in beta and provide excellent feedback.

ABOUT THE AUTHOR

In addition to The Last Oracle series, Melissa McShane is the author of more than twenty-five fantasy novels, including the novels of Tremontane, the first of which is *Servant of the Crown;* The Extraordinaries series, beginning with *Burning Bright;* and *Company of Strangers,* first book in the series of the same name.

She lives in the shelter of the mountains out West with her husband, four children and a niece, and three very needy cats. She wrote reviews and critical essays for many years before turning to fiction, which is much more fun than anyone ought to be allowed to have.

You can visit her at her website **www.melissamcshanewrites.com** for more information on other books and upcoming releases.

For news on upcoming releases, bonus material, and other fun stuff, sign up for Melissa's newsletter at http://eepurl.com/brannP

ALSO BY MELISSA MCSHANE

THE CROWN OF TREMONTANE

Servant of the Crown

Rider of the Crown

Exile of the Crown

Agent of the Crown

Voyager of the Crown

THE SAGA OF WILLOW NORTH

Pretender to the Crown

Guardian of the Crown

Champion of the Crown

THE EXTRAORDINARIES

Burning Bright

Wondering Sight

Abounding Might

THE LAST ORACLE

The Book of Secrets

The Book of Peril

The Book of Mayhem

The Book of Lies

The Book of Betrayal

COMPANY OF STRANGERS

Company of Strangers

Stone of Inheritance

Mortal Rites

Shifting Loyalties

Sands of Memory (forthcoming)

THE CONVERGENCE TRILOGY

The Summoned Mage

The Wandering Mage

The Unconquered Mage

THE BOOKS OF DALANINE

The Smoke-Scented Girl

The God-Touched Man

Emissary

The View from Castle Always

Warts and All: A Fairy Tale Collection

CPSIA information can be obtained
at www.ICGtesting.com
Printed in the USA
LVHW052355071019
633408LV00001B/67/P